PROP 485

Story By: James Casey

jamescaseybooks.com

Cover By: Shauna Marshall

shaundrawn.com

Author's Notes:

I just want to say a thank you to anyone who purchased this book. It means so much to me. I came up with the idea for this book my senior year of high school, back in 2011. It started off as a first-person kind of very high school oriented take on if murder was made legal. I even had the tagline picked out, "…and you thought high school was rough?" I scrapped it in 2012 because I did not have enough grasp on creating a full-fledged novel. I picked it up in 2014 when I took a creative writing novel course at Cal State Long Beach. My professor, and amazing author, Tyler Dilts taught the class that had me getting back into this idea. The basis of the story remains, but the approach is much darker, and not so fixated.

With that said, to anyone reading, thank you, and I hope you enjoy.

Acknowledgements

♥ Amy, from the bottom of my heart thank you, thank you, thank you. From staying up all night till the sunrise editing the story night after night as I wrote it to encouraging me every step of the way, you are the reason I have this to show. You kept me accountable with chapter deadlines (even though we both know I never met them) and continued to cheerlead me the entire way. I love you so much Amy!

♥ Shauna, thank you so much for the cover art! It is exactly what I wanted. I seriously admire your work so much and am so happy and appreciative that you drew the art for me. I cannot wait to draw out another horrid sketch of what I want, and you do your magic to make it actually amazing. We've been friends since kindergarten and this almost feels full circle in a way because of our sixth-grade books. I love you!

♥ Jessy, thank you for being there for the entirety of this novel. I believe you were the first person I told the idea to and you have been cheering me on and waiting for the final product ever since. I remember in 2012 when I sent you the first 40 something pages of the first draft and you still encouraged me to keep going even after reading that mess. That's true love right there. I love you!

♥ Nessa, thank you for talking this book out with me and helping me with the pricing and other aspects that I needed help on. That weekend you came over and we spent the entire time working on this book was so much fun. I cannot thank you enough for that. You are an amazing person and I am so happy to call you my friend. I love you!

- ♥ Erika, my sister. I know reading my book and editing it over your winter break home from Berkeley probably was not your favorite thing in the world, but I needed someone smarter than me. And we both know that you have been correcting my grammar and spelling since you got into kindergarten. You* are so smart and talented and I am so appreciative of you for fine tuning it for me and helping. I love you!

- ♥ Tyler Dilts, my favorite professor ever and mentor. I really wanted to drop out of college but being able to take your class three times kept me in it. Twice I was fortunate enough to get you for novel and once for short story. The critiques and way that your classroom was set up made for nothing but growth. You accepted every work as equal and never shamed anyone. You allowed students the openness to really be creative and I thank you so much! This book would not be finished if I had not taken your courses.

- ♥ Dr. Monica Jackson, thank you so much for teaching the course on self-publishing. Those three weeks were so informative and so helpful. I wouldn't know anything about publishing if not for you. Thank you so so much! Check out Dr. Jackson at lifeskillsenterprise.com

*yes, I did that on purpose to bug my sister.

Prop 485

PROLOGUE

It was snowing outside as he played with his toy car, vrooming it up and down the hallway as his dad stayed plastered to the television in the living room. The news was on, an anchor explaining that this election would change everything depending on what was decided. He was only eight years old and had no idea what was being said, he only cared about his racecar.

"The counts are in," the anchor said. His father sat up in his chair, leaning forward. "With a fifty-two percent lead, Prop. 485 has passed." There was a tone of sadness that he could detect from the woman on the television. "I can't believe," she said, trying the best to compose herself. "It's legal."

"Holy shit," his dad shouted. "Roxanne, it's legal!"

"What's legal?" the boy asked, not understanding the word.

"It means we can go do it without getting in trouble," his dad said, turning back to the screen.

"Murder is now legal." The anchor's voice shook as she spoke.

The boy looked up and cocked his head, confused. Wasn't murder bad? His mom stepped out from the kitchen and walked up behind his father. With a quick swipe of her hand she pulled a pistol out of her apron and held it up, firing the gun into the back of his head. Before he had time to react, his mom turned the gun on herself and pulled the trigger.

He was completely alone.

CHAPTER 1

There was a gun pointed at him and he didn't know why but his feet wouldn't move, wouldn't run. It was as if his brain shut down out of fear and none of his limbs would work. He was paralyzed, staring down the barrel of a shiny silver pistol. There was a clicking noise and he knew it was the gun being cocked, knew it was all going to end now. He accepted it, because it had been eleven years since Proposition 485 had passed and he hadn't been killed...yet. Not that the entire country exploded into a violent rage or anything, but murder wasn't an uncommon occurrence at all.

Jeff's palms were sweaty, and his breathing was ragged. He never really thought much about his death, because, why would he? He was sixteen and death seemed like a distant dream that would never come. But the reality was death could happen at any minute, to anyone, he just happened to avoid the inevitable for sixteen years. Other's weren't as fortunate — eventually everyone dies.

Everything seemed to move in slow motion as he watched the hooded figure's finger against the trigger. The black gloves giving a sharp contrast between the shine of the silver. He watched as the man's finger pulled back along with the trigger. There was a bright flash directly in front of Jeff's face and he could literally see the bullet releasing from the chamber, heading directly for his forehead. This was it, this was the end of his life as he knew it.

Beep. Beep.

Jeff's eyes shot open and he let out a terrified gasp. His face was riddled in sweat and his sheets were sticking to his arms and legs. *It was just a dream*, he thought. *A damn well realistic dream.* The beeping continued, and he could finally catch his breath enough to realize that it was his alarm, blaring.

Propped up on his elbow, he slammed his hand down onto the snooze button, silencing the room of the annoying wailing. All he could hear was his breathing accompanied by the rhythmic banging of his heart in his chest. That was by far one of the worst, if not the worst, ways he'd ever woken up for his first day of school. Junior year was starting, and he wasn't ready.

Who would be when anyone could kill anyone at any time? Jeff had always seen the older movies depicting high school as some horrid environment where the mean girls and popular jocks would make your life a living hell, but those movies were nothing compared to what he had to go through.

Once Proposition 485 had passed, people tried to stop it, tried to repeal the decision, but to no avail. Anytime someone would feel like they could do it, stop the madness, they would be shot dead, or stabbed, or tortured; the people doing it weren't picky. That was the problem. Before the vote no one believed it would pass and on the rare occasion it did they had all expected a repeal, making it but a very short and disturbing time in the country's history. But what they had failed to think of was once the law passed, anyone could kill anyone.

So, people would go on their noble mission to stop the unjust law and they would be accompanied with death. Every single person who tried ended up six feet in the ground. Eventually it slowed down until less and less people attempted to stop the law and then one day it ceased to be a talked about issue, at least in politics. No one would touch Proposition 485 with a ten-foot pole.

But the politics of it all is not what affected Jeff on a daily basis. Instead, he was plagued with crippling fear that some kid was going to come to school with a gun and start picking everyone off one by one. Or, the more realistic scenario, a bully would beat him to a bloody pulp.

Jeff heard his phone buzz next to his pillow and he turned to see who was texting him this early in the morning. It was Mal. He should have known.

Mal, short for Mallory, was his best friend. They had known each other since they were in third grade and they had been inseparable since. She was the one person he could be completely honest with and vice versa. There were moments when she would put up a wall and keep him out, but he never let that deter him from staying friends with her. Besides, he figured a good friendship was one that could always be improved, and they had continued to improve theirs every step of the way.

Taking his phone, Jeff swiped to the side to display his messages.

Mal [7:30am]: Don't even think about going back to bed.

Jeff [7:31am]: did you read my mind or something?

Mal [7:31am]: Yes. And don't forget you're my ride!

Jeff [7:32am]: yeah yeah I know. imma shower and then ill leave!

Jeff put his phone down and hopped out of his bed, grabbing his already picked out outfit from his dresser. He still liked to pick his clothes out the day before school, it made life easier for him in his groggy morning state. The warm shower was a welcomed friend because fall was just beginning, and the weather already felt like full blown winter, frigid and relentless.

His skin had already started to lighten as the sun stopped shining daily. The summer tan was washing away, and the paleness of his face was beginning to match the rest of his body. With a sigh, he swiped some gel through his medium length black hair, put on deodorant, brushed his teeth quickly, and grabbed his empty backpack off the floor. It was the first day, what teacher would actually assign work?

"Jeff, sweetie." his mom called from the end of the hallway. "You want some breakfast?"

"Nah, I'm good!" he said, heading down the hall while slipping on his black knee length coat. His room was across from his parents, the bathroom the last door at the end of the hallway. Family pictures riddled the walls. "I have to pick up Mal and I'm already running late. I'll text her to bring me a granola bar or something."

"Okay," his mom said, a smile gleaming on her face. His mom had a beautiful smile, but her lips were as thin as a few sheets of paper lying on top of each other. He knew she was self-conscious because she would apply too much lipstick when she went off to work, attempting to make them look fuller. The red lipstick she had on then was so bright and deep that it contrasted dramatically against her pale skin, almost as if she was desperately trying to both detract from her lips but also only attract attention there. Her hair was cut short in the front, bangs across her forehead and shoulder length blonde hair in the back. "Have a great first day of school." Her face hardened as she grabbed his arm as he waltzed past her. "Be careful."

Jeff knew what she meant. Don't piss anyone off who could kill you and if anything happens, run. His parents went over that with him at a young age. His dad sat him down and started the talk with telling him to always vote Democratic and finished it with explaining what the proposition meant for his life. They never went into too much detail, they knew the school would teach him, but they gave him the basics.

"I'll be fine, mom," he said, leaning forward and giving her a kiss on the cheek. "Don't worry about me."

"It's my job to-"

"Worry." Jeff finished the sentence, rolling his eyes. "I know, I know. Love you."

"Love you, too!"

As soon as he opened the front door Jeff shoved his hands in his pocket and buried his neck down, trying to sustain as much warmth as he could. The cold air nipped at his exposed skin and sent an icy cold chill down his spine. Winter was his least favorite time of the year and if the weather was already that cold, he knew it was going to be a long three months. He half jogged to his car that was parked at the curb outside his house, unlocking it and slamming the door behind him. His hands were already held up against his mouth and he breathed into them, trying his best to warm them. He turned his car on and let it heat up as he shot Mal a text letting her know he was leaving.

The heater in his car took a long time to start to make an effect and he was already almost to Mal's when the air started to shift to a more reasonable temperature. At least the defroster worked quickly. Jeff drove down the street and watched as some of the kids were waiting for the bus stop. The memories of scanning the school card and filing into the bulletproof glass protected bus stop before his license filled his thoughts. That was something he did not miss at all.

His parents had bought him the car after he got his license earlier that summer. It was a birthday gift. He had gotten his license the day of his sixteenth birthday and when he came home the car was waiting for him. He always wondered if they would still have given it to him if he had failed the test.

Once he was a block away from Mal's house he texted her telling her to come out. As much as he loved her, he learned quickly that she was never quite on time. Texting her a block away was Jeff's way of making it so that as he pulled up she would be coming out.

With his brakes squeaking, Jeff came to a stop outside of her house and waited. He decided he would text her two blocks away the next time he picked her up.

Her front door opened and she rushed out, a blue scarf wrapped completely around her neck. Her dark hair was pulled up into a bun, her natural coils shining in the light. Since Mal had discovered the art of makeup, not a day that went by that she did not highlight her cheekbones, accentuating their beautiful sharpness against her tawny brown skin. She had on long brown boots, jeans and a giant jacket with UC Berkeley written across it. It was her dream school. Jeff reached over and unlocked the passenger side door, getting ready for the cold air to invade his car.

Mal was quick with getting into the car, unwrapping her scarf and folding it in her lap. She let out a loud huff and turned to Jeff, giving him a flashy smile. She had on a dark raspberry matte lipstick that contrasted against her white teeth. She looked like a model from an ad for toothpaste.

"Ready for school?" she asked, flipping down the visor and checking herself in the mirror.

"Not in the slightest." Jeff drove forward, and a sudden feeling of anxiety filled his stomach.

"You worried about Adrian?"

Jeff shuddered at the name. Adrian. The piece of crap who thought torturing kids every day at school was his job. He had never had a personal encounter with him, but Jeff was well aware of the damage he was capable of. From far away, Adrian looked mean, with a constant scowl on his face and a walk that could only be described as a stalk.

"He's a senior this year," Jeff said, not looking over. "You know what that means, right?"

"He's leaving at the end of the year?" Jeff could hear her trying to be positive and he appreciated it.

"That, yes," he said, sighing. "But that also means he won't ever have to come back. You think he's gonna actually kill someone this year? I mean, he always threatens it, and I've seen him beat kids and stuff, but I don't think he's ever actually killed someone."

"We're just gonna do what we always do," Mal said, reaching over and patting Jeff on the shoulder. "Keep our heads down and survive another year of hell."

"I just have a bad feeling."

"Me too."

The rest of the car ride to school was quiet, except for the beating of Jeff's heart in his eardrums.

CHAPTER 2

The double doors leading into the school swung open as a crowd of kids came rushing out, faces pale. Jeff and Mal were walking up as the group of kids rushed past, shoulder checking Jeff and making his backpack fall to the ground. He cussed under his breath and went to pick it up, Mal beating him to it and handing it to him.

"That's pretty light," Mal said, and Jeff could feel her eyes fixed on him. "Not even a folder, Jeff?"

"No one assigns work on the first day, Mal." Jeff could feel himself getting defensive and he wasn't even sure why; he bit back and stopped at the first step leading up to the school. "I will bring a folder tomorrow, okay? But for now, can we focus."

"Fine. What are we focusing on?" Mal tucked her hands deep in her jacket pocket and burrowed her neck deeper into her scarf.

"Well for starters," Jeff said, starting to walk up the stairs. "We're about to embark on our first day back to school and an entire stampede of kids just barreled by. Now I don't know about you but that seems a little sketchy."

"Why do you think they were running?" Mal's eyes looked worried and they shifted from Jeff's gaze to the front doors leading into the school. "There's no way anything is happening on the first day. Right?"

"I don't know."

Jeff took a step forward and his legs felt like they were made of lead. His eyes were focused on the doors, but his legs did not want to go. Taking in a deep breath of cold air, Jeff took another step, his palms sweating inside his coat pocket. The steps were glistening from the melted snow and Jeff took each step cautiously, making sure not to slip. That would be a great way to start his junior year of high school, with a broken tailbone.

Mal was by his side, walking at the same pace. Jeff wanted to reach out and hold her hand as they walked up together. Not because he liked her or wanted to stay warm but simply because it would make him feel more at ease, even safer. It was a childish sentiment to think that simply holding Mal's hand would somehow make whatever was waiting for them behind the doors better, but it would calm his nerves.

"At the first sight of anything," Mal said, grabbing a hold of Jeff's forearm, "we run."

"Agreed." Jeff said and felt his shoulders ease at her touch. "Are you ready?"

They both stood in front of the doors and Jeff could see someone had painted a pistol with a red x over it. The red contrasted against the old black doors with their chipped paint and frost from the cold. Jeff sighed and took in one last breath before reaching out and placing his hand on the handle.

He thought about how he could turn around at that very moment, not go into the school, not see what was waiting ahead of them, and simply drive home. His parents would most likely understand, and he would just have Mal stay with him because her dad would not understand.

Mal's dad had been struggling with alcohol and his anger ever since his wife died. He blamed the proposition, but he also blamed Mal. At least that is what Jeff believed. Mal never actually said it, but the way she talked about how hostile and mean her father was was all the proof Jeff needed.

Jeff hated her father.

"Okay," he said, not even sure if he was saying it for Mal or to calm himself down. "Here we go."

Jeff pulled on the heavy black doors and they swung open, letting out the heat from the school. The air felt like a sudden wave of relief against his icy bare skin. Mal and Jeff walked into the school and looked around cautiously, ready for any sign for them to leave. The doors slammed loudly behind them and Jeff let out a strangled yelp and jumped. Mal covered her mouth, laughing.

Jeff turned back and glared at her but watched as Mal's face morphed from humor into something that Jeff could only describe as horror. Her smile went slack, and her eyes widened as they watched something behind Jeff. His heart began to pound in his chest and he could feel his knees going weak and he wanted more than anything to leave and not look back but before he could force himself to, his head turned around to see what made Mal react that way.

About fifty feet down the hallway Jeff saw what made Mal's expression change; down the long stretch of blue lockers, Jeff could see a boy slamming another boy into the lockers and then throwing him across so that he barreled into another set of them, falling. The boy crumpled in on himself on the floor and Jeff could see he was small, scrawny. The other boy had broad shoulders and from what Jeff could see was much taller than the other.

There was a moment where Jeff felt paralyzed and couldn't move as he watched the boy stalk forward and kick the other one in the face. Jeff recognized the bigger guy as he shifted and slammed his foot back down on the other kid. Adrian.

He should have known the minute he saw a fight that Adrian would be the one involved. Not knowing if he should help or turn a blind eye, Jeff turned to see Mal, her hands cupped over her mouth as she too watched in horror.

"What do we do?" Jeff asked, feeling his voice come out frantic and high pitched.

"I don't...I don't know!" Mal's eyes were wider than Jeff had ever seen them, her enlarged pupils taking over the almond brown of her eyes and turning them black.

Jeff wanted to run up and yell for Adrian to stop, to get off the kid and leave him alone, but he knew how that would end. Adrian was a senior and had always scared Jeff, but now that he was the top dog of school, Jeff had a feeling things were going to get much worse.

"Help!" The boy shrieked, his voice high and cracking. Most likely a freshman, Jeff thought.

Adrian kneeled down and shoved his hand against the boy's throat. Jeff could hear a strangled off cry as the boy's head smashed against the metal locker, a bang echoing down the hallway.

He watched in muted horror as Adrian leaned forward and put his mouth next to the boy's ear, seemingly whispering something. Then, without warning, Adrian yanked a knife out of his jacket pocket and shoved it directly into the kid's chest.

Mal let out a shriek and Jeff felt his stomach twist in knots, causing him to dry heave. If he had eaten that morning it would have been expelled from his body. Adrian turned his attention to Jeff and Mal, a vile grin stretched across his face.

Adrian wiped his hand across his forehead, moving the strands of hair that had fallen forward during the attack and Jeff could see a streak of blood stretch across his forehead. Before he had a minute to think, Jeff grabbed Mal's hand and began to run.

Jeff could hear Mal's footsteps behind him as he ran down the school's corridor, turning and twisting the further they ran. His legs were burning, and his lungs felt like they were on fire, but he didn't stop. The other hallways were full of students so Jeff and Mal were pushing their way through, too scared to look back and see if Adrian was behind them.

As Jeff reared a corner he slammed into a tall and plump man; Mr. Shan, his social justice teacher. With his usual colorful argyle vest atop a maroon button up, he pushed his glasses up and smiled.

"Jeff, Mal," Mr. Shan said, his voice cool and calm as always. Jeff had never seen Mr. Shan raise his voice even when he was stopping a fight in school. "Why do you guys look like you saw a ghost?"

"Well," Jeff started but hadn't yet caught his breath. "It's kind of a long story and I don't think we should talk about it here." Jeff's eyes were darting around, checking to see if Adrian was coming towards them. "Or ever, really. Yeah. It's nothing. Come on, Mal." Jeff reached out and grabbed Mal's hand and pulled her forward with him.

Mal pulled her hand away from his and said, "what the hell?"

"What?" Jeff did not stop and neither did Mal. They kept up a consistently quick pace, maneuvering around students.

"Why didn't you tell Mr. Shan?" Jeff could hear the frustration rising in her voice. "I mean really, Jeff? He could have helped us!"

"Helped us how?" Jeff stopped dead in his tracks and pivoted around, face to face with Mal. "We tell Mr. Shan what we saw and what? Adrian gets expelled? You think someone who is willing to kill at *school* isn't going to come back and exact some sort of revenge on the two idiots who turned him in? If we tell we're as good as dead."

"Well he could have at least hid us in his classroom!" Jeff could see in Mal's eyes that she knew he was right, and knowing Mal, she didn't want to admit this. Because admitting Jeff was right would be admitting that they were sitting ducks waiting to be killed.

"Listen," Jeff whispered, leaning in. "Maybe Adrian didn't see our faces, okay? It doesn't look like he followed us and honestly, he probably had bigger things to deal with, like killing someone. So, here's what we do." Jeff just wanted this to be another nightmare that he would wake up from at any minute, but he knew it wasn't, knew this wasn't going to end with him waking up in his bed. "We keep our heads down like we always do. We tell no one what we saw."

"Okay," Mal said, nodding along to the plan.

"It's messed up, I know, but we have to survive. And if we tell anyone and it gets around, then Adrian will know it was us." Jeff's entire body was shaking from adrenaline and he could see Mal's legs were shaking.

"So, what do we do now? Go home?" Mal was gnawing at her nails and Jeff wish he knew how to ease her mind.

"No." Jeff put his hand on her shoulder and let out a sigh. "We go to class and pretend everything is fine."

CHAPTER 3

The rest of the school day was a blur. Jeff went to each class and listened to his teachers explain what the expectations were for the classes, but it was all background noise. The only thing he could bring himself to focus on was Adrian. Adrian and that poor kid. He had witnessed an innocent boy getting murdered and he had done nothing. Jeff felt like a coward.

Even as he drove Mal home he didn't say much. A few nods here and there, and some one worded responses, but no conversation. Mal didn't talk much either. He assumed she was also replaying the image of the kid being beaten and stabbed, over and over again. Every time Jeff closed his eyes, the images of the boy's helpless face would flash in his mind.

How old was the boy? What did he do to make Adrian *that* mad? Jeff wished he could go back and stop it, go back and tell the kid to run, do anything to help. It was no use though. He had witnessed a murder, not his first, but still just as disturbing.

When he was ten years old he had seen a man shoot another man in the parking lot of a grocery store. The bang was so loud that Jeff had latched onto his mom, who instinctively wrapped him in her arms to shield him.

The shooter had only been a few feet away from them and Jeff remembered looking up into his eyes and seeing nothing but anger. The man had dark brown eyes, almost black, and his mouth was curled into a vicious smile. He was happy with what he had done.

Jeff had watched as the other man, who looked much younger, fell to the ground clutching his chest as blood began to pour out in between his fingers and stain his white button up. The blood was so vibrant against the white and Jeff and his mother were frozen in terror. He could feel her legs shaking against him and he wanted nothing more than to get in the car and leave, but the man turned to them both and cocked his head.

"Please," his mom had said. "I won't say anything."

"So, what if you do," the man said, sticking the gun into the back of his pants. "It's legal, remember?"

And with that he strode towards the entrance of the grocery store as if nothing had occurred. Jeff's mom let out a strangled cry and fell to the floor, holding onto him tighter than ever before and wept into his shoulder. She kept repeating that it was okay and that they would be too, but Jeff knew nothing was okay about that situation.

Even at ten he knew how utterly wrong it all was — the murder *and* the law — and yet they could do nothing about it. An ambulance would come and take the body and the family would be notified, not even knowing who had killed their son or father or husband. It didn't matter at that point because all that remained of him was his crumple body, lying in a pool of blood.

Jeff waved as Mal walked into her house and as soon as she was out of sight he yelled, banging his fists into his steering wheel. He had to let his emotions out before he went home. There was no way he was going to tell his parents about what happened. They would make him be home schooled and although it had seemed like a nice idea before, he was not about to leave Mal alone at school.

As he pulled up into the driveway, Jeff saw that his dad's car was not in the driveway and neither was his mom's. A rush of relief came over him. At least now he would be able to go inside, take a hot shower and calm down. His entire body felt like a wooden board, stiff. He opened up his car door and stepped out, turning back to grab his backpack from his passenger side. As he turned around there was a bang, and someone was in front of him yelling "boo!"

Jeff yelped and dropped his backpack, falling against the car, his knees buckling from fear as his heart plummeted to his stomach.

"Whoa there," Marc, Jeff's boyfriend, said. "I thought it would be funny to scare you. Sorry."

"Jesus!" Jeff pulled himself up and tried to catch his breath. "Don't do that."

"All right, I won't." Marc reached for Jeff's bag and gave him a kiss on the cheek. "Rough first day back?"

"You have no idea." Jeff started walking towards his front door; Marc followed. "I saw a kid get killed."

"Damn," Marc said, "did you know them?"

"No." Jeff opened the front door and the heater had been left on. It felt amazing.

Marc closed the door behind him and grabbed Jeff by the arm, pulling him in close.

"Anything I can do to make it better?" Marc wrapped his arms over Jeff's shoulder and kissed him. Marc's lips were soft and never chapped, which Jeff loved because the cold weather always made his lips chapped.

"Thanks," Jeff said, pulling away as he rested his head on Marc's shoulder. "It was awful."

"I bet."

Jeff had only known Marc for a little over a month. They had met during summer. Marc was working at the kiosk at the mall that sold phone covers and had flagged Jeff down, convincing him that he not only needed a screen protector, but his number. Jeff couldn't resist Marc's smile. His teeth were perfectly straight and white, which Marc had told him before, "four years of braces better pay off."

Marc was twenty-four and had already graduated college. He was a little taller than Jeff and had light brown hair that was buzzed on the sides and long in the middle. He wore it in a top knot, although sometimes he would let it loose, making sure to comb it over to one side.

Jeff was not too sure how his parents would react to this, so he hadn't told them about Marc just yet. Besides, what was the rush?

They hadn't known each other that long and it was not like they were planning on flaunting their relationship. Murder may had been legal, but statutory rape was still a thing. Although, Marc was pushy on the subject of meeting his parents. He would come over unannounced, like he had just done, and it would make Jeff worried that his parents would see.

But with everything that had happened that day and the fact that his parents were not home, he was happy that Marc was there. It somehow made him feel safe.

Jeff walked Marc to his room because he had never been in the house yet. As soon as Jeff let him in, Marc started walking around and exploring the bedroom. It was pretty plain as far as rooms can go. The bed was in the middle and directly across from it, next to the door, was his dresser with a tv on top of it. There was a walk-in closet at the other end of the room and a wide window that had a lovely view of the driveway. He had a work desk with his laptop on it which he made sure to face away from the door incase his mom walked in when he was exploring areas of the internet that his mom would deem perverted.

"No posters?" Marc asked, eyeing the walls. "How… not what I expected."

"Well, I'm not that interesting." Jeff sat down on the edge of his bed and watched as Marc kept looking around. It felt like he was being judged solely on his room's appearance.

"I highly doubt that," Marc said, sitting down next to him on the bed. "You were interesting enough to catch my eye."

"And here I was thinking all along it was my phone you wanted."

"I want much more than your phone." Marc's eyes softened. "You're pretty pale, you sure you're okay?"

"Oh, that?" Jeff said, pulling at his skin on his forearm. "I just become the color of the snow during winter, nothing to do with the events of today, simply life."

"Ah, I see," Marc said, a devilishly handsome grin rising on his face. "I don't have to worry about that," he said, seductively running his hands down his body. "My beautiful brown skin stays like this through the blazing sunny days, and through the dark winters."

"I just burn in the summer and then whiten up in the winter."

"It's cute," he said, chuckling.

"You're cute."

Marc smirked and pushed Jeff back on the bed, lying on top of him. "You think your parents will think I'm cute?"

"This again?" Jeff said. It wasn't that Jeff was never planning on introducing his parents to Marc, but the constant questioning of it was a nuisance. He attempted to sit up, but Marc wouldn't let him. "Seriously, Marc? Can we not do this?"

"I just don't get it." Marc's eyes were locked on Jeff's. "Just tell your parents you're gay and we can be together."

"I'm bi," Jeff said, his voice coming out coldly. "I've told you that. Plus, my parents know I'm bi. I told them a while ago."

"Then why haven't you told them about me?" Marc leaned forward and kissed Jeff's neck.

Jeff wanted to get up and not have this conversation. He was not in the mood. Today had been long enough and Marc was not helping. All Jeff wanted to do was go shower off how filthy he felt after witnessing the murder and just be left alone. But he knew if he told Marc that, then Marc would try to go in the shower with him and Jeff did not want to take their relationship to that level. Not because he was worried about losing his virginity to the right person, but because he wasn't sure if he wanted to stay with Marc much longer. And if sex was added into the relationship it would just make it more complicated.

"You're twenty-four," Jeff said matter-of-factly. "And I'm underage. My parents, no matter how open minded, won't go for that."

"Okay," Marc said, sounding cautious. "Well then, can you at least just admit you're gay? I mean that's a good first step."

"I'm not gay, though," Jeff said, this time pushing Marc off him and sitting up. "I'm bi."

"Oh, come on," Marc said, standing up and glaring down at him. "I said the same thing when I came out. That way I wouldn't have to throw away the chances of having a 'normal' life, but trust me, you'll feel better once you admit it."

Jeff could feel his anger starting to rise and he wanted to stand up and yell in Marc's face and shake him and get his point across, but instead he took a deep breath and gnawed at his lower lip.

"Bisexuality is real," Jeff said, and he could hear his voice coming out as if he was talking to a child. He could see by Marc's face that he wasn't amused. "People can like both genders. In fact, there is even something called pansexual. I'm surprised you, being as you're older than me, don't know this."

Marc was not smiling, in fact, he looked pissed off. His nostrils were flaring as he stepped forward, pushing Jeff back on the bed and wrapping one of his hands around Jeff's neck.

"Don't be a smartass," Marc whispered in his ear. "It isn't cute."

"Well neither is you trying to say I'm lying about who I am." Jeff didn't move an inch. He wanted to swat Marc's hand away from his neck, but Marc's grip was actually pretty tight. "Can you let go, please."

"Isn't it funny," Marc said, as his eyes surveyed over Jeff's body, his grip loosening, just a little. "I can end up in jail for being with you and consensually fucking you and yet if I murdered you right now, I would walk free."

A chill shot down Jeff's spine and a pang of terror made his heart beat as if he had just run a mile. Marc's eyes were still looking him up and down and his hand was still wrapped around his neck. Jeff was about to push him off when Marc got off of him and strode to the window.

"Sorry," he said, bowing his head into his neck. "It's just so dumb to me that our relationship can end with me going to prison, but Joe Shmo down the block can kill some innocent person and walk away."

"Life's unfair." Jeff said quietly, not sure if he even said it loud enough for Marc to hear. "I still don't understand how the law even passed? It just doesn't make sense to me."

"Shit, your parents are home," Marc said, stepping away from the window. "I should go." He gave Jeff and quick kiss and walked to the bedroom door, turning back around. "Oh, and murder has always been legal. You just needed to be a cop before Prop 485 to get away with it."

And with that Marc was gone, leaving Jeff to mull over what he meant by that.

CHAPTER 4

The words repeated in Jeff's mind like a mantra. "You just needed to be a cop." What did Marc mean by that? It had to mean something. Unless Marc just said it to make Jeff obsess over it in the hopes he would move past the creepiness of Marc holding him down on the bed. Either way, Jeff needed to know.

It was midnight and Jeff was supposed to be asleep but with everything that had happened, and the cryptic way Marc left, Jeff got out of bed and went to his desk, opening up his laptop and immediately dimming the brightness.

"Okay," he said to himself. "Time to figure it out."

Jeff clicked open the internet and waited for it to fully load, then typed his question into the search engine.

"Was police brutality the reason for Prop 485?"

There were over two hundred thousand results. He clicked the first article and began to read.

There are no definitive answers as to how Proposition 485 was passed. There are conspiracy theories commenting that congress was blackmailed into it. There is a conspiracy theory that claims when Barack Obama became president, that was the start, but here at LogicalNews.com, we find that theory to be overwhelmingly popular among racists. But one thing is for certain, in the years leading up to its passing, police brutality was at an all-time high. New bills were being drafted to continue to marginalize groups of people, disproportionately black Americans. Laws that began to bend the definition of murder, making it okay to 'accidentally' murder a protester and not get any jail-time. Laws that were founded solely to continue the rampant corruption and racist ideologies that plagued Washington.

It was not the rich who were affected though, and the new laws made it even easier for police to kill with impunity. More and more news stories arose of police misconduct, brutality, and even complete videos detailing accounts of murders. The 2016 election did not help the problem. Instead it fanned the flames to the society we know today.

In order to fully understand, we broke down a timeline:

1. *Trump is elected President of The United States (before its new name, America United).*
2. *With the lowest approval rating in history, along with being the vile, racist, hateful, and downright treasonous man he was,*

the public was outraged after Congress did nothing to impeach him.

3. *As more and more people began to demonstrate their first amendment right, police killings began to rise, and the Department of Justice turned a blind eye.*

4. *By 2018 the public was outraged, and the Trump regime had begun to make more and more lax laws about murder and what police had the right to do.*

5. *By 2020 when Trump was voted back into office and the country shifted to only federal law and no more state law, the police violence was an epidemic.*

6. *Cut to 2024 when Prop 485 became legal.*

7. *The belief still is that Russia hacked into the election that year and changed the votes.*

8. *There was overwhelming evidence, just like in the 2016 election, and just like then the Government did nothing.*

9. *The public was terrified and after the law nothing was the same.*

10. *Police brutality is not uncommon today either, it just is easier to clean up when you can literally blame anyone for murder now.*

Jeff felt sick, physically sick. The fact that Marc had not been lying also made him worry just how ignorant he was about the world he lived in. Closing his laptop, the darkness engulfed his very being. He became the darkness.

Jeff [12:09am]: I cant sleep. I just googled about police and how it basically caused prop 485 I cant believe it!

Marc [12:10am]: Yeah it's pretty fucked up. But, hey, look at the bright side, now you can kill people! :)

Jeff [12:12am]: ha ha not funny. I would never kill someone.

Marc [12:15am]: Why not? Sometimes you have to.

Jeff [12:16am]: ive gone 16 almost 17 years without killing anyone I think I can make it a lifetime. have you ever killed anyone?

Jeff sat still and watched his cell phone and waited for it to light up with a reply from Marc hopefully saying that he had never killed anyone, but after ten minutes, he realized he was not going to get a reply. His stomach tightened, and his mind was pole vaulting from one thought to the next, hoping his boyfriend had just fallen asleep and was not evading the question.

His thoughts were disrupted with the sound of an ambulance siren in the distance. Knowing better, all Jeff could think was that someone had died. While he was sitting in his room, researching on his laptop, someone had been getting murdered. Who is to say it was not a child or an innocent person, and now Jeff's mind went straight to the police. *Were the police responsible for the death that most likely just occurred?*

CHAPTER 5

The next morning Jeff was awake before his alarm clock. All night his mind had been mulling over the array of information that he had absorbed. When he finally did fall asleep he would find himself waking up every thirty minutes unable to pinpoint the exact reason. Part of him believed it was because his eyes had just been opened to the injustices that plagued the country, but somewhere deeper he knew that was not quite it. He already knew how awful the world was first hand, everyone in the country knew. Murder cannot be legal unless the society it abounds in is okay with the death of individuals on a national scale.

Jeff did not move from his bed for quite a while. He sent Mal a quick text letting her know he would be late to get her and then he stared up at his ceiling. His mind was racing but the main thought that found its way down to his stomach and twisted it around was Marc not replying to his text. As juvenile as that felt, Jeff could not deny himself the anxiety of wondering if his boyfriend had killed before. The thought alone sent a chill down his spine, but he was not entirely sure if it would actually affect his outlook on Marc.

Admittedly, Jeff knew eventually the older he got the more people he would meet who have murdered. It was inevitable. The issue Jeff was having was if he was ready to accept that he was getting to the age where life and death walked hand in hand, and if he was willing to accept Marc after hearing his answer. Marc was Jeff's first boyfriend and it wasn't that he was afraid of being with someone who killed, he was afraid that he could end up numb to it all.

Jeff forced himself out of bed and got ready. His parents were both in the kitchen eating breakfast — his mom had her usual of toast and oatmeal while his dad "watched his cholesterol" with Cheerios — and waved for him to come over.

The dining room table had a perfect view of the front door which made it nearly impossible for Jeff to get out without talking to his parents.

"How was your first day back?" His father asked while blowing on his coffee.

"It was fine," Jeff said, not daring to tell them about the murder he witnessed the prior day.

"Nothing happened?" The tone in his father's voice hinted that he wanted Jeff to admit to something, but there was no sure way of knowing what exactly it was.

His father had a permanent crease across his forehead which matched his crow's feet that were becoming more and more defined with every year. With a still stare and pursed lips, his father stared at Jeff, his sea green eyes not hinting at anything. The only thing that seemed slightly off was that his cheeks were slightly more red than usual.

"No. It was pretty uneventful. But listen, I'm running late, and I have to go."

"Here," his father said, pulling out a small object and placing it on the table. "Keep this in your car. I know you can't bring weapons onto school, but that doesn't mean you shouldn't have protection around."

Jeff walked to the table and looked down at the object. It was a navy-blue pocket knife. Picking it up, Jeff flicked the blade out. It was not a big knife which meant he would be able to hide it easily, and with knowing Adrian saw him yesterday, the thought of having a knife on him brought a sense of calming.

"Thanks," Jeff said, leaning forward and giving his mom a kiss on the cheek. "I hope I don't ever need to use this." Jeff fiddled with the closed knife in his palms.

"Us too, sweetie." His mom closed her hands over his, covering the knife. "Be safe, okay?"

"I will." Jeff could see the stress in his parents' eyes. They found out about the previous day, they had to have. His father had never once told him to bring a weapon to school and his mother was first to advocate for peaceful ways out of situations. The school must have called them If Jeff played it like he didn't know maybe they would not badger him about it. "I promise I'll be safe."

With one last nod and a shove of the knife into his pocket, Jeff made his way to the front door. He knew he could technically bring the knife onto school grounds. Unlike public school which was riddled with police, metal detectors, and locker checks weekly, the private school Jeff's parents sent him to was much laxer in their approach. Sure, they had locker checks once a week, but police were not patrolling the halls, and metal detectors had not been set up, yet. Instead, beautiful Oak Valley Academy employed five security guards to monitor the entirety of the school. Jeff understood there had never been an incident — until the day before — but he still found it strange just *how* laid back the school's approach was to the law.

The academy, however, did have a waitlist that parents were willing to kill for, possibly even had. The rumors surrounding how students got into the academy seemed farfetched to Jeff when he first was accepted, but the more aware he became the more questionable everything around him became.

He could feel the knife in his pocket and as he pulled up to Mal's house, he still did not know if he was going to bring it into the school with him. The idea of having to use it on Adrian was enough to send a chill down his spine, but he also knew that Adrian was now the first kid at Oak Valley to kill another student, and faculty was not going to simply move on. As Jeff's mind began to contemplate all that could go wrong, he did not see as Mal walked up to car and yanked open the door. Jeff gasped, and his right hand collided with his chest in fear.

"Jesus," he said, sighing. "You scared me."

"Did I?" Mal laughed, playfully bringing her right hand up to her chest and her left hand to her forehead.

"Oh, wow, I didn't know I was checking my temperature, too."

"Oh, you didn't?" Mal grinned, shutting the car door. "Good thing I'm here to show you since you don't seem to have control of your arms."

"Good thing," Jeff said, shifting the gear to drive. "It's also a good thing the guy with no control of his arms is the one driving."

"Oh, totally," Mal continued. "Can you imagine if I drove? We wouldn't have to worry about *if* we're going to make it to school."

"Yeah," Jeff said, turning and making eye contact. "We'd just have to worry if we'll make it out of school."

"Jeff," Mal said, "don't joke."

"It's not a joke."

The academy seemed quiet. No one was out in front, the doors to enter were closed like they had been yesterday. Jeff was half expecting a group of teenagers to come barreling out in fear, but nothing happened. Maybe the administration was simply trying to keep the murder out of the public's eye. It would not surprise Jeff. Every school had a reputation, he knew that, and Oak Valley was known to be the safest school to send children to. The idea of a freshman being stabbed to death could potentially ruin the name that administration had worked so hard to sell.

Mal opened up the door into the school and Jeff felt his jaw drop. The inside was swarming with security guards: some had guns, others simply had portable metal detectors, but every single one wore a solemn look on their face.

"Shit," Jeff said, realizing the knife was still in his pants.

"I guess they're taking it seriously," Mal said.

"I have a knife."

"What?" Mal's voice was sharp and quick.

She grabbed Jeff harshly by his inner arm and he winced as her purple nails dug into his skin. Jeff saw a stocky, bald security guard starting to walk over to the two of them. The man did not have a gun, at least from what Jeff could see, but Jeff could see there was a taser and a baton attached to his belt. The bald man's shirt seemed a little too tight and his head glistened, reflecting the luminous fluorescent lighting. Jeff's chest tightened along with Mal's grip.

"Go," Mal said under her breath, "now."

With ease, Mal led the way, her hand — or better yet, talon — did not cease in its relentless piercing of flesh. Jeff was almost positive he was bleeding but knew he couldn't react. He had to put on his best poker face, which was extremely hard. One of his most defining qualities was his complete lack of control over his reactionary facial expressions.

Jeff attempted to nonchalantly pivot and see if the security guard was following the two of them. The man's head was a beacon for Jeff to see, and a beacon that was closer than before.

"What are we gonna do?" Jeff whispered.

"Oh, I don't know," Mal said, shifting her hand so it twisted in Jeff's skin. "Not bring a fucking knife to school."

"Jeff! Mal!" Mr. Shan exclaimed, standing in front of the two in the hallway. "Crazy stuff, right?"

"Yeah," Jeff said, looking back one more time and seeing the guard distracted with another student. "Can we talk to you in your class?"

"Sure," Mr. Shan said, placing a hand on Jeff and Mal's shoulder. "It's all a bit surreal."

"Totally," Mal said, letting go of Jeff's arm. She turned her gaze and glared at Jeff. "Never know who might have an agenda, right, Jeff?"

Mr. Shan nodded and turned around walking towards his classroom. Jeff felt his face heat up and he turned to Mal, rolling his eyes. Without another word the two of them followed Mr. Shan down the crowded hallway.

Jeff counted at least seven guards as he walked across the campus to Mr. Shan's classroom. He had never seen so much security in Oak Valley, let alone any school he had gone to. In fact, Jeff had only ever gone to private schools his entire life, and he had never really had to witness anything other than a few fights here and there. Was this going to be how the rest of the year would go? No trust. Being forced to deal with daily checks, knowing that every security guard would be on high alert. Had his entire educational platform shifted?

"Oh, no," Mr. Shan said, stopping and pivoting to face the two. "I just remembered that I have a staff meeting about what happened. What a tragedy."

"Yeah, the way he was stabbed like that," Jeff said, flashbacks of witnessing the murder came flashing through his conscious.

"How did you know that?" Mr. Shan asked. He was taller than Jeff and had a perfectly round belly that made him look like a cartoon character. A copper flat top was where Jeff's eyes would go to until Mr. Shan would talk and then he would stare at his luminescent smile. His briefcase strap rested on his left shoulder and crossed his chest. Jeff watched as his glasses rose with his scrunched nose and furrowed brow.

"What?" Jeff could hear his voice as it quavered.

"You said he was stabbed. How do you know that?"

"Mr. Shan," Mal said, her voice coming off condescending. "Do you know how fast information travels? I heard it from some girl who got a text from her boyfriend because his dad works for the city."

"Oh," Mr. Shan said, nodding and cocking his head still trying to wrap his head around it.

"Yeah," Jeff said, letting out a — hopefully realistic — chuckle. "It's basically like we knew before the knife even got pulled out."

"Jeff!" Mal elbowed him in the side. "That's not funny."

"Sorry," Jeff said, making eye contact with Mal and trying his best to let her know he realized how badly that came out.

"Well," Mr. Shan said, half smiling, but also looking disheartened. "You two can still wait in my class, if you want?"

45

"Yes, please," Jeff said. "I'd feel safer."

"Of course," Mr. Shan nodded. "I'll let you guys in and then I'll get to my meeting. Don't do anything devious while I'm out."

"Mr. Shan," Mal said, resting her hand on his shoulder. "Even if we wanted to, we have you first period."

Jeff watched as she winked and grinned, and Jeff could not help but grin himself. Mal was always good at defusing situations. If it had just been him he would have been suspended, possibly expelled, because he would have panicked and gotten caught with the knife.

He needed to get rid of it.

Mr. Shan unlocked his classroom, nodding to both of them as they entered. The room was set up in an unconventional kind of way. The desks were put in a circle around the classroom, with Mr. Shan's seat towards the top of the circle, next to the whiteboard. There were a multitude of inspirational posters that littered almost every visible space along the walls. Directly across from the entrance, the wall had windows, finding home to a view of the track field.

Every day there was an inspirational quote on the board. Jeff turned to see what it said that day. Written on the board in cursive the quote read: *The life of the dead is placed in the memory of the living - Marcus Tullius Cicero.*

Jeff sighed.

"What the hell, Jeff," Mal intersected the silence. She was standing across the classroom, next to the windows, her right hand on her hip. "Are you trying to get expelled?"

"No," Jeff said, leaning against the board. "My dad gave it to me and I forgot, okay? Can you get off my back?"

"Get off your back?" Mal stepped forward with an incredulous look — that bordered on anger — plastered on her face. He had only seen that side a few times, and never directed at him. It felt bizarre that the expression he had always attributed to people being rude to Mal was now being used on him. "Are you joking, Jeff? Please tell me you're kidding."

"Wrong word choice," Jeff sighed, running his hands through his hair. "But, I mean, we didn't get caught."

"You mean *you* didn't get caught." Her voice was haughty as it came out.

"Mal, why are you getting so worked up about this?" Jeff knew he had screwed up, but it was a mistake. There had to be something else going on, because this sudden burst of disdainful feelings worried Jeff.

"Listen," Mal said, taking a deep breath and holding her hands up to her mouth like a prayer. "Your dad gave you the knife, right?"

Jeff nodded and waited for her to continue.

"Well," Mal walked to a chair and sat down. "My dad isn't like yours, Jeff."

"I know." Jeff had seen the bruises, known when she wasn't actually sick, and he hated that there was nothing he could do. Even if he called Child Protective Services, there was a waitlist for a worker to come to your house. Jeff had researched it when he had first seen the bruises. Even if he was able to get someone to come out, all that would do was force Mal into the system, and as disturbing as it was, Mal was better off with her father. "I get it."

"No," her voice rose, "you don't. You don't get it, Jeff, and that's fine, it is. I don't expect you to get it. But, I do need you to understand this. If my dad finds out about yesterday and finds out that I saw it, well, uh, he's going to be mad. To say the least."

"I'm sorry, okay?" Jeff pushed himself from leaning against the board and stepped forward, jokingly putting his hands up to surrender; Mal laughed. "Listen, I'm going to get rid of the knife, okay."

"Just leave it in your car," Mal said. "That way if, God forbid, Adrian ever confronts us, you can still have some form of access to it."

"Yeah," Jeff said, agreeing without an actual plan of carrying through. Sure, the idea of having a knife in his car seemed appealing, but Jeff knew there would be no way, if it ever were to happen, that he could run, get away from an attack, make it to his car, and get the knife in time. It was a death sentence.

He needed to hide the knife somewhere he could get to it. He needed to feel safe.

CHAPTER 6

Jeff and Mal sat next to each other as the rest of the class began to funnel in. The faces of most students seemed to be a mixture of fear and annoyance. Jeff could hear whispers about what had happened as they began to fill the silence of the classroom. Something deep inside him wanted to let them know what actually happened, not for any moral reason, but rather for the attention. He knew it was pathetic, but the thought of knowing something the entire school wanted in on was tempting. The name Adrian came out of someone's mouth to Jeff's right, and simply hearing it caused his face to heat up.

Telling everyone was not an option.

Mr. Shan was the last to rush into the room, his sneakers squeaking against the checkered — white and blue — tiled floor. Jeff was eager to start class. After all, he was a junior, and he knew what that meant. At this stage in his high school academia he would now be able to learn about Proposition 485.

An entire period dedicated to discussing the violence, political views, and reasons why the proposition even became a ballot, and how the country survived. It was the most exciting aspect of junior year, to Jeff.

"Hello, class," Mr. Shan said, pulling his briefcase off his shoulder, and sitting down in his chair. He reached in and pulled out a three-ring binder that read on the cover: Sociology/Social Justice. "Who knows what we learn in the first week of this year?"

Before anyone else could, Jeff's hand rocketed into the air. Mr. Shan nodded at him and Jeff said, "we learn about Prop. 485."

"Precisely." Mr. Shan licked his thumb and began to flick through a stack of papers, counting. "We are going to learn," he licked his thumb again and continued, "the history of the most infamous proposition. The exact reason most of you," he looked up, "have gloomy faces today."

Mal leaned to her left and whispered to Jeff. "How are we doing better than some people?"

Jeff shrugged and looked around, taking a quick survey of the room. There were a lot of empty seats in between his classmates, who, if Jeff didn't know any better, looked like they had seen it happen themselves. There was a guy directly across from Jeff in the circle who would not stop bouncing his leg up and down while biting at his nails. A girl a few seats over to him had glossy eyes as if she had been crying all night. Jeff scoffed and turned back to Mr. Shan.

"The teacher's union and I fought extremely hard to be able to teach this which is why we only have one day to cover it. If I had my choice we would study it for an entire semester, but of course it's not up to me." Mr. Shan half smirked and finished counting his papers.

"What caused it?" Jeff said, forgetting to raise his hand.

"I would love to discuss that with you," Mr. Shan said, splitting the pile of papers in half and handing one half to each student on his side. "But like I said, we fought long and hard for this, so we have to do it right. I just passed around permission slips that your parents need to sign and return back to me by Thursday. Then," Mr. Shan made eye contact with Jeff. "I will be able to answer all your questions."

The girl next to Jeff handed him the permission slips and he took one, passing it to Mal. The slip read that over the course of the period, the students would possibly be exposed to talks of violence and other triggering content. Due to the nature of the discussion, it was entirely up the parents' discretion if their child would be able to participate and attend the course material. Underneath all of the topics it could open up to, there was a note saying the students would not be tested on the material.

Jeff figured that was an incentive for parents who did not feel comfortable but were also worried they would miss out on information for a test.

"I don't think my dad is going to sign this," Mal said as she looked over the permission slip. "I know he can be an ass sometimes but he's still my dad and he wants to protect me."

"Don't you think being knowledgeable of the world you live in is protection?" Jeff said, annoyed at the thought of Mal missing out on an important discussion about the world they're blindly living in, or at least Jeff is.

The action from earlier in the day had distracted him, but now his mind decided to trudge up the question left unanswered by Marc. Had he killed anyone?

"I guess," Mal said, "but my dad isn't the type to change his mind."

"Just forge it."

Mr. Shan audibly cleared his throat, causing Jeff to shift in his seat and divert his attention back to his teacher, who raised an eyebrow at him. Jeff lipped sorry and sunk into his seat while Mr. Shan began explaining what exactly they were going to be learning that day.

The bell rang, and first period was over. Jeff knew that after third period, he would end up going to first lunch, which Mal did not have. They actually only had the first three courses together. They had tried their best to fit their schedules together, but freshmen year had lent to part of the issue when Jeff was put in Health while Mal was placed in Art. That difference in one class shifted their schedule immensely due to the fact that all the students needed to take Health by the end of their junior year.

Jeff wished they had never been split up in freshmen year because then they would be able to have their classes together.

Before getting up from his seat, Jeff turned behind him where a bookshelf was against the back wall of the classroom. Without thinking it through, he slipped his hand into his jeans pocket, hid the knife under his jacket sleeve, and then slipped it in between two encyclopedias. He knew from experience that no one even took a double look at encyclopedias. Why would they when all the information was online?

As they shuffled through the crowded school hallways, Jeff was keenly aware of his surroundings, not diverting his attention from trying to spot Adrian. The hall was filled with the noise of slamming lockers, shoes squeaking against the tile, mixed with the smell of hundreds of wet sneakers. Besides the addition of security guards, Jeff could not see anything out of the ordinary, or Adrian lurking.

As he looked over he could see that Mal, too, was looking around them. There was no going back to being ghosts in the hallway if Adrian really had seen them. Jeff knew that eventually they would be confronted about it. He just prayed that Adrian would understand and leave them alone.

He did not want to fight.

Jeff eyed the clock at the head of the classroom. His backpack was already zipped up, his folder put away, and his feet rapidly tapped against the floor as his gaze became fixated on the second-hand ticking. Doing a countdown in his head, Jeff tried his best to time the bell with exactly when he expected. With closed eyes, Jeff counted down from five, reaching the end only to be unaccompanied by the bell. He huffed and opened his eyes, turning to see if he was the only one ready to go.

Jeff's eyes shifted to the side and he peered over at the girl sitting next to him. She had three different colored pens on her desk, her notebook was still out, and he was able to hear her pen scribbling on the paper. *What could she possibly be taking notes on?*

"...and that's why the formula is going to be very important for the test." Jeff caught the last sentence and began to reach into his bag to copy the formula down when the bell rang, and his teacher started erasing the board.

"Shit," he mumbled to himself.

The girl next to him closed her binder and placed all of her pens into a carrying case — which was home to a plethora of colorful drawings — before gliding out of her seat and walking away. Jeff was not sure why he didn't ask her for her notes, but instead he stood up and sighed, looking forward and seeing the entire board cleaned.

"Mr. Braen," the teacher said as Jeff walked by. "You seemed out of it, are you okay?"

"I'm fine," Jeff said, nodding his head and walking out before the conversation could continue.

As he stepped into the hallway his eyes locked with the blackness of Adrian's. His heart felt like someone punched it as it stopped pumping blood for a second before continuing at a quicker rate. Wiping his palms on his pants, Jeff forced his gaze down and focused on his breathing. He knew Adrian must have seen his reaction: the blood draining from his cheeks, his eyes widening, while his mouth pursed up. There was no maneuvering his way out of this, and Adrian took a step towards him.

Jeff's mouth went dry and his lips felt like they were being glued together. His stomach instantly pulled taut and made him want to puke right then. He felt his gag reflex kick in and held his lips tight together, forcing down the bile that rose and burned his esophagus.

"Hey," Adrian said, his voice oozed with confidence as he stood directly in Jeff's path. "So, I think we need to talk."

Jeff stood still and felt his lips twitch into a half smirk as a fearful chuckle escaped his mouth. "About what?" he asked.

"Events," Adrian said, leaning in until his mouth was inches from Jeff's ear. "I know you're on lunch, and I know you know what I mean."

Jeff felt his knees begin to shake, but he forced himself to nod in agreement. "What is there to talk about?" Jeff could hear his voice, quivering, while his eyes began to burn.

"The economy." Adrian smirked, and Jeff was taken aback. His smile was gorgeous: straight white teeth that shined against the light, enclosed in plump pink lips and an attractive five o'clock shadow. His eyes had a darkness to them, yes, but being that close, Jeff could see how high his cheekbones were, how Adrian's hair fell effortlessly down and framed his face; he was beautiful.

"What?" Jeff said, emerging from his thoughts.

"I'm joking," Adrian said, placing his arm around Jeff's shoulder and pulling him in close. His arms were a bit tanner than Jeff's, but it looked like the Fall weather was also reverting Adrian back to ghost status. Jeff could feel Adrian's muscles tighten against his neck as he was forced to stand directly next to him. Adrian started walking and Jeff had to follow. "I know you saw."

"No," Jeff said without hesitating. "I mean, yes, but I won't tell anyone. I swear."

"You swear, huh?" Adrian kept his grip tight around Jeff as the two of them sauntered past a cluster of security guards.

The men turned and watched them pass but did not do anything. Jeff tried his best to make a pleading face with his eyes, but Adrian did a quick wave to the guards and they nodded back, not realizing that they were witnessing Jeff's walk to the grave. Jeff cursed at himself in his mind for leaving the knife in a classroom on the other side of campus.

"So," Adrian said, as they made it to the doors that led to the field. "You swear."

"Yes," Jeff said, his answer sounding more like a gasp. "I swear. I don't care enough to tell, plus I'm smart."

"Oh, well, shit, if you're smart." Adrian opened the door and gestured for Jeff to go outside.

It was not snowing at the moment, but the ground was slippery from the melted flakes that had whitewashed the vibrant green field. Jeff did not move as he felt the cold air nip at his face, or as Adrian gestured again. He was not sure he *could* move.

"Why?" Jeff asked, stalling.

"Why, what?" Adrian gripped Jeff's forearm with strength and jerked him forward, slamming the door behind them.

"Why are we going outside?"

"So, we can talk, of course. I thought you said you were smart." Adrian pushed his back against the wall and rocked on his heels. "Let's get to know each other first, okay?"

"I don't...." Jeff sighed and rubbed his hands against his face. His nose was already frigid and hurt as his palms wiped down on it.

"Never really seen you around so I know you're not a senior," Adrian said, his breath filling the air in front of him. "And you came out of Mr. Laherie's class so I'm taking it you're a junior." Jeff watched as Adrian nodded, even though Jeff had not said anything back. "Your expression tells me I'm correct. What's your name?"

Jeff went to answer but his tongue would not work, it felt numb. With a deep breath, Jeff licked his bottom lips and tried to say his name again. "Je...." His voice cut out and the dryness in his mouth caused it to hurt as he swallowed. "Jeff, my name is Jeff."

"Jeff," Adrian pushed himself from blocking the door and stepped forward. Since he was taller than Jeff, it always felt like he was looking down on him. "I'm not a killer."

Jeff heard himself gulp before realizing he had done it.

"I know, I know, 'but what about yesterday, Adrian?'" Adrian grinned and again Jeff could not help but look at how beautiful his smile was. "Now listen," Adrian's front teeth hooked onto his bottom lip and he slowly dragged it across. If Jeff did not know any better, he would say Adrian was flirting. "What happened yesterday was not what I wanted. I need you to understand that."

"I, I do," Jeff said, nodding his head repeatedly. "I get it."

"Do you?" Adrian shoved both his hands into his pocket. "I don't know," taking his right hand out of his pocket. "I mean, I don't really know you, Jeff, so you can see how I wouldn't know if you actually did, in fact, get it.'"

"You can trust me." Jeff could feel his eyes burn and he was glad it was windy so he could blame any tears on that.

"But, Jeff," Adrian took his other hand out of his pocket, reaching forward and placing his hand against the nape of Jeff's neck, pulling him in until they're bodies were almost touching. "You also have to be able to see it from my point of view." Adrian let out a small laugh and before Jeff could blink there was an icy blade against the left side of his neck. "I am placing my entire academic career in the hands of someone," Adrian pulled Jeff until they're bodies were against each other, "who I don't know."

Jeff could feel himself shaking against Adrian's brick body. His arms were statuesque, his jawline looked like it had been chiseled from marble, and somehow, he still found a way to smile through it all. Maybe if Jeff focused on Adrian's grin, he would not feel the blade enter into his skin and tear the life out from him.

"I'll do anything," Jeff said, his eyes frantically shifting from Adrian's eyes, to his mouth, to the door leading back into the school. Maybe he could somehow kick Adrian's shin and bolt for the door. He had to try something, right? If he did nothing, then the outcome was one grim slash away.

"Anything?" Adrian's eyebrow rose, and his hand tightened around Jeff. "What could you possibly do that would guarantee you not to tell anyone?"

Adrian stayed quiet and Jeff waited for him to go on, only he didn't.

"Not a rhetorical question, Jeff," Adrian said, pushing the blade slightly harder against Jeff's jugular. "I mean, I can name one thing that I can do that will guarantee, without any doubt, that you won't be able to tell anyone."

Jeff started to wrack his mind with different ways to get out of it. He felt like Adrian was flirting but that would only make him whore himself out without any actual guarantee of living after. *Think, Jeff, think.* His mind was racing, but there was not enough time. Jeff could feel the warmness from the blood that was dripping down his throat from the tip of the blade pressed against his skin. That was all he could feel. His legs felt as though he was floating, unable to actually tell if his feet were connecting with the grass. The heaviness his arms felt weighed them down, making his fingertips feel like accessories and not a part of his body.

"Time's ticking, Jeff."

Adrian put one of his legs behind Jeff's Achilles tendon and applied pressure, causing Jeff to howl as Adrian then forced him to his knees. The pain shooting through his leg was unbearable, and he was now looking up at Adrian's blade, a drop of crimson blood dripping off and staining the white ground.

"Please don't do this," Jeff said, gaining control of his arms, trying to push the knife away.

"Don't," Adrian barked, taking the knife and slamming the handle into Jeff's nose. There was not a popping noise, which Jeff assumed meant his nose did not break, but that did not stop the blinding pain to explode across his face. Blood began to flow down, and he could taste it seeping into the cracks of his lips and onto his taste buds. His vision came to accompanied by a throbbing through his temples. "I'm sorry, Jeff, but you're not giving me any reason to believe you, and I'm not going to ruin my life because some loser who can't even fight knows something about me."

"You don't have to do this," Jeff said, spitting blood onto the floor next to him. "You're making a huge mistake."

"Oh, really," Adrian said, "who's the one on their knees begging? That's right, Jeff, it's you. So, if anyone made a mistake, I think you and I both know who did simply based on the predicament that has unfolded."

"Please," Jeff said, wiping blood from getting in his mouth. "Listen to me. If you kill me," Jeff closed his eyes and tried his best to think of an excuse. Nothing. Poor, Mal, was all he could think, and that in turn formed a solution. "I wasn't the only one who saw!"

"What you don't think I know that?" Adrian's finger tapped against his waist while his hand that held the knife stayed perfectly still in front of Jeff's eyes.

"Think about it," Jeff said, adrenaline coursed through his veins, making him able to talk without his voice shaking. "You kill me and it's going to be around the school so fast."

"What's your po—"

"On the off chance you're able to get away with killing two people in two days, security saw us walking together."

"So?" Adrian did not look impressed with the information. "Kids walk together all the time, Jeff. It's high school."

"They'll question you because that's what happens." Jeff took a moment to formulate his thoughts. "They haven't questioned anyone about the kid you killed yesterday because as far as their concerned there were no witnesses. Now, let's say you kill me and get away with it. When they pull you into question, my best friend will be there to let them know that we saw you yesterday, and really, you think anyone is going to listen to you."

"What does that mean?" Adrian's sly smirk was replaced with a venomous glare.

"Everyone knows that it's just a matter of time before you start killing people." Jeff could hear the anger in his own voice emerging out from the fearful quietness that strangled him earlier. "What I mean is, everyone expects you to kill. Everyone knows that you're a psycho, and no one likes you."

"Is that so?" Adrian said, sticking the blade back against Jeff's throat.

"It is."

"Okay," Adrian said, lifting his hands up and backing away. "I won't kill you, yet."

"You won't kill me, period."

"Don't get cocky," Adrian said, squatting in front of Jeff with the knife wielded in front of him. "Cockiness is everyone's downfall, Jeff."

"I'm not cocky," Jeff said. "I'm smart."

"We'll see," Adrian said, standing up and placing the knife back in his pocket. "See you around, Jeff."

With a wink, Adrian turned around and walked back into the school, leaving Jeff bloodied and on his knees in the freezing cold, and wet, grass. Jeff closed his eyes and tried to breathe but his entire body was shaking. He did not move.

"You're okay," he repeated to himself like a mantra.

Ultimately it was the bell that snapped Jeff out of his fear ridden daze and to his feet. He wiped his nose and upper lip, hoping it was not stained with blood. The collar of his shirt was the only place his blood dripped down to, so with a quick zip of his jacket, his neck was hidden from anyone's view.

His phone buzzed in his pocket and he pulled it out, expecting it to be Mal.

Marc [11:52am]: Let's not talk about it over text. Hope you're having a good day though. I'll see you later on today?

Jeff angrily shoved his phone back and stormed through the doors back into school, back to class, and back to acting like everything was normal. The hallways were full of kids bustling from room to room, but no one even took a second glance at Jeff. He knew he wiped up the blood, but there was no way his nose was not swollen, and how could people not notice the grass stains on his knees? It was as though he was a ghost.

Student after student would walk past him without so much as a nod. Most had headphones in and were looking down as they walked, but others were simply keeping to themselves, seemingly not wanting to talk to anyone. Jeff's eyes darted from face to face, seeing if he could find Mal and warn her, even hoping that he would run into Mr. Shan.

As Jeff turned the corner he walked directly into a security guard who was facing the other direction. Jeff collided with his broad back and knocked the man forward. He had to stop himself by reaching out and holding onto the open locker of a student in front of them. Turning around, the security guard surveyed Jeff up and down, while Jeff did the same.

The guard had a nametag that read "Michaelson," and on his belt Jeff could see mace, a baton, and handcuffs. He was stocky, about the same height as Jeff, and had piercing green eyes. The beard that covered half his face only made his eyes stand out more.

"Why do you look like you've seen a ghost?" Michaelson asked.

"I, um," Jeff looked to the side and saw Adrian standing across from the two of them. Without skipping a beat, Adrian lifted his hand to his throat and made a slitting motion. "My grandma died," Jeff said, the lie making it out before his mind could process.

"Oh," the guard said, furrowing his brows as his gaze went down to the stains on Jeff's knees. "And that?"

"I went into the field and cried," Jeff said, not even sure how he was able to lie this well. "I didn't want anyone to bother me, so I knelt in the grass. I know, dumb, right?" Jeff let out — what he hoped was — a convincing chuckle.

"Sorry for your loss," Michaelson said. "I know what that's like."

"Oh, I'm sorry," Jeff said, praying the encounter would cease after that.

The bell rang for everyone to be inside class and Jeff saw that Adrian was no longer creeping in the background. Jeff let out a sigh of relief and Michaelson smiled, patting him on the shoulders.

"I'll walk you to class," the guard said.

"Thank you," Jeff said, feeling safe for the first time that day.

CHAPTER 7

Jeff [12:00pm]: adrian just almost killed me!!! im shaking I cant breathe. Listen we need to meet up and walk out of school together!

Mal [12:04pm]: Oh my god what! Are you okay?? Did he hurt you? And oh no my dad took me out of school early! I'm sorry! Please be safe

Jeff [12:30pm]: ill be fine. Okay ill talk to you later I need to figure something out and mr ericson keeps looking my way and I cant lose my phone.

Mal [12:31pm]: Jeff I'm so sorry! Please be safe and text me when you can and call me when you get home!

Jeff [12:32pm]: Marc can you come and pick me up after school?

Marc [12:34pm]: Yeah, of course. I'd love to show everyone that you're mine.

Jeff [12:36pm]: youre so weird lol but okay thank you so much! I almost got killed today at school and im just really scared

Marc [12:37pm]: Who am I killing?

Jeff [12:39pm]: Dont joke about that when you never even answered my question

Marc [12:43pm]: Call me old fashioned, but I believe any serious question should be asked in person. When it's in person it's so much more meaningful because you can see the person's emotions and know if they're lying.

Jeff [12:45pm]: I never thought of it that way. But anyways cool so please come and get me from school. I get out at 2:35

Marc [12:46pm]: I will be there.

Jeff [12:55pm]: Thank you by the way it means a lot

Marc [1:20pm]: I care for you, Jeff.

Jeff [1:21pm]: I care for you too

Marc [1:26pm]: Go focus on learning now so that maybe, one day, you can text with proper grammar. I will see you after school. Stay safe and know I care.

Jeff [1:30pm]: Maybe for you, I will write better.

Marc [1:33pm]: I just got hard reading that beautiful sentence.

Jeff [1:35pm]: There's plenty more where that came from.

Marc [1:37pm]: Don't tease me with grammatically correct sentences if you're only going to end up reverting back.

Jeff [1:45pm]: That's a personal matter. I would much rather discuss it in person. You know? So I can see your emotions.

Marc [1:50pm]: Clever. See you in a little.

Jeff [2:00pm]: Mom I'm going to hang out with a friend for a little while after school. I won't be late.

Mom [2:08pm]: What friend and where? You know I worry. Please be safe! Love you.

Jeff [2:10pm]: It's just with Mal mom don't worry we will be fine.

Mom [2:15pm]: Tell her I said hi! Be home at a reasonable time.

CHAPTER 8

As the bell rang for the final class of the day to be over, Jeff attempted to seem unbothered, but that failed the minute he heard the ringing. Without skipping a beat, Jeff was out of the classroom door and barreling his way through the hallway to the front doors. If he could just make it outside and be with Marc, then he knew he could at least live to see the next day, or long enough to come up with a plan.

The day had been consumed with contemplating whether or not to disclose all of the information to Marc or to just give him the very watered-down version of the events. Logically speaking, if Jeff wanted to have protection he would have to explain the entirety of the story to Marc, Jeff knew that. But the thought of anyone else getting hurt, especially Marc, made him question the idea of telling him. Not to mention, Marc had now evaded the question of if he had killed someone, twice, and Jeff needed to know.

He had not seen Adrian in the hallways since his run in with the security guard. Jeff saw that as an advantage to get out of the academy safely, and he took it. As he reached the front doors he did not hesitate to slam them both open, dramatically, and dash outside, hoping to see Marc standing there, arms crossed with a cool set of shades on.

Instead, Jeff gaped at all of the parents standing outside the school waiting for their children. *They called home,* he thought. And he knew exactly what that meant: his parents did know about the death when they sent him to school today.

On any typical day, there were a few parents to pick up their children. Most kids who went to Oak Valley took the bus to and from school. The school bus consisted of complete bullet proof glass, a bullet proof exterior, along with a metal detector when the students entered. Jeff remembered back to when he would have to take the bus with Mal and the two of them would sit in the far back, trying their best to stay away from anyone.

Thinking back to how scared he was, Jeff almost laughed out loud. Two years ago, he would have been quietly huddling, waiting for the bus with Mal, afraid that anything he did wrong would get him killed. He was not sure if he was becoming more of an adult, or if having a knife against his throat made him realize how not scary being outside was, but for the first time Jeff was not in a state of trepidation, but rather in awe of how many parents came to pick up their children.

Jeff took a moment and closed his eyes, listening. The leaves in the trees above him exhaled a small rustling noise into the background as parents greeted their children. The double doors would bang closed in between, and Jeff was not afraid. He kept his eyes shut and listened more: there were birds calling to one another high in the tops of the oaks, the wind caused a whirl that blew across Jeff's face, and he felt the slight warmth of the sun landing on his exposed skin. In some strange way, Jeff was at peace.

"Jeff," Marc's voice broke through all the sounds surrounding him and Jeff opened his eyes.

Marc was standing directly in front of him, and he looked gorgeous. His hair was pulled up in a bun, the sides of his head must have just been cleaned up because the edge work was masterful. A navy-blue coat that came down to his thighs covered Marc's upper body but was tight enough to accentuate his arm muscles. Jeff's eyes felt heavy as he surveyed Marc up and down, a goofy smile rising to his cheeks.

"Hey," Jeff said, stepping forward and holding out his arms for a hug. Marc's lips curved into a beautiful smile, more so than Adrian's, and he pulled Jeff into his embrace.

Marc held Jeff tightly in his arms, rubbing up and down on his back. With pressure, Marc's hands slowly maneuvered across Jeff's upper and lower back. The feeling of Marc against Jeff mixed with the smell of clean clothes and Marc's cologne — a very light smell that was not overpowering but smelt as if it costs a fortune — made Jeff unsure if his arms would actually release Marc.

"Are you okay?" Marc asked, pulling away to meet Jeff's gaze.

"I will be," Jeff said, leaning forward and kissing Marc.

"What happened?" Marc's voice bordered on caring but there was a quick hint of anger that found its way to the forefront.

"Remember how I told you," Jeff leaned in and whispered, "about the kid getting killed yesterday."

Marc nodded, "yeah."

"Well," Jeff said, taking a breath and looking at his surroundings. All he could see were students exiting the building where they were either met by their parents or left. There was no sign of Adrian. "Here let's just walk to the parking lot and I'll tell you. Where did you park?"

"I walked," Marc said, wrapping his arm around Jeff's shoulders and pulling him close. "I know you drive to school and I figured I would walk so we could hang out and your car wouldn't get towed."

"Thanks," Jeff said, looking down, suddenly feeling shy. "You didn't have to walk, though. I would have picked you up."

"Jeff," Marc said, as they began to walk towards the parking lot. "You specifically asked me to come pick you up, you realize that, right?"

"I thought you would drive." Jeff rolled his eyes. "Besides, it's unsafe just walking around."

"Don't worry about me," Marc said, flashing Jeff a toothy grin. "I can take care of myself."

"Speaking of," Jeff said, half smiling because he could see Marc's eyes roll. "Don't roll your eyes. You have an answer for me."

"Okay," Marc said, taking a pause.

Jeff waited for his answer, but the pause alone was all he really needed. So, Marc had killed someone before. Jeff wasn't entirely sure how he felt, seeing as he had not heard it actually be said from Marc, but also because Marc came to get him. Marc was making an effort, and sure, Jeff was worried that maybe the answer would somehow change their relationship, but he also wasn't.

In some way, after Adrian had him on his knees and his life had been in the control of another person, Jeff understood that sometimes it was not a choice. He did not know if he would've been able to kill Adrian if their encounter had kept going, but the fact that it was a thought in his mind made him understand it is not so black and white.

"I want to be honest with you," Marc said, his hand squeezing Jeff's right shoulder as they continued to walk side by side.

"I want that, too," Jeff said.

"Yes," Marc said.

"What?"

"Yes, I've killed before."

"Okay," Jeff said quietly.

"Okay?" Marc asked, letting go of Jeff as they made it to the car.

"I don't know," Jeff admitted, unlocking the doors and sliding into the driver's seat. "If you had answered this a day ago maybe I would've had a different reaction but, honestly, after today…." Jeff could feel the icy blade against his throat and his jeans were still damp from being slammed into the snowy grass.

"Yeah, what happened? You never told me."

Jeff turned the engine over and let out a sigh. "The guy saw Mal and I, yesterday." Jeff looked behind the car and shifted to reverse, easing his foot off the break. "So, he, um, he found me, and he threatened me." Putting the car into drive, Jeff slowly followed the line of parent's, who had decided to park in student lot, out of the parking lot. "By the way, where are we going?"

"I was thinking my apartment," Marc said, shrugging.

"Okay," Jeff said, "you lead the way."

"I will," Marc said, pointing for Jeff to make a left. "And you tell me what happened because that told me nothing. Besides, seeing as your nose is bruised, something else definitely happened."

"I knew my nose would end up bruising," Jeff said angrily. Now he would have to explain it to his parents. Granted, they already knew, but this would make them put two and two together and Jeff would be taken out of school.

"Hey," Marc said, interrupting Jeff's thoughts. "You can trust me."

Jeff nodded and decided that he would tell Marc everything. If he couldn't trust the person that he was dating, then what was the point? Jeff's parents had been together for eighteen years, and Jeff knew that they were always honest with each other. Honesty was the foundation for a healthy relationship.

"Okay," Jeff said as he began to explain the story to Marc.

Marc's apartment was not too far from Oak Valley, so Jeff's story took up the perfect amount of time. The complex was not in a bad neighborhood, in fact, it was a gated community. There was a guard on watch at the gate which eased Jeff's mind, even though he was not the one who lived there. The community was small: there was a pool that was next to the clubhouse where potential buyers could be found sneaking free coffee, the buildings themselves were two story and painted blue. A sign that read "no animals" was posted down each road Marc had Jeff turn. As Jeff expected, no one was outside.

While Marc was mulling over the details that Jeff had given him, he turned the car off and shifted in his seat, facing Marc. It was the quietest either of them had been together, and Jeff was starting to feel a sense of uneasiness take hold of his shoulders, knotting them up. The windows began to fog up as they sat in silence. Jeff watched as Marc gnawed on his bottom lip while his right hand tapped vigorously against the side of his thigh.

"Let's go inside," Marc finally said, unbuckling his seatbelt and opening up the door.

Jeff did not say anything, he simply followed him up the stairs.

Marc lived on the second story. There was a welcome mat outside of Marc's door which Jeff found to be refreshing, until he read it. "Yes on Prop 485." As he read it, Jeff felt a twinge of anger fill his blood. How could someone be for the proposition, not to anything that would show their support. The law was made legal the year Jeff was born. It wasn't changing.

"Oh, that," Marc said, looking back and seeing Jeff's face. "It's vintage, you know? People actually had these on their doors."

"Like you?" Jeff said, raising his eyebrows.

"I do it to be ironic," Marc said, stepping on the mat. "Besides, it's the equivalent of having a 'beware of dog' sign. People see you support the law and they won't try to steal from you." Marc leaned in and Jeff could feel Marc's lip against his earlobe. "Who'd want to cross a killer's path?"

With that, Marc unlocked his door and walked into his apartment. Jeff took a moment before taking a step into Marc's place. The layout was not what Jeff had expected. Jeff had anticipated that the inside would be a mess and it would be darkly lit, but the inside was the polar opposite of that.

Across from the front door was a mirror on the wall, next to a coat hanger. Jeff peered at himself in the mirror and saw what Marc had meant about his nose. It was not overly bruised or swollen, but there was a minor cut along the bridge accompanied by a small puffy reddening. The bags under his eyes, from lack of sleep, were more alarming to Jeff than his nose.

The living room was directly to Jeff's right, where there sat a black leather couch across from an extremely big flat screen tv. There was a glass coffee table in front of the couch and Jeff did not see a single smudge on the glass. The apartment had wood flooring and Jeff watched as Marc took his shoes off before walking further inside, so he followed suit.

The apartment smelled like clean linens and Jeff could feel his eyes shifting from side to side trying to take it all in. As he made his way further, he realized the kitchen was at the far end of the apartment, a dining room table — also glass and also completely wiped — was grounded next to the living room. The kitchen itself was pearly white with a large titanium refrigerator in the middle. On top of the counter next to the fridge, Jeff saw a large bulky grey boombox.

"Is that?" Jeff pointed, not wanting to sound like an idiot.

"A CD player? Yes." Marc sounded proud.

"Holy shit," Jeff said, scurrying across the wooden floor before halting to a stop in front of it. "I've never seen one in person."

"They're an eyesore, sure," Marc said, coming up behind Jeff and wrapping his arms over his chest. "But I love older things."

"I've always been fascinated with them," Jeff said, running his fingers along the boom box: the felt speaker covers, the buttons that made an audible click when pressed, the cassette slot. It all felt so surreal.

"You know," Marc said, putting his hands on Jeff's hips and turning him around, planting a quick kiss the moment they were face-to-face. "I also have a VCR."

"What?" Jeff's jaw dropped.

"And," Marc said, leaning in and kissing him again, this time slowly, his hand on the nape of Jeff's neck. "I have VHS's."

"Do you really?" Jeff said, biting Marc's lower lip. His thoughts were beginning to flee his mind with each passing second in Marc's arms. His back was against the counter and before he knew it, Marc lifted him up, with ease, and put him down on the counter, gliding forward and filling the open space between Jeff's legs.

"Yeah," Marc exhaled on the side of Jeff's neck, his mouth sweeping along Jeff's skin, sending goosebumps exploding across his arms. "I can show you."

"Show me what?" Jeff asked, feeling Marc against his thigh.

Jeff forgot what they had even been talking about as Marc's right hand slowly inched up Jeff's thigh. The pressure being applied caused Jeff to let out an audible moan. Marc smirked as his hand continued its path. He did not have to time to think because Marc's mouth closed over his, his eyes closed, and he leaned back, propping himself up on the counter with his arms.

Marc had a way of kissing that drove Jeff insane. It would always start off slow, tender, and would devolve into a sloppy mixture of roughness, including lip biting and sucking, and Jeff wanted more. His mouth felt magnetized to Marc's, only releasing to shift their faces, and then immediately connected again. Marc's tongue filled Jeff's mouth and he felt empty without it.

Marc's hand reached Jeff's hard on and Jeff groaned out as Marc wrapped his hand around the head in his pants, slowly grinding his palm up and down. Jeff took his legs and wrapped them around Marc's lower back, yanking him forward, making them as physically close as possible. Jeff felt Marc's other hand dig into his back while he began to rock on his heels, working his hips forward.

"Marc," Jeff exhaled, not sure he would be able to stop them from taking it any further, because he wanted to. He wanted Marc to lift him up and throw him onto his bed and for them to have sloppy sex, but he knew he shouldn't. At least not after everything he'd been through that day. He needed a sense of stability more than he wanted Marc inside him.

"Yeah?" Marc asked, pushing his body forward slowly, his forehead touching Jeff's.

"Can we watch a movie on your VHS?" Jeff could hear his voice quaver.

"Is that what you want?" Marc eyed Jeff's pants. "Is that what you," his grip tightened on Jeff's pants, "really, really want?"

"No," Jeff admitted, "but it'll make me feel better."

Marc took a step back and closed his eyes, taking in a deep breath. "Okay," he said, smiling at Jeff. "Go get on the couch and I will get a movie."

"Really?" Jeff asked, beaming.

"But just know, this," he pointed to his crotch, "it's not getting what it wants."

"Hey, neither is mine," Jeff said, purposefully grabbing his with his hand.

"Don't say no and then tease me," Marc said, charging forward and slamming Jeff's back against the kitchen wall behind the counter, spreading Jeff's legs apart further than before. Jeff let out a yelp but was immediately silenced by Marc's mouth overtaking his.

Just as quick as it started, however, Marc pulled away and winked, sauntering out of the kitchen and down the hallway straight across from them. Jeff took a moment to compose himself, and readjust his pants, before making his way into the living room.

The couch was more comfortable than Jeff had imagined, and the idea of watching a movie on it seemed like an equation for him to fall asleep. His legs were hanging off of the edge as he leaned back, grinning, his lips still tingling.

Marc emerged from the dark hallway with a box that was bigger than anything Jeff had ever seen a movie sold in. Usually they were small, palm sized cases that held the digital download in them. Jeff's eyes stayed focused on the video cassette in front of him.

"I figured something fun." Marc made his way to the couch and sat next to Jeff, holding up "Lady and the Tramp" on VHS. "What do you say?"

"Oh, I love this movie. I have the seventy-fifth digital anniversary copy on my laptop." Jeff eyed the box. "Can I see it?"

"Sure," Marc said, handing the case over.

Jeff held the movie in his hands, examining it, surprised at how much lighter it felt than what he imagined. When he opened it up, the blandest looking film was presented in front of him. A rectangular black olive covered box with wound up film on one side, an empty see through blank circle on the other, and a basic white font of the movie's name in the middle. Jeff wasn't entirely sure why he expected it be something oddly fantastic, but with the way his parents' generation often became nostalgic of the nineties, he figured they would have been more thrilling.

"I thought…." Jeff took a moment and reexamined the VHS. It was definitely something he would never imagine seeing at any store he went in, and somehow that made it seem more exciting than before. "I just didn't expect it to look like this is all. My parents told me you have to rewind it? How can you tell which side is the right one?"

"Well, you see," Marc said, placing his hands over Jeff's. "If you flip the cassette like this," Marc shifted the box in Jeff's hands and he allowed it, smirking. "Then you can read the name correctly, so if that lovely, long, tape is on this side," Marc's left hand rubbed across Jeff's. "Then you know it's been rewound and is ready to go."

Jeff could only hear the sounds of both of their breaths, coming out quick and quietly. Jeff cleared his throat and turned to Marc. "So, how do you put it in?"

"You just walk up and slip it in," Marc said, standing up and walking over to a dark box, thicker than any laptop, or video player he had ever seen before, and slipped the VHS into a slot that ate it. "Then you turn the TV on," Marc rushed over, grabbing the remote off the coffee table and hitting the power button before crashing down on the couch next to Jeff. "And voila, the movie just starts."

"No piracy warnings you can't skip?" Jeff asked.

"Nope," Marc said, grinning.

"No wonder our parents' generation all hate internet ads."

"They grew up in a time when ads were yet to infiltrate every menacing corner of the internet," Marc said, dramatically twitching his eye.

"Simpler times," Jeff said, matching the dramatics by mimicking a cross along his chest.

"To a bett—"

Jeff's phone began to ring and cut Marc off, almost causing Jeff to shriek. He figured it would be his mom checking in on him.

"Just give me one," Jeff held his finger up and grabbed his phone, checking the screen. "Mal." Jeff silenced his phone and then held the power button until it turned off.

"Why didn't you just pick up?" Marc asked, pausing the movie at the first scene.

"I don't want to talk to her right now," Jeff said, crossing his arms over his chest. "I know it's technically not her fault, but I texted her and told her we needed to stick together at school, after it all happened, you know?" Marc nodded in agreement. "Well, her dad took her out of school but, I don't know, it was just the way her text came off. I just don't want to talk right now. I'd rather be here, with you, watching an old ass movie on an old ass machine."

"Fine by me," Marc said, clicking play, and pulling Jeff into his arms to watch the movie.

Jeff felt a soft nudging against the side of his head, forcing him to slowly open his eyes. There were credits scrolling down the screen in front of him, illuminating the dark room which he then realized was Marc's apartment. That realization made Jeff peer to his right and see that the very thing nudging him was in fact Marc.

"Movie's over," Marc said.

Jeff propped himself up and let out a chuckle. "First time seeing a VHS and I fall asleep."

"You lasted for at least two minutes," Marc jested.

"Okay, it was at least five!" Jeff joked.

The two of them laughed, Marc looking more at ease and happier than Jeff had ever seen him before. Jeff was pretty sure if he held a mirror up to his own face, he too would have that same grin and those same eyes.

The two of them eased back, Marc grabbing the remote and explaining to Jeff how to rewind the movie in a salesman's voice. He got up and turned on the light, continuing to describe what was happening, even as his phone began to ring. "And you see, this, this beautiful device that is currently interrupting my entire spiel, yes, this beauty was sold to me for a mere $100, with a twenty-four-month lease, but it can be yours for," he looked at the contact. "Hold on," his voice back to normal.

Marc walked out of the room as he said hello, and Jeff sat quietly and still trying his best to not focus on who it could be. He could hear Marc whispering something from the other room, but he couldn't make it out. Jeff could hear him say "bye" and then Marc came back into the living room.

"Everything good?" Jeff asked.

"What? Oh, yeah," Marc said, pointing to his phone. "That was my friend Alena. She's cool and all but usually she calls me when she's going through some stuff, you know?"

Jeff nodded.

"So, I figured instead of subjecting you, to what could have been the worst, crying phone call, I would leave the room." Marc sat down on the couch, wagging his phone in the air. "But, turns out it was a good call."

"Oh, really?" Jeff said.

"Yeah. I mean at first it was about work and stuff, but then she told me she's having a party tonight." Marc made his eyebrows do a little dance.

"You want to go?" Jeff asked, figuring Marc was asking in order for Jeff to leave so he could go.

"Only if you want to, of course," Marc said, looking with a face of anticipation.

"You want me to go with you?"

"No shit." Marc furrowed his brow. "Why would I not want to show off my man."

"Shut up," Jeff said, looking down and shyly grinning. "I'll go."

"Really?" Marc looked shocked.

"Why that face?" Jeff asked, offended at how incredulous Marc looked at Jeff's answer.

"I don't know," Marc said, shrugging. "It's just, well, you tend to stay in a lot. Which is cool, I get it, with the law and protective parents, I do. I just thought, maybe, it wasn't going to be your thing. No offense meant."

Jeff took a second to take a breath and see it from Marc's side, because he felt like he got slapped with a passive-aggressive backhand. "I guess."

"I'm sorry," Marc said, his puppy dog eyes were more adorable than Jeff could have anticipated. "I swear I meant nothing by it, okay?"

"Okay," Jeff said, taking Marc's lower jaw in his hand. "I can have fun."

"Okay, Mr. Fun," Marc said, his hand grappling onto Jeff's neck and pushing him back against the leather. "Let's go."

Marc let Jeff leave his car in Marc's parking space while he drove them to the party in his old Toyota. Jeff liked that Marc didn't have a car with autopilot. He knew how to drive without autopilot and he admired other people who did too. The defroster was on full effect as the heater warmed up the car.

Jeff prayed the party was inside because he did not want to have to stand out in the cold. The car's thermostat said it was twenty degrees Fahrenheit.

Marc drove according to the speed limits, not slamming on the acceleration, or trying to show off to Jeff through his driving. It was nice. Jeff felt safe as he watched the houses pass by, most surrounded by gates or walls.

Eventually they parked in front of a two-story house surrounded by a tall, black spiked gate. Jeff got out of the car after Marc and tailed behind him cautiously. The house was on a cul de sac and Jeff could see that there were already quite a few cars piling along the narrow street.

Marc informed Jeff that the way in was around back. Jeff followed Marc and saw a muscular man standing at the gate leading in. Marc casually walked up and did a sort of handshake, fist bump with the guy, turning back to Jeff and waving for him to come. Jeff couldn't help but be the one now gaping in shock.

Marc smirked.

Jeff made his way past the guard, nodding his head and half bowing as he did, and entered into a walkway. There were vines above and around him that formed into a cylinder which led to the back door of the house. Jeff had never seen anything so beautiful and yet so confining before.

Marc's hand warmly wrapped around Jeff's that was limp by his side.

"Come on," Marc said, motioning towards the door with his head.

Jeff nodded and followed Marc, keeping their hands intertwined. As they followed the walkway, Jeff could begin the hear music make its way through the walls. The closer they got to the door, the louder it became.

Marc opened up the door, holding it open for Jeff as well. As Jeff entered the party he felt like he was transported into something he would have seen from older films that his parents enjoy watching.

To his left was the kitchen which was swarming with party goers refilling their drinks. One boy was actually doing a keg stand and Jeff felt a feeling of exhilaration watching him being held up while chugging beer. Everything felt surreal about this life that Marc was exposing Jeff to.

There was a strong scent of weed that quickly made itself known and present. Straight across from Jeff were a group of individuals sitting on the couch, and floor, surrounded by a cloud of smoke.

The staircase was to his right and it was being used as a rest spot for the ones who looked like they had a few too many. As Jeff made his way further in he noticed that behind the staircase was a game room with a pool table in the middle.

Jeff made eye contact with a girl who was leaning against the wall, a pool stick in her grasp, and a joint hanging out her mouth. Her hair was aqua blue and styled in a pixie cut. She had on a white tank top which showed of a plethora of tattoos that covered both her arms. With muscular arms and a build that made him not want to ever get on her bad side, Jeff watched as she furrowed her brow as they made eye contact. The pit of his stomach sank as he watched her throw the pool stick down and come charging forward. Jeff flinched and closed his eyes as she barreled past him and ran into Marc's arms. Jeff peeked open his eyes and realized what had happened, trying his best to seem normal.

"You made it!" The girl, who Jeff assumed was Alena, said, joint in hand.

"Of course, I did," Marc said, beaming. "This is my boyfriend, Jeff."

Marc pointed to him and the girl let out a gasp. "He's even cuter than you made him out to be." Jeff blushed, trying not to show how happy he was at that comment. "I'm Alena by the way."

"Jeff," he said. Now that she was closer he could see that her face was riddled with tiny orange freckles, lining across her cheeks and nose. There was a tattoo with white ink across the side of her neck. He almost missed it because it blended with her skin, but all that was written was *survived* in cursive. "Nice to meet you."

"You too," she said. "Listen, how about I clear us out a room for us and a few close friends and we catch up, get to know each other?" She took a hit of her joint and handed it to Jeff.

"Oh," Jeff said, looking down. "I've never smoked before."

"Hold on," Alena said, gasping louder than before. "You've never? Marc where did you find him?"

"Hands off," Marc said, "he's bi. He might just try and get with you."

Alena laughed along with Marc, but Jeff stood quietly, waiting for them to stop. He didn't want to make a scene of it right when they got to the party, but that didn't mean Marc wouldn't be hearing about it later.

"Anyways, sweetie," Alena said, and Jeff almost rolled his eyes but was able to catch himself and keep a poker face. "You just put it in between your lips, inhale, and hold it in for as long as you can."

"I, um, I still need to drive later," Jeff said worried at the thought of being pulled over.

"If you just smoke a little," Marc interjected, "it should be out of your system within a couple of hours. Promise."

Jeff turned his gaze to Marc who had a hopeful look in his eyes and Jeff realized this was a test. Maybe not consciously, but if Jeff said no to smoking it would prove that he was not fun. Besides, the look in Marc's eye was enough to make Jeff's decision.

"Okay," Jeff said, smiling as Marc rushed forward and grabbed the joint.

Marc stood behind Jeff and held the joint up to his mouth. Jeff could feel Marc's chest pressed against his back, could see people staring, could hear Alena cheering, but all that faded away the moment Marc lit the end of the joint. Jeff closed his eyes as he inhaled, taking in as much smoke as he could, instantly feeling his entire throat burning. He began to cough, keeping his mouth closed the best he could, trying not to let any smoke escape. He held the smoke in between the coughing for at least ten seconds before having to exhale it all out, hacking.

Jeff could hear Marc clapping over the sound of his chest being attacked. His lungs felt as if they were home to a forest fire that would not go out. Having a completely dried out mouth did not help the fact that his throat was still burning. As he was hunched, head in between knees, coughing, he felt a tap and looked up to see Marc holding a drink in a red cup.

"Here," Marc said, "it's water. It'll help."

Jeff nodded and tried his best to smile as he coughed some more, grabbing the cup and sipping on the water. Jeff wanted to not try and down it all at once, knowing most likely he'd only cough it up. Instead he would sip it and let it work its magic down his throat. As for his lungs, with each inhale, the burning hurt a micro less. He would just need to wait for that to go away.

"Yeah," Alena said, "the first time is always the toughest. Not to mention this has wax infused in it."

"Alena," Marc said, eyes widening before going back to normal. "Wax?"

Jeff didn't know what that meant, but the water felt amazing for his throat. He stopped focusing on the two of them and his gaze began to wander around the room.

A guy made the first shot on the pool table, the loud bang of all the balls scattering along the green felt drew Jeff's attention. The background noises became nothing but static as Jeff continued to survey the pool table. His vision seemed to tunnel and all he could focus on was the man who took the shot. He watched as the guy, who had on a denim jacket with torn off sleeves, did a victory fist pump to his side before leaning over, lining up the pool stick, and taking the shot.

Jeff's eyes felt heavy.

"Jeff," Marc's voice pulled him out of his spotlight focus. "You good?"

"Totally," Jeff said, turning his head back to face Marc, only feeling like his vision had to catch up. "This is fun."

"Yeah?"

"Yeah," Jeff said, grinning. "Can I take another hit?"

Alena had the joint in her mouth, taking a puff. "That's up to your boyfriend," she said, purposefully blowing a cloud of smoke at Jeff.

"Why is that?" Jeff said, his smile fading.

"Because he's the one who's going to have to babysit your ass if you get too high."

Jeff was not sure if that was to be meant as an insult or if she genuinely was concerned about him getting too high. He looked over to Marc and gave him a quizzical look. Marc smiled, and Jeff gaped at how beautiful he looked. His hands came down on both of Jeff's shoulders, instantly loosening his muscles.

"How 'bout this," Marc said, his eyes shining like diamonds. "We wait, see how you're feeling in a little. It's got wax so it's a little stronger and I don't want you not able to drive home."

"Oh," Jeff said, nodding. He continued to nod in agreement and could see that Marc look like he was going to laugh. "You're right."

"I know," Marc smirked, pulling Jeff into his arms. Jeff's face was nuzzled against Marc's coat and he wanted to stay in Marc's embrace for the rest of the party.

Jeff felt connected to Marc in a way he had never before. He could feel Marc's heart beating against his chest, he could feel the blood being pumped in his veins, he could hear the sound of Marc gulping. Somehow, he felt as if he and Marc were the same person, connected through their contact.

It was then he realized how high he was and indefinitely decided against smoking anymore.

Alena had stayed true to her word and cleared out a room for them and a few people to sit in and relax. It was Jeff, Marc, Alena, and two other people who Jeff had yet to meet.

The room was small, only big enough for a twin sized bed — which lay against the middle of the wall, plain white sheets — and nothing else in the room: no posters, no scrapes against the black wallpaper, not even a cellphone charger on the night stand. Something felt off to Jeff, but he chalked it up to the weed and sat down on the edge of the, perfectly pressed sheeted, bed.

Marc sat next to him, on his left, who was next to Alena. The two others, a guy and girl, were seated on the floor.

The guy had on dark eyeliner, a silver lip piercing — towards the left side of his mouth— with a chain that followed to his earing. He had short wavy hair that faded up on the side, a design of three lines was buzzed into his hair on the left. His clothes were a mixture of business meets goth, with a black leather blazer, accompanied by ripped black skin-tight jeans. He sat with one leg up, his elbow rested on his knee while his jaw rested on his hand, and his other leg lay flat outwards on the floor. He looked like a model for an edgy clothing ad.

The girl had a different look. She had on a short plaid skirt, which was met with fishnet stockings. Her shirt was a white, skin tight, blouse. Blonde flowing hair swooped down over her shoulders. Her legs were crossed as she sat. They looked like they could be siblings.

Jeff could not help but stare at both of them. They were stunning, each in their own way. The lighting that came from the lamp to Jeff's right, made them look even more beautiful against the black wallpaper.

"Hi," the guy said, looking at Jeff. "I'm Peter."

Jeff realized he had actually been staring for an uncomfortable amount of time at the two of them, and Peter was now trying to break the ice.

"Hi," Jeff said, nodding. "I'm high, I mean Jeff, but also high, I'm that too." Jeff shut his mouth and mentally beat himself up over that Freudian slip.

"Hey," the girl said, "Robyn."

Jeff did a curt nod and tried his best to remain semi normal, even though he felt like he could hear her voice echo when she said her name. He felt as if he was permanently squinting.

"Okay," Alena said, "now that we're all acquainted, let's play a game."

"What game?" Peter asked.

"Never have I ever."

"That game gets too passive aggressive," Robyn said, letting out a sigh. "Someone always gets upset."

"Is someone in here afraid of skeletons in their closet?" Alena made eye contact with Robyn, as if she was testing her. "Maybe afraid someone might say something?"

"Where are you going with this?" Robyn said, glaring.

"I'm just sayi—"

"I'll start," Jeff said, cutting her off. He just wanted to focus on something other than the tension building in the room which was causing his heart to pound in his chest. He had never felt this strangely worried and anxious in his life. "Never have I ever…." Jeff paused, racking his brain on something he figured no one would get, that way they could see it could be fun. "Um, how about, okay, got it. Never have I ever done heroin."

Jeff held up his ten fingers, eyeing everyone else in the room. The tension was still there, but there was also an easing that Jeff could sense. Marc was the first to hold up his ten, looking around at everyone else. Peter was next, followed by both of the girls putting their fingers up.

"Okay," Jeff said, "so now whoever did it drops a finger, right?"

"Yes," Alena said, lowering her right thumb; Peter and Robyn also did.

Jeff's eyes widened. He felt horrible. His chest started to tighten, but then Alena began to laugh.

"Look at your face," she said, pointing to Jeff. "You look like you've just seen a mass shooting. You're so cute." Alena smirked and then cocked her head with a devious smile. "Speaking of, I want to go next. Never have I ever witnessed a mass shooting."

Peter put his index finger down, followed by Robyn. Jeff felt his mouth gape open in shock at how nonchalantly they put their fingers down. Alena let out a giggle, and Jeff turned, his eye sight still slower, to see her watching him.

"Okay," Peter said, a smirk rising. "Never have I ever committed a mass shooting."

"Fuck you," Robyn said, immediately standing up. "This is what I'm talking about. Fuck you, too, Alena."

"Robyn, calm down," Peter said, putting his hands up. "I didn't think you'd admit it, Jesus. Have you ever heard of a lie? Besides, we all know the story."

"So, what? You still knew I'd react," she shouted, "how could you not?"

Jeff felt as if his face was being stabbed by an alarming number of small needles, while simultaneously losing breathe with each passing second. He had never felt like this before, this paranoid that something awful was imminent.

"He has a point," Alena said, casually shrugging. "You did react. You could have just not, nobody would have questioned."

"Okay, guys," Marc said, clearing his throat. "Let's all calm down. Okay, Robyn, you've done that. It's legal, right? Plus, you're the only one who reacted. Nobody else cared."

Jeff wanted to interject and say that he cared, that the idea of a mass shooting was alone disgusting and horrific, and to be in the same room as someone who had committed one was terrifying. But all that he could do was listen in mute horror as his boyfriend somehow spun it to sooth someone that awful, and to make them feel okay about it. It all felt so wrong.

Robyn nodded, and Marc continued. "So just sit down, and let's play until someone goes out. What do you say?"

"Okay," Robyn said.

"Besides, you're already almost halfway there." Marc belted out a laugh and everyone else followed. Robyn flipped him off but also started to get in on it and chuckle. Jeff tried to let out some semblance of a laugh, but all that came out was a weak, forced sounding ha.

"I'll go," Marc said, "and then we'll go counter clock wise, and actually go in order." He looked around at everyone and nudged Jeff, flashing him a quick wink. "So, never have I ever fallen in love."

Jeff didn't move a muscle, nor did he put a finger down. Everyone else did. They unanimously formed a combined orchestra of groaning as they did so.

"Your turn," Marc said, grabbing Jeff's hands and planting a kiss on each one. "What hasn't my man done."

Jeff blushed and thought about it, closing his eyes as he did. "Never have I ever been caught sneaking out of the house."

Everyone put a finger down and Jeff felt triumphant in that moment.

Marc leaned in and whispered, "I didn't know you sneak out."

Jeff leaned forward, until they were inches away. "There's a lot you don't know about me."

"I can see that."

"Okay," Alena said, "do you guys need the room for a moment alone, or?"

"Shut up," Marc said, pointing to Robyn. "You're next."

"Fine," she said, only having five fingers left. "Never have I ever been in foster care."

Jeff looked around and saw Marc and Alena put their fingers down. A feeling of shock came over Jeff with the realization that Marc had been in foster care. He had heard all of the horrific things that happen in the system, and how most kids end up there due to the death of their parents. Suddenly, Jeff's heart weighed heavy at the idea of Marc scared in foster care.

"Now who's being a bitch," Alena said, rolling her eyes at Robyn.

Jeff whispered in Marc's ear. "I didn't know you were in foster care."

"Yeah," Marc said, nudging Alena's shoulder. "We were taken into the same house, grew up together."

"Damn straight," Alena said. "We've been through some shit together, haven't we Marcy Marc."

"Yes, we have," he said, grinning. Jeff wanted to kiss him.

"Okay," Robyn said, "Peter, your turn."

"All right," Peter said, cracking his neck from side to side. "Never have I ever stabbed someone to death."

Everyone, except Jeff and Peter, put a finger down. Robyn was now down to four fingers left, Marc had seven, and Jeff had all ten high and up. He felt out of his element, unsafe. Everyone in there seemed to feed off this energy that made them laugh and gloat about killing, about taking the life of a human, who could be anyone, really. Jeff was beginning to feel sick as he thought about how everyone is born into the world and has no say in where they end up, and how everything since that moment is leading to death.

His heart began to race, he could see Alena saying something, but the words were not registering. He felt dizzy and nauseous all at once, the room felt as though it was spinning. He needed to leave. Without thinking, Jeff tried his best to spring off the bed and into action, but his legs felt as though they were floating, and he wasn't entirely sure he could walk.

"Jeff," Marc said, standing next to him and placing his hand on Jeff's shoulder. "Are you feeling all right?"

Jeff's eyelids felt as though small weights were tied to his eyelashes, pulling them down. His mouth puffy and dry, and his stomach was constricting in on itself.

"I don't know?" Jeff whispered, his hands clinging to Marc's arms.

"You're okay," Marc said, turning to the others and motioning something. They all got up and collectively told Jeff to feel better.

The door shut, and Jeff was now alone with Marc in the black room. "It's just the weed hitting you really hard, okay?"

"Okay," Jeff said, not letting go of Marc. How could he drive like this?

"I swear, in a couple of hours, you'll be fine."

"Okay," Jeff said, Marc lowering down and sitting on the bed, Jeff following.

"Do you want to lay down?" Marc asked. His voice was soft and soothing, and Jeff wanted to simply close his eyes and listen to Marc speak.

"Yeah," Jeff said, shyly smiling.

"Okay." Marc lied on the bed, knees bent, perfect for Jeff to be the little spoon.

Jeff leaned forward — much further than he thought — and Marc's arm reached out and held him from falling face first into the ground.

"I'm just taking off my shoes," Jeff said, slowly untying his laces and sliding the shoes off. Marc's grip a constant.

"Come here," Marc said, gently pulling Jeff onto the bed.

Jeff lied next to him, their bodies together. Marc's warm arm wrapped around Jeff's chest, Jeff holding to it with both his arms. Their feet were next to each other and Jeff took his and knocked them into Marc's. Marc countered back. And just like that, all the panic rose from him and was replaced with a warmth that made him smile from ear to ear.

"Thanks for taking me out," Jeff said. "It was a good distraction."

"Anytime," Marc said, kissing Jeff's ear. "Now just relax and breathe in," Marc breathed in, his chest against Jeff's back. "And breathe out."

Marc did that a few more times, but Jeff was already asleep by the second time, happy and warm in Marc's arms.

CHAPTER 9

There was a crashing sound, as if someone had dropped a glass on the floor, that had Jeff's eyes shooting open, realizing he had fallen asleep. The party was still going on. Jeff could hear laughter, the pool balls colliding together, and faintly behind all of that, he could hear Marc breathing on his neck, suddenly feeling the light tickle that accompanied it.

Jeff's eyes began to droop, a tired feeling taking over. *What time is it?* he thought, carefully reaching into his pocket — trying his best not to wake Marc — and slipping his phone out. He clicked the button on the bottom of the phone, but nothing happened, just a blank screen. Pressing it again, it did the same thing. Jeff knew there was no way he was out of — and that's when he remembered that he had shut off his phone when Mal called.

"Shit," he hissed, holding the power button down.

The screen illuminated and started its process of turning on. First, the screen was simply white, and then it would dim, and the words "powering on" shown on the screen. After that Jeff's lock screen appeared and he saw that it was twelve thirty am. His phone began to buzz, repeatedly. There were a total of twenty missed calls from his mom, fifteen from his father, and twelve text messages from Mal.

"Oh, no." Jeff sat up, forgetting Marc's arm was over him, face nuzzled on his shoulder.

"What the...." Marc rubbed his eyes and squinted at Jeff. "What time is it?"

"It's 12:30," Jeff said, hearing panic in his voice. "I was supposed to be home hours ago! My parents probably already have a search team out for me."

"Okay, relax," Marc said. "Just call them and tell them you fell asleep at your boyfriend's house."

"I can't tell them about you."

"Why do you have to get into details?" Marc said, raising an eyebrow. "Just say I'm someone from class. It's not like you have to introduce us."

"I don't even know if I'm still high." Jeff wanted this night to be over with. How had his day gone from being so bad, to so good, back to bad? His luck was running out.

"You're not," Marc said matter-of-factly. "Trust me you were pretty gone earlier. I'd be able to tell."

Jeff sighed, looking down at his phone. His eyes still felt heavy, but his vision no longer had to catch up, plus his body didn't feel numb anymore. He knew he was most likely still high in some capacity, but he also knew getting home was more important. "Here goes nothing."

"Just sound tired and apologetic and tell them you'll be right home." Marc got up off the bed. "I'll go start the car and that way we can leave right away."

Jeff nodded, already dialing back. "Sounds good." The phone rang. Jeff's heart raced. The door closed behind Marc, and the phone rang again. Jeff wanted to hang up, but his mother picked up.

"Jeff?" Her voice sounded hoarse, but she still managed to shout it out with so much pain.

Jeff wanted to curl up and die for making his mom go through that. "Mom, I'm so sorry. I fell asleep and my phone died! I'm so, so sorry."

"Mal called the house," she said, sniffling. "You weren't with her. You lied. Do you know how worried we all were?"

"I know. I'm sorry."

"Where were yo—yes it's him. Your father just came back from driving around looking for your car."

Jeff pulled the phone away from his mouth and cursed.

"Where the hell were you!" This time his mom sounded angry.

"I was, uh, well," Jeff took a deep breath and sighed. "My phone died while I was asleep because I, kind of, fell asleep at my boyfriends." Jeff ended the sentence as though it was a question.

"I," his mother stopped. "We will discuss this when you come home."

"I'm going to go to the bathroom and then I'm heading home."

"Come home now," his mother said, hanging up the phone.

Jeff put his phone away and stood up, taking a few steps to see if he was okay. His body felt as though he was in a perpetual state of sleepiness, but not actually ever succumbing to rest. He had driven like this plenty of times before — tired but needing to stay awake — when him and Mal would sneak out — taking his parent's car with the newest bullet proof glass available — and park and talk. He could do this.

Brushing aside any self-doubt, Jeff grabbed the knob and opened the door. The room had been dimmed, causing Jeff to squint as he stepped out into the party. As his eyes readjusted, Jeff realized the party now appeared much different than before. When he first arrived, there were people his age, Marc's age, all letting loose and having fun. Now, there were grown men, scruffy and dirty, some had sunken in cheeks and the look in their eyes of an addict looking for their next fix. As Jeff surveyed the rest of the party, he saw a few people who looked his age still, but it no longer was the same.

Alena appeared next to him, eyes glazed over and red, a smile plastered on her face. "Hey," she said. "You wanna know what these tattoos are for?"

"What?" Jeff asked, not sure how drunk or high she really was.

"They're," her voice slurred, "for," she leaned in, "every kill. I get a new one when I kill someone." Her eyes widened, and she mimicked an explosion next to her head. "Mind blown, right?" She laughed, placing her hand on Jeff's shoulder, trying to balance herself. "Didn't expect that, did you?"

"You and Marc work together?" Jeff said, completely ignoring her and remembering Marc said there was a work issue.

"No." Her brow furrowed. "I would never work at a mall stand. Please."

"Oh," Jeff said, "he said there was work issues when you called earlier."

"That?" She smacked her lips as her eyes drooped almost fully shut. "That wasn't at that mall." She lifted her head up and put her hand to her mouth, suddenly heaving.

"Oh, shit," Jeff said as he watched her try her best to run to the bathroom.

Jeff knew he should go and help her, but he also didn't care much for her. She rubbed him the wrong way and made him uncomfortable. He wasn't sure if that story about the tattoos was true, but he didn't doubt it. He couldn't understand why Marc would still want to be associated with her. Not to mention the fact that they did not work together. Everything about the encounter made Jeff uneasy.

He made his way out of the party, cautiously. The new attendees seemed to have a much different reason to be there. Jeff saw — as he walked from the room to the living room — two of the men lying with their heads back on the couch, needles by their side. Without making eye contact with anyone, Jeff was able to make it out the back and through the vine shaped walkway. He stepped out and saw Marc sitting in his car, the engine on, ready to go.

Marc was too good for Alena.

Jeff got into the car and grabbed Marc by the neckline on his jacket, kissing him. Marc's mouth formed to his, and just as soon as it started, it ended. Marc pushed his palm against Jeff's chest, but kept one arm around the nape of his neck, forcing him to stay close but not touch.

"That was hot," Marc said, his breath against Jeff's mouth, heavy. "But don't forget," Marc pulled him a little closer, but kept his hand firm on his chest. Their lips barely met, and Jeff had never been more turned on. "I'm in charge."

Jeff let out an audible moan.

"Say it." Marc grabbed the back of Jeff's hair and pulled his head back. "Say I'm in charge."

"You're in charge," Jeff groaned, feeling his Adam's apple against the tightness of his throat.

"Again." Marc's mouth swept across Jeff's throat.

"You're in charge."

"That's right," Marc let go off Jeff's hair and slammed his lips against Jeff's. His mouth felt tingly and numb as Marc aggressively forced Jeff's mouth open. He wasn't sure if he was still turned on from it or starting to get scared.

Marc slowed down and then pulled away, his tongue gliding across his bottom lip. "Don't you forget it."

Jeff leaned his back against the headrest, a grin on his face, unsure if his lips were in pain or still numb.

Marc put the car in drive and they drove out and away from the party. Jeff wanted to ask him about why he lied about working with Alena, but he realized there was a lot he didn't know about

Marc. Up until then he didn't know he was in foster care, let alone had a foster sister. Maybe whatever was said on the phone call was personal and if he asked about it, it might come off untrusting. That was the last thing Jeff wanted Marc to think of him. They had been really clicking lately and Jeff attributed it all to them starting to be honest with each other.

With heavy eyes, Jeff's head nodded off against the window and he was fast asleep, feeling completely safe with Marc.

"Hey," Marc's voice coaxed Jeff out of his sleep. "We're here. Let's get you in the car and home before your parents freak out anymore."

"Thank you," Jeff said.

Marc was holding the passenger door open for Jeff. He held out his hand for Jeff to grab onto as he stepped out of the Toyota. Jeff stood up, let go of Marc's hand, and stretched. He moved his neck from side to side and wiggled his arms awake.

"I'm ready," Jeff said, reaching into his pocket and pulling out his keys. "Tonight was fun. It got a little creepy at parts," he chuckled nervously. "But otherwise I really had a good time."

"So did I," Marc said, giving Jeff a hug and a quick kiss. "Now go get home safely so you're not grounded for an eternity. Although," Marc smirked. "After what I learned tonight, you could just sneak out."

"You'd like that wouldn't you?" Jeff winked.

"Go before I get greedy and keep you to myself a little longer."

"See you later," Jeff said, unlocking his car and getting in. He turned the key in the ignition and backed out, looking in the rearview mirror and seeing Marc parking his car. Jeff wanted to be old enough to go out and stay out all night, he wanted to be an adult.

But, before he could become an adult, he first needed to face his parents at home. The dashboard said it was one in the morning. Jeff knew his parents would be upset and worried, but he had never done anything like this before. Plus, he said he was with a boyfriend, which also had never happened before. There was a twinge of hope that his parents might go easy on him, but surrounding that spec was every negative outcome that could possibly happen.

Jeff parked in his driveway. The living room light was on in his house, along with the porch light, and his own room. His stomach did a quick somersault while he heart weighed heavy, knowing his parents were up all night worried and they still had work in the morning. He felt awful.

With a flip on his hand, Jeff hit his visor down and inspected himself in the mirror before going in. His nose had a small cut on the bridge, which was surrounding with a light red and puffiness. It didn't look too bad and he could say it was an accident. As for the cut on his neck, he simply needed to wear jackets and collared shirts for a small while. His eyes were bloodshot, but Jeff saw that he looked, if anything, tired. This was doable, he could spin his appearance to not look like he had been threatened at knife point, and then later smoked weed at a house party. He would be okay.

With one last huff, Jeff got out of his car and closed the door quietly. Each step he took towards the front door caused his heart to drum faster. The inside of his palms were clammy and he realized he really had to pee.

This would be the worst lecture.

With his house key in hand, Jeff reached the front door and did his best to talk himself up. He unlocked the deadbolt and before he could even reach for the knob, his mom flung open the door and threw her arms around him. Out of all the scenarios that had went on in his mind, Jeff hadn't really viewed this as even being remotely possible.

His mom pulled away, took a long stare at Jeff's face, while her hands were placed on his cheeks. Jeff awkwardly smirked and then blurted out he was sorry.

"You better be," his mom said, stepping into the house. Jeff followed. "We were worried sick."

"I know," Jeff said.

His dad was sitting on the sofa, arms crossed. It was passed one in the morning and both of his parents were still in their work clothes. They hadn't changed all day.

"What were you thinking?" His dad stood up, yelling. "You can't just wander off without us knowing. We don't get the privilege of living in a country that is sane and humane."

"I swear I didn't realize. I fell asleep and my phone died and—"

"I don't care! You could have told us where you were and how to reach you beforehand. That way if something like this happened we wouldn't be up in the middle of the night, biting our nails, and thinking how our only son is most likely being killed and there's nothing we can do."

Jeff stayed quiet, his head bowed in a mixture of emotions that was making his insides twist together. His father was standing in front of him now and his mom was trying her best to diffuse the situation, telling his dad to take a breath and the important thing was Jeff being safe. It was all in the background as he contemplated telling them the full truth. His parents would most likely homeschool him and make him stop seeing Marc. He could live with being homeschooled, although he never wanted to before. After that day, it didn't seem too awful of a choice. The not seeing Marc, however, was not an option.

Jeff really liked Marc.

"Leo," his mom said, putting her hands on his dad's shoulders. "Look at his nose. He's had enough fighting for today." She turned to Jeff. "I saw it the minute you walked in. Is that why you went to your boyfriend's? Which is the first I knew about any boy."

Jeff took a moment to collect his thoughts and think of a lie. "Yes, but it wasn't a serious fight or anything. I don't want you thinking the school's unsafe and homeschooling me or anything, but yeah, I got in a fight. I'm sorry I didn't tell you guys I was seeing anyone it's still new."

"We're not gonna homeschool you," his dad said. "We've put too much money into all the private schools to take you out now. That's why I gave you the knife."

"And," his mom said, furrowing her brow at his father. "We want the very best education for you. With that said, you're not going to school tomorrow. You need a day to cool off. No cellphone, no laptop, no tv. You are going to sit and reflect."

"But I need to turn in a permission slip by Thursday for my social justice class," Jeff said, worried he was going to miss out on the most exciting topic discussed in class.

"Good thing tomorrow, or better yet today," his dad said, groaning, "is only Wednesday."

"Goodnight," his mom said, turning and heading down the hall.

"Don't you ever do that again," his dad said, pulling him in for a tight hug. "I'm glad you're safe."

And with that his parents shut off the hallway light and went into their bedroom, closing the door behind them. Jeff grabbed his phone and figured his parents had forgotten to take it away. Their threat was most likely a bluff.

Clicking on messages, Jeff decided to read Mal's messages.

Mal [3:45pm]: Hey I just tried calling you and it went to voicemail. Let me know you're okay!

Mal [4:15pm]: What are you mad at me?

Mal [5:30pm]: Okay now I'm worried! This isn't funny Jeff. Please let me know you're okay

Mal [6:00pm]: I just called your mom and she said you told her you were coming to my house???? What??

Mal [6:01pm]: I love you and I just really hope you're okay!!!

Mal [6:01pm]: <3

Mal [6:22pm]: If you don't call or text me back by tonight I'm telling your parents about Adrian.

Mal [6:39pm]: Also my dad's in one of his moods so I probably won't be at school tomorrow which makes this even worse.

Mal [6:39pm]: I'm really worried!!

Mal [6:40pm] Please be safe!!

Mal [8:00pm] Your parents keep texting me and asking if I've heard anything. I'm giving it till the morning and then I'm telling them

Mal [10:58pm]: Goodnight. Please be safe wherever you are!

Jeff sighed and felt even worse for making Mal go through all of that. It wasn't her fault her dad took her out of school, he knew that, and he also knew how his moods sometimes got the better of him. Jeff clicked on his screen and began to type a message.

Jeff [1:28am]: im so sorry!!! my phone died and I was at marcs house and I fell asleep. my parents are so pissed im grounded so I wont be in school either. at least well both be away from adrian! again mal im so sorry I put you through that :(hope youre okay. love you

After clicking send, Jeff went into the kitchen and opened up the cabinet next to the fridge for a small cup. He put the glass under the water spout on his refrigerator's door and filled it. Within a moment it was empty. He hadn't realized how thirsty he was.

As he made his way into his room, he placed his phone on its charging port next to his bed. There was no way his parents would actually go through with it. Jeff took off his clothes, sleeping in his

110

boxers, and shut off the light. He lied in bed and started drifting off. The day had caught up with him and in that moment his body finally succumbed to the sleep it so desperately wanted.

Jeff squinted at the sunlight that was forcing him awake. Throwing his hand up, he blocked the immediate cast of the sun and was able to see that his blinds had been opened, completely. *Mom,* he thought. With an automatic reaction, Jeff reached for his phone, fully expecting it to be in his grasp. Only his hand closed around nothing, pulling his gaze from the blinds to the spot where his phone used to be.

"Are you kidding me," Jeff muttered, throwing his blankets off of himself angrily and closing his blinds.

With a huff, he crossed his arms and shifted his eyes to his desk. No laptop. Jeff cursed under his breath. His parents had truly kept their threat and he was now void of any interaction with the outside world. At least he had told Mal he was safe. Since they were both grounded anyway, Jeff wasn't too concerned with not having his phone since she most likely had hers taken away also.

Rubbing his hands up and down his arm, Jeff hurried back into bed and under the safety of his comforter. His toes were already cold enough to hurt when he rubbed them together for warmth. Jeff closed his eyes and attempted to fall asleep, but his nose hurt when he rubbed it and he remembered the day before. Sure, the night before he was able to fall asleep at the drop of the hat, but now his mind began to race: the threat, the making out, the party.

Marc.

Jeff had forgot to text him that he was grounded and now he couldn't. The idea of Marc texting him about the night before and getting no reply made Jeff's eyes burst open and his heart race. Maybe Marc would put two and two together and come to the realization that Jeff was grounded. He doubted that though.

"Oh, no." Jeff shot up in bed. If his mom had his phone and Marc were to text him about the night before, his mom would be able to read the preview message. *Anyone* who texted him today would show a preview on his home screen. Jeff's stomach plummeted at the thought of his mom reading anything about all that had happened the day before.

Jeff pinched the bridge of his nose and immediately reeled his fingers back from the sharp pain that shot up. This was the first notable nose injury Jeff had ever received and he wasn't entirely sure he could get used to the pain, which eventually devolved into an annoying throbbing.

Once again, out of frustration and lack of being able to fall back to sleep. Jeff tossed his blankets off himself, flung open his door, and left his room. He cut across the hallway to his parent's room, knowing they both were at work.

His parents room, since being the master bedroom, had a bathroom connected directly to it. The California King mattress was center in the bedroom, and a plasma TV hung on the wall across from it. A sliding glass door across from the hallway entrance led to the backyard. The beige curtains were drawn giving the room a certain darkness to it, with small lines of light slipping through the slits where the two curtains connected.

Without skipping a beat, Jeff strode into their bathroom — which was in the corner of the room next to the TV — and opened up the medicine cabinet above the sink. He didn't need the lights, he knew exactly where the bottle was.

His mom would never admit to it, but Jeff knew she had a pill problem, or better yet coping mechanism to the law. She had a friend who was a pharmacist and was able to get Vicodin. Some lie about chronic pain. Jeff would occasionally sneak in and take a pill here and there to help him relax when he was tense. In that instance however, he really needed them for his nose.

Jeff poured two pills into his hand, placed them on his tongue, and then turning the faucet on, leaning over for water. He slurped up as much as he could and swallowed the pills. Placing the bottle back, he turned around, returned to his room and lied in bed, slowly feeling his muscles relaxing, and the throbbing subsiding.

Jeff felt semi-happy about how everything had gone yesterday. He now got to stay home and sleep all day. It was starting to feel like more of a vacation than a punishment, and with that last thought Jeff was able to fall back to sleep.

Knocking came from the front door, causing Jeff to squint one eye open, waiting to hear if it was a one-time thing. It wasn't. Jeff huffed and got out of bed, reached for a gray hoodie that was hanging over his desk chair, and slipped on a pair of sweatpants that was lying on the floor. With his arms crossed, Jeff made his way down the hallway, walking quietly up to the door, and looked through the peephole. Immediately, he unlocked the deadbolt and swung open the door.

"Mal!" Jeff said, too happy to notice the pain in his nose when his entire face scrunched in excitement. "What are you doing here? I thought you were grounded?"

"I am," Mal said, stepping inside. Jeff closed the door behind them. "I told my dad how you got hurt by Adrian and explained how serious it was. I asked him if he could drive me here really quick to make sure you're okay."

"Mal, that's so nice." Jeff felt guilty about dodging her call the day before. "Are you okay?"

"Me?" Mal asked, furrowing her brows. "Why wouldn't I be?"

"I just mean," Jeff shrugged, "your dad has a temper."

Mal's face went slack and Jeff saw her guard being put up as her lips pursed. "I'm fine."

"I didn't mean to offend you. I just wanted to make sure you were okay, too." Jeff saw her take her sleeves and discreetly pull them down into her palms. He knew that meant something was up, that her father most likely hit her. He wished she would open up.

"I just came to make sure you were okay, now that I know you are, I'll leave." Mal turned on her heel and Jeff made a split decision call.

Without fully thinking it through, he said, "wait," and pulled her in for a hug. He knew if she was in pain she would wince, and although he felt semi-manipulative, he needed to know. As his arms wrapped around her and he squeezed, Mall winced and pushed him off.

"You're an asshole," she said, stomping towards the door.

"Are you okay, Mal?" Jeff asked, completely sincere. "I just want to make sure you're okay."

Mal stopped, and Jeff saw her shoulders were tense. She sighed, and they relaxed.

"He just had a little too much to drink. He apologized immediately this morning." Mal still wasn't facing him.

"He's an abusive alcoholic, Mal."

"No," Mal said, turning around. Her arms were down by her side. "He's not an alcoholic. He just hasn't dealt with my mom's death. It was hard."

"Mal…" Jeff trailed off because what he was going to say wouldn't fix anything, it would just cause an argument. Instead he thought about what would be good for Mal, in the moment. "Um, do you want some Vicodin? For the pain?"

"You have Vicodin?" Mal squinted a skeptical glance.

"My mom, well, let's just say you're not the only one living with someone who uses a coping mechanism."

"Gotcha," Mal said, doing a quick nod.

"I'll go grab you two pills. One for now and then one for tomorrow," Jeff said.

Jeff made his way down the hallway and into his parent's room. He wanted to tell Mal to stay with him and for her dad to leave, but he knew that was unrealistic. Mal's dad was a big man — well over six foot with a stocky build that made him look like the perfect bouncer for a club. Jeff had not admitted it to Mal, but her dad scared him, and he didn't even have to live with him. How Mal did it was a mystery to Jeff.

As Jeff was putting the pill bottle back into the cabinet, a loud and aggressive knock came bellowing from the front door. Sighing, Jeff knew that meant Mal's dad was coming to get her. He rushed back into the living room, handing her the two pills. They did a quick goodbye, Jeff making sure not to squeeze when he hugged her goodbye.

"Be safe," he said, as she turned and opened the door.

"Let's go," her dad grunted, doing a stern nod — and one over — at Jeff.

The front door closed behind them and Jeff locked the door, returning to his bedroom. The day was almost half over. All he needed to do was get his parents to sign his permission slip and then he was good to go for class the next day. With all the awful stuff that had happened the past couple of days, Jeff was ready to sit and learn about a topic that intrigued him.

He was ready for some semblance of normalcy.

CHAPTER 10

Jeff had his permission slip in hand as he walked into first period with Mal. His parents had come home from work the previous day and gave him back his cell phone, along with a lecture about charging his phone and telling them where he will be. They hadn't seemed mad though. Sure, they were not happy, but it felt more of a plea from them for Jeff to stay safe and aware. He left with a melancholy feeling, knowing that he had caused his parents unnecessary worry.

After the talk with him, his parents looked over the permission slip and signed it, telling Jeff to really listen during that class. He whole heartedly assured his parents he would listen and ask any questions that came up. After all, he had been looking forward to this class since he started high school. Sex Ed was boring. The internet taught him all he needed to know, but being able to ask any question about Prop 485 made him more excited than he wanted to admit. And he knew he could have searched about it at any time, but he also knew himself better, and besides not knowing where to start, Jeff was accustomed to falling down rabbit holes, going from one site to the next until he was nowhere near where he had started.

When he had picked Mal up she thanked him for the Vicodin, and that was all that needed to be said. The subtext was there. She was thanking him for not prying into it the day before, Jeff could tell. He nodded, and they listened to the radio.

Everything felt like it was taking abnormally long. The drive to school became the "let's see how many red lights we can hit in a row" game. And even then, as Jeff sat in his chair, permission slip clutched in hand, everything felt slow. His eyes glanced back and forth from the clock, at the head of the classroom, to the door, waiting for Mr. Shan to enter in, and class to start.

The chairs were not set up in their usual circle, but rather in rows, a podium in the front of the classroom. It was very formal, nothing like Mr. Shan. Luckily, no matter if the classroom was in a circle or rows, Jeff's seat was still in the very back corner by the books.

Class started in two minutes. Jeff surveyed the room, noticing a few empty chairs dispersed throughout, but still no Mr. Shan. His leg tapped vigorously under his desk as the thought of something awful happening to Mr. Shan crossed his mind, and that single thought sent his thoughts racing down a kaleidoscope of different scenarios that could have happened to — Mr. Shan entered the room and all of Jeff's worries exited his mind.

"Hello, class," Mr. Shan said, placing his things down on his desk before turning his attention to the class. "Does anyone still have a permission slip to turn in, or if you did not get it signed, something to read? You will be across the hall; the classroom is empty for first period."

Jeff's arm shot up with his permission slip and Mr. Shan nodded as he glanced around the room.

"Okay," he said, starting down the rows and collecting the permission slips. "Looks like everyone who's here got theirs signed."

Mr. Shan came by, taking Jeff and Mal's slips. Jeff turned and raised his eyebrows in excitement towards Mal. She did a nod back, not looking as excited as Jeff was. As Mr. Shan gathered the last of the papers and walked to the front, the bell rang for class to begin. Attention set forward, Jeff was ready.

"So," Mr. Shan began, "before I get into everything, I want a show of hands of how many people actually understand the law."

Jeff furrowed his brow, *what was there not to understand?* He thought.

"Don't be shy," the teacher coaxed. "Trust me, the law and the ramifications of it on our justice system are pretty convoluted."

After that, a few students put up their hands, or better yet raised them barely above their heads. Jeff turned and saw Mal even had her hand semi-up. He felt like he was missing something. Murder is legal, done and done.

"I thought so." Mr. Shan clapped his hands together and nodded. "So, we all know the basics, right? Murder's legal. Still saying it out loud just doesn't sound anywhere near okay for me, but here we are." He walked to his podium, set up in the middle of the classroom, and rested his arms on it. "Let's see. Who can answer this question? When police find a dead body, what do they do?"

Jeff put his hand up, assuming he knew the answer. Mr. Shan pointed to him and nodded.

"Well," Jeff said, trying his best to not sound like he was not entirely sure. "Don't they call paramedics?"

"You would assume so, yes, but no."

Jeff sunk a little lower into his seat.

"And you would do so rightfully because why would they do anything else?" Turning to the white board, Mr. Shan began to draw a circle in the middle, with the word crimes, adding smaller, blank circles connecting to it. "With murder off the board, what are other crimes you guys can think of?"

Hands began to raise around the room and as Mr. Shan called on each answer, the web grew larger and larger.

"Okay," he said, putting his marker down. "That's enough. Now, take a look at these and you now know what police do when they find a dead body."

"What do you mean?" Someone in the front said.

"They find a dead body and they check to see if anything else occurred. For instance, they would see if the person's wallet was still there, if not it was most likely a robbery and they will do an investigation into that. They will check for any sexual assault, they will see if drugs were involved, check if there was some sort of gambling on human life happening. Long story short, murder is legal, if, and only if, it's completely devoid of *any* other possible crime that's punishable."

Jeff suddenly realized there was a lot to Prop 485 he did not know and felt a twinge of guilt for judging everyone else.

"So," a girl in the back said. "Basically, a weird way of population control?"

"Okay, well I'm not inclined or allowed to make those types of judgments, but that's not to say there are not theorists out there who do say it is a form of population control. What I'm saying is, the justice system now cracks down harder on every crime, especially if it has to do with a murder. Just because this law passed," Mr. Shan stepped out in front of his podium and started to pace. "Does not mean people are happy, and there are plenty in the justice system who have such strong hatred for it, making it their own personal mission to find anything they can on a murder case."

A guy's hand in the front rose up and Mr. Shan pointed to him.

"If people hate it so much, why is it still a law? Like, can't we just make it not a law anymore?"

"I'm glad you asked. To answer that, we must look back at the past and see what even caused this law to pass."

Jeff rose his hand. "I read that it was because of police brutality."

"That was definitely a component." Mr. Shan nodded in agreement. "Police brutality was one of the many factors that contributed to a vote even being cast for the legalization of murder.

But, that was not the only thing. Does anyone think they know what year most historians say was the start to the society we have now?"

Jeff started to think. He knew the law was passed the year he was born. Figuring that there would have had to have been years before that he thought maybe 2018 but decided not to answer in case he was wrong again.

"No one," Mr. Shan said, looking across the room. "Well, it was 2016. That's when most historians say there is evidence of a shift in societies desensitization of violence. Police brutality videos became so normalized, that on any given day, videos of unarmed, mainly black men, being killed by police were viewed at rates as quick as new music videos. 2016 was also an unprecedented year in history for mass shootings, marking the first year where there were more mass shootings — with more casualties — than there were calendar days. 2016 was the election year where Trump won, and an entire global shift happened. That year felt like an honest to God nightmare. Ask your parents. The world felt like it was ending.

"But those also were not the only factors that makes 2016 the year. Politically speaking, there was voter fraud happening, deliberate attempts to undermine candidates in people's own parties, Russian spies were leaking information exposing the political injustices, and people were stirred up. America was built on a principle of a country being for the people by the people, and that year the people felt like they were being silenced.

"After Trump took office, many allies across the globe backed off supporting us, and the U.N. had to step in when Trump was threatening to possibly cause a nuclear holocaust. Everything compiled together into a perfect storm, and as society began to stir, more and more violence began to escalate.

"By 2019, the country was at its worst and it seemed like a civil war was going to happen. Either that, or a complete uprising of the citizens. With everything so tumultuous, a change happened, politically, that sent the first domino into what we now know today."

No one in the classroom spoke. Jeff had never seen an entire classroom this intent on listening to every word being said by the teacher, and yet he too could not turn his attention anywhere else. He had no idea how much he did not know.

"In 2020, the people voted to make the country one state. Only federal laws. No more state laws, no more electoral college, no more party system. The United States of America became America United, and it was now mass voting on any law.

"And since, before, there were elections every two years. That now meant the President was up for reelection every two years. In 2022 a man named Ivan Hughes took office."

"Wait," Mal said, raising her hand. "Isn't he President right now?"

"Yes, he is." Mr. Shan sighed. "He presented Prop 485 to the public. Hughes promised them that the country would not break into mass violence, but that this would help make a dent in the overcrowding of prisons, help the economy get back on its feet, and ultimately save America.

"Sounds crazy, and yet it passed. I guess when a country is at its worst, full of fear and anger, they choose an option that they normally wouldn't. But since it was mass voting, somehow it happened, and shockingly, the economy did get better, there was a dent in overcrowding, but it was not a saving option at all.

"Funny thing is, everyone was so worked up over Prop 485 they never really paid attention to the other propositions being put on the ballot, and because of that, a few other laws changed. Hughes also fought for the law that removed term limits for Presidents.

"He had his way after that, and he kept to his promises. The economy boomed almost immediately after the law. Bullet proof glass, bullet proof accessories, weapons, protection for houses, security, insurance, et cetera were all everyone was buying. Hughes kept his word all right. We came out of our national deficit as people used every bit of money they could scrounge up to protect themselves.

"We were already an extreme capitalistic society before, but after Prop 485, businesses were rolling in money. But, remember the number one rule of my Social Justice class."

"Look at the world around us with an intersectional lens." Everyone said together.

"Exactly! Now, when we look at Prop 485, who is left at a disadvantage?"

"The poor," someone said.

"Low income families," Mr. Shan said, "exactly. The homeless were the most disadvantaged and because of that, there was a decline in homelessness."

"But," the same person said. "There are a lot of homeless people today."

"Today, being the key word. In 2025, a year after Prop 485, the middle class was thriving and support for Hughes and Prop 485 was rising. But, like most good times, it comes to an end.

"Outsourcing happens, and just like that, the economy begins to sink, the middle class diminishes, and now we have today's society. Businesses closing, homelessness at its highest in years, and violence starting to rise again. I'm not saying this to scare you, I'm saying this in hopes that maybe there will be another shift soon and this law can be a dark shade in our nation's history."

A girl towards the front raised her hand, and Mr. Shan called on her.

"Aren't you not allowed to take a side, legally? Because my dad says Prop 485 saved the country."

"I'm allowed to not like murder, Becky." Mr. Shan looked like he wanted to say more, but he left it at that.

Jeff turned his gaze to see if Mal was listening or if he could roll his eyes at Becky's remark with her when he saw someone outside the classroom. Adrian's face was perfectly in view through the glass in the center of the door. Their eyes met for a brief second, but Jeff diverted his away, trying his best to act like he did not see, but he knew Adrian saw him.

Jeff felt his palms begin to clam up, a ball forming in his throat. Trying his best not to draw attention to himself, Jeff shifted his eyes back to see if Adrian was still there.

He was.

Adrian motioned, aggressively, for Jeff to come out of the classroom. Jeff's pulse began to race, and he could feel his forehead beginning to sweat. He had to think. If he stayed in class until the end, he could inform Mr. Shan and get security. Besides that option, he didn't see any other way. There was no way he was going to go outside.

Jeff very lightly shook his head no to Adrian. He could see Adrian flick his tongue across his lower lip and run his hands through his hair.

Without realizing it, Jeff had tuned the lecture out and now had no idea where in the history lesson they were. He sat, faced forward, trying his best to stay focused on Mr. Shan and not glance at Adrian. As he listened to the lecture, he also quietly breathed in and out to calm his nerves. Adrian had looked infuriated when Jeff refused and there was no telling what he would do. No matter how hard he tried though, Jeff's stomach did not ease up on the queasiness.

There was a buzzing against legs as his phone vibrated in his pocket. Jeff slyly used his right hand to slip his fingers in and gently pull his phone out. A preview of the message shined on his screen from an unknown number.

[Unknown 7:55am]: get out her now or ill kill your friend and then you

The world around him felt as though it stopped. His feet nonexistent. Blood drained from Jeff's face as a light-headed feeling took over him. How had Adrian even gotten his number? His vision tunneled out for a second and he no longer could count on his plan. Different scenarios sprung into his mind, but there was only one option that would guarantee Mal's safety.

The only option, and it wasn't even his own. If he could choose he would stay in and tell Mr. Shan what was going on, and hope that they found Adrian, but there was no guarantee. If Mal died because of Jeff, he would never forgive himself. He needed to know she would be safe and he knew what that meant, what he was forced to choose.

Jeff had to go out and face Adrian.

CHAPTER 11

Everything was background noise, all Jeff heard was his heart beat, all he felt was his chest getting tighter with each breath. *Think, think, think.* His right hand felt numb as it was wrapped so tightly around his phone that he had not even realized his left hand was white knuckling the side of his desk. He needed to think of something fast.

Adrian had a knife, at least he did the other day when he had attacked Jeff. Assuming he still had that, Jeff needed something to be able to defend himself. He really did not think that Adrian would be ignorant enough to believe he could get away with two killings, mere days apart, but Jeff also knew that people were capable of unexplainable actions.

Think, think, think.

The knife! The knife his dad had given him. A rush of relief flowed over him. His desk was in the back, directly in front of the encyclopedias. If he could manage to reach behind him and grab it, he would at least have some sort of chance.

Mr. Shan was writing on the board significant dates and court cases that were all factors into the law. Jeff really wanted to learn about it all, understand the history. That was all he had been looking forward too, and now he had to miss it. Anger filled his bones as he thought of it. Any other day, it could have been any other day. But no, of course it was the only school day that Jeff had ever actually cared about, besides finally graduating next year.

Unclenching his left hand from the desk, Jeff carefully — and slowly — maneuvered his arm behind him, blindly placing his fingers down on top of the encyclopedias. When he had put the knife in, he made sure to insert it in the middle of the book so he would be able to spot the gap between pages. Since he could not see however, Jeff was now using his touch to rub down the pages and feel for the gap.

His fingers gently swiped across the encyclopedias, anxiety setting in with the idea that someone had found the knife and he was now all out of options. The phone buzzed again in his hand, but he did not read it or turn his focus away from his left arm. Two encyclopedias and nothing. Another buzz. His fingers finished another and with each passing moment, Jeff felt panic begin to set in.

Buzz.

Still no knife.

Jeff was about to give up when his index finger glided across a gap in the pages. He let out a long sigh, not realizing he had been holding his breath as he worked his hand in between the pages, finally feeling the handle to the knife. His fingers closed around it and he attempted to casually lift it up. Once he slid it up into his palm, he pulled his hand out of the encyclopedia, hiding the knife in his sleeve, and then raising his hand.

"Yes, Jeff?" Mr. Shan pointed to him.

"May I go to the restroom," Jeff said, and he could hear the shakiness in his voice. "I don't feel well."

"Yes, of course. You look pale, are you sure you don't want to go to the nurses?"

"I might," he said, standing up and keeping his hand held around his sleeve.

"Feel better."

Jeff nodded and turned to Mal, whispering, "I think it's just my breakfast, I'll be okay."

Mal nodded and told him she'd let him know what he missed. He thanked her, taking an extra moment to detail her, not knowing if it would be the last.

Her hair was pulled up into a bun. She had on small hanging diamond earrings that shimmered in the sunlight. Blue lipstick, matching the light blue eyeshadow, made Mal look as beautiful as ever to Jeff. She had on a black leather long sleeve coat that came down to her knees. Her arms were covered, a turtle neck covering her neck, and Jeff knew it was because she was hiding the bruises from her dad.

All he wanted was for her to be safe, and that was why he needed to stand up and go outside. At least he'd know he did everything he could to keep her out of harm's way.

His knees felt wobbly underneath him as he walked from the back of the classroom out into the hallway. He imagined how bad he must have looked to the other students: shaky, pale, sweating, and walking like an old man. Jeff needed to get control over his nerves.

As he stepped out into the hallway, Adrian was leaning against a locker, arms crossed, glaring at Jeff. All the security guards from the other day were gone. It figures, as most establishments do: react immediately and then stop caring. Adrian stepped forward and strode towards Jeff, his eyes locked and lowered.

"You're coming with me," Adrian snapped, gripping his hand around Jeff's right arm. His fingers felt locked into Jeff's skin, only getting tighter, never looser.

Jeff kept the knife right where his sleeve met his palm.

"Where are we going?" Jeff said as he was forced down the hallway. Adrian did not reply.

As they turned a corner, Adrian shoved Jeff through the entrance to the bathroom. His knees collided with the tile, causing him to curse out in pain. As he pushed himself up, Jeff heard the bathroom door closing behind them. He turned to see Adrian propping a metal foldable chair against the doorknob.

"Do you know how easy it was to sneak a chair into this school?" Adrian stepped forward.

The bathroom wasn't big. Directly across from the door were the sinks. Two to be exact, and in that moment, Jeff had his back against one of them. To his left were the urinals, and across from them were three stalls. Jeff's eyes shot down to see if anyone was in the stalls.

No one was.

"What do you want?" Jeff said, trying his best to sound unafraid. There was no quavering in his voice and he felt like that was an improvement already. He knew in his head that it was most likely the adrenaline that was coursing through him.

"I want to know why the fuck you told." Adrian didn't move. He was between the sinks and the door, blocking the only way out.

"I didn't tell anyone, okay." Jeff was getting irritated. The reason he was missing out on class, and having his life threatened was because Adrian thought he told someone. Jeff slid the knife into his palm.

"Then why the hell did I have a detective at my house?"

"Maybe they know you're a psycho and just assumed it was you. You're proving it right now, I mean, Jesus Christ. I didn't tell anyone."

"Oh really?" Adrian lurched forward, reached into his pocket and flicked out his knife. "This detective came all dressed to impress with his coat and boots to my fucking house saying he knew I attacked you, saying it was only a matter of time before he links the two."

Jeff refused to believe his parents would have told. They would never put him in danger, and they hadn't even known about Adrian. The only people who knew were Marc and Mal. Jeff knew Mal wouldn't have said anything, but he didn't know about Marc. Had Marc called the police? Was he in danger because of Marc?

"I swear to God I didn't tell anyone!" Jeff started to evaluate the situation. Adrian continued to step forward, brandishing the knife in front of him, and Jeff saw no indication of him stopping. His fingers rolled the knife around in his palm and he decided what to do next. Adrian took another step forward and it was now or never.

Jeff revealed his hand from behind his back and flicked the blade out, aiming it at Adrian.

"I'm guessing the chair was as easy to sneak in as this," Jeff said, watching Adrian raise his eyebrows.

"You ain't gonna do shit," Adrian said.

"You sure about that?" Jeff did not want anything more to happen. He wanted it to end at that moment with Adrian backing off and letting him go. That would be ideal. No one would get hurt.

Adrian simply nodded his head and held up his hands. "Okay," he said, "okay. I guess I wasn't expecting you to fight back."

"That's because you don't kno—"

Jeff was cut off as Adrian jutted forward, catching Jeff off guard. Before he knew it, Adrian ducked, his arms open wide — completely evading the blade — and slammed into Jeff, colliding his back into the sink behind him.

The wind was knocked out of Jeff's lungs as his entire back lit up like a fuse while a web of pain radiated down his spinal cord and into the rest of his body like a virus, causing him to drop the blade onto the floor. Adrian stepped back as Jeff's body collapsed. His head was leaning against the porcelain sink as he tried to regain control of his breathing.

"Officer he came after me," Adrian mocked, squatting in front of Jeff. "You made killing you and not getting expelled so easy."

Jeff inhaled, his vision blurry from the pain. He shifted his sight to the knife that had bounced on the tile and was now a few feet away. He needed to get it back. Adrian saw what he was looking at and smirked.

"You're gonna try and grab that?" Adrian leered, standing up and stepping over, the tip of his shoe next to the blade. "Have fun getting it," he said as he kicked the knife across the tile and under a stall door.

 Jeff closed his eyes in frustration, not sure if he was going to be able to get out of the bathroom alive. That was his one way of defending himself. He had never been in an actual fight before, and as he sat there, he realized he did not have any time to ponder options. He needed to act and there was only one thing he could come up with.

Jeff coiled his right leg back, and as Adrian went to squat down again, he kicked as hard as he could into Adrian's shin. His leg connected and jolted back. Adrian groaned in pain and fell forward, his hands opening up to catch his fall, dropping the knife. Jeff honed in on it as it fell and bounced next to the urinal at the end of the row.

Before he even had time to think, Jeff scrounged to his feet and charged for the knife. Adrian's hand latched onto his ankle and Jeff fell face first onto the floor. His already sore nose hit the tile and he let out a shriek as he heard a pop which was accompanied by pulsating pain and a nose full of blood. He could taste it dripping into his mouth, the warm iron. His vision became spotty and the room felt as though it was spinning in that moment.

Adrian began to drag Jeff back and climb forward, making it hard to wiggle out of. Latched onto Jeff, Adrian crawled on top of him, trying to force Jeff onto his back. Jeff's arms were stretched out in front him, the knife almost at his fingertips. Adrian grappled onto both of Jeff's arms — his hands constricting Jeff's wrists before banging them down. Jeff's entire body was throbbing as he continued to try for the knife. Adrian's grip was still just as tight, only then he started to raise Jeff's arm upwards.

There was an intense sharp stabbing that started to increase the more Adrian pulled back, and Jeff was certain Adrian was going to tear his arm sockets out. Jeff screamed out in pain as loud as he could.

"Help!" Jeff shouted, and Adrian let go of his arms, only to grip a handful of hair from the back of Jeff's head and use that to slam his face into the floor.

Jeff's vision blacked out and he lost feeling of his body. When he came to, he was lying on his back and Adrian was on top of him, his legs holding Jeff's arms down.

"You put up more of a fight than I expected," Adrian said.

Jeff tilted his head sideways and looked behind him. The knife was still there. There was still hope.

But that thought quickly vanished as Jeff felt Adrian's hands wrap around his throat, squeezing out any air left in Jeff's lungs. He tried his best to breathe in, but nothing happened. He could hear the strangled wheezing, the sound of his sneakers screeching against the floor as his legs flailed. His eyes burned, and his face felt like it would pop from the pressure at any second, and all he saw was Adrian's face, above him, grinning.

This couldn't be it. Jeff was not going to let himself die on the bathroom floor in his high school. He focused all his energy and got control of his legs, making his last attempt to fight back as his vision began to blur. Jeff kicked his knee up and connected with Adrian's crotch.

The grip was gone, and Jeff heaved in as much air as he could, coughing. Adrian fell to the side cursing, and that was Jeff's opportunity. He pushed himself up and scooted far enough back until he could reach the knife. The moment his hand closed around the course handle, Adrian yanked him back by his legs.

Jeff fell back against the cold floor once more as Adrian attempted to do what he had done before and force Jeff down by climbing on top of him. As he tightened his grip on Jeff's leg, he pulled again and was now almost completely above him. Jeff didn't want to stab him, but he didn't see another option.

Adrian's eyes were bloodshot, and Jeff could see the rage in them. His brows were aimed downward, as though pointing to Jeff, and his lip was curled up, snarling. Jeff had to act now, or else Adrian would overpower him.

With one swift motion, Jeff swung the knife forward and felt it collide with the side of Adrian's neck, felt it as it sliced through his flesh, puncturing deeper into his throat, until he twisted the handle. Red, thick and warm, blood began to pour out of the wound, coating down the handle and dripping onto Jeff's hand. Adrian gargled and spit up blood, his eyebrows no longer aggressively pointing down, his eyes no longer harboring such a hateful expression.

Jeff found himself not able to turn his gaze from Adrian's eyes. Even as more blood began to coat down his arm and stain his clothes. Adrian almost had a confused look on his face as his arms gave out and his full weight collapsed onto Jeff. His eyes fluttered in a strange way, blood bubbling out of the corner of his lip. Jeff wanted to puke, but he could not bring himself to move. Adrian's body, heavy and limp, was all he could seem to register. His own body was nonexistent to his mind; he wasn't there.

All that he saw, were Adrian's eyes. All that he felt was Adrian's chest against his, the breathing becoming more and more shallow. All that he heard was the sound of Adrian's breath wheezing out of his slack lips.

Jeff watched the life leave Adrian. Everything ceased to exist at that moment. Jeff had expected his eyes to shut when he died, but they stayed open, his upper eyelid hovering in the middle, in a state of perpetual openness. Jeff could not turn away, no matter how much he wanted to, his eyes were transfixed on Adrian's lifeless ones.

The dead weight began to register in Jeff's mind though and he became keenly aware that he was covered in Adrian's warm sticky blood. Jeff needed to get out from under him.

His entire body throbbed in pain as he used all his strength to try and push Adrian off of himself. Positioning his hands underneath Adrian's chest, Jeff started to lift Adrian off. The pressure began to ease off of Jeff's chest until his hands slipped from the blood and Adrian collided back down on top of him.

Any relief was stripped away along with Jeff's breath. He wheezed out and coughed, rethinking the strategy. Jeff still kept his hand on Adrian's chest, but aimed them to his left now, sliding his body off. Jeff figured the blood would help slide Adrian.

Jeff pushed off sideways, and slid out from underneath Adrian, whose body lied face first, bloodied in the center of the bathroom. The sight made Jeff dry heave. He was glad he had not eaten breakfast that morning.

Sitting up, Jeff pulled himself up by the urinal, gagging. His knees were sore from the fall causing him to limp forward. The only noise in the bathroom was the sound of his blood coated sneakers squeaking against the tile. With his arms out to hold him up against the wall, Jeff slowly limped towards the door.

As he made his way closer to the door, Jeff had an irrational fear that somehow Adrian was still alive and would attack him, but all he saw as he turned around were blood smeared tracks leading back to Adrian's lifeless corpse. Jeff's gaze moved upwards as he looked at himself in the bathroom mirror. His face was crimson and bruised against his petrified pale skin.

He did not recognize himself.

There was a dark red blood stain above his lip. His nose did not look as bad as he would have assumed, but his left cheek bone however seemed to have gotten the most impact when his face met the tile. The cheek was swollen, a shiny purple and red welt pushed up under Jeff's left eye. At the head of the welt there was a gash from the hit, which bled down his chin and onto his neck where it was met by both the forming hand marks that were manifesting on Jeff's skin, and Adrian's still fresh blood.

The chair was lodged under the doorknob as Jeff grabbed the cold metal frame and yanked it out from underneath. With a desperation to finally get out of the bathroom, Jeff tossed it, causing a loud bang and echo to fill the silent room. The noise did not register with Jeff who was already turning the knob and getting out.

The hallway was empty as Jeff leaned his right arm against the white wall. Every action placed a strain on his body. He trudged down towards the Principal's office, smearing bloody hand marks as he went, stopping every few steps to catch his breath. When he swallowed, an aching would radiate in his throat.

A security guard turned the corner and stopped in his tracks, reaching into his pocket and pulling out a black handgun. He was a hefty looking bald man who harbored a soul patch underneath his lower lip.

"Stop right there," the security guard said, pointing the gun at Jeff.

"Help me," Jeff said hoarsely before his vision began to tunnel, causing him to collapse onto the thin carpet that covered the school's floor.

CHAPTER 12

Jeff regained consciousness as his eyes fluttered open to the brightness of fluorescent lights above his face. Squinting, he shifted his head to the side, hearing the sound of paper rustling underneath him. As he eyes adjusted to the light, he was able to peer around and figure out his surroundings.

To his right, was a bland colored tan counter, which was home to a silver sink in the middle. Next to the high faucet was a box that had disposable purple gloves, a glass jar full of cotton balls, and a red container that said, "biohazardous waste." Not entirely sure how long he had been passed out, he assumed he was in the hospital.

As he turned his head to his left, he realized he was still in school. There was a glass window that had a view of the front office where he could see the principal, the school nurse, and a man with a long leather black coat huddled together, seemingly discussing the events. Jeff watched as the nurse shifted her gaze to the room, making eye contact with him.

Jeff instinctively turned away, knowing that it wouldn't change anything. She noticed that he was awake and now he had to actually deal with what happened. Closing his eyes, flashes of Adrian's slack lips with red bubbles forming as his life wheezed out of him came barreling to the forefront. A tear escaped out of his closed eyelids, running down his cheek, sideways.

"Jeffrey," a woman's voice infiltrated his thoughts.

Jeff opened up his eyes and met the gaze of the school nurse. She had on a form fitting white blouse with a black ankle length skirt. She had very short black hair, almost a buzz cut, with pink side bangs across her forehead. He had never really seen a haircut like that before, but she was able to pull it off effortlessly. She had full lips, a wide nose, and when she smiled to talk it almost made everything fade away for a second.

"How are you feeling? Can you talk?" Her voice was calming, easing his mind and relaxing his muscles.

"I..." Jeff started but coughed, his throat sore. "He tried to kill me." His eyes welled up as he felt the tears starting to fall, his vision a blurry mess.

"Okay, let's just relax for now." She turned around and grabbed an ice bag that was lying inside a cooler on the floor. "Here, put this up to your cheek."

Jeff reached out and held the ice pack in his hand, shivering as he placed it on his gash. The cold hurt at first and he pulled it away, taking a breath before slowly putting it against his welt again. This time he held it and did not move the bag, knowing if he did not do something for the swelling, his face would be bruised for weeks to come. If he could at least bring it down to where his eye did not look like it was disappearing behind a bloody mountain of skin, he would be all right.

"I'm nurse Bolt," she said, garnishing a sympathetic look in her eyes. "How does your nose feel? I popped it back into place and then put some strips to keep it in place and stop the bleeding. You're lucky, it could have been much worse."

Jeff hadn't even realized that his nose was not throbbing in pain like it had been earlier. Cautiously, he attempted to wiggle his nose. It still hurt, but the pain was not as excruciating as before, and he could get air in through his nostrils.

"Thank you." Jeff managed a small smile but grimaced as his cheek flared with discomfort. His mind kept replaying the fight over and over again. Maybe he could have stopped it somehow? Did he have to kill Adrian? He sighed, "what happens now?"

"Well," Nurse Bolt began, "we called your parents, so they are on their way."

Jeff groaned and closed his eyes, wishing the day never happened.

"Just keep the ice on your cheek to make sure that swelling goes down."

"I didn't want to kill him," he said, staring forward. "He wouldn't stop, and I didn't have any other choice. I don't know what —"

"Shhh," the nurse said, sitting down on a rolling stool. "Don't stress yourself out more than you already are. You survived."

"I killed." Jeff exhaled, licking his lower lip and tasting blood. "I killed Adrian."

"Jeffrey," Nurse Bolt said, cupping her hands together and leaning her elbows on the patient table he was currently lying on. "Between you and I, you did this school a favor."

Jeff shot the nurse an incredulous look. How could she say that killing someone was a favor? Sure, Adrian had tormented kids, but that didn't mean killing him was the solution. If the school really wanted its students safe they would have figured out a reason to expel Adrian before it escalated and people got killed. Instead, like most teaching establishments, it all came down to money. Jeff knew that, he did. Private schools thrived because people wanted the best for their children, and no institution would risk losing money, and a potential lawsuit, over a troubled kid.

Part of being a teenager was being troubled.

"Jeff!" His mom's voice came booming in as her and his father came rushing into the nurse's room. "Oh, my God, your face." His mom was by his side in a second, her hands instinctively going to cup his cheeks. She stopped before she grabbed his face and kept her hands at bay.

"What happened?" His dad's voice filled the room.

"Jeff, are you okay? My baby. I was so worried when they called. They wouldn't tell me anything." Her mom glared at the nurse. "Just, 'there's been an accident.' This looks worse than just an accident!"

Jeff watched his father pacing across from where he was lying down. His dad had his thumb in his mouth as he gnawed at his nail. Pausing, his dad turned to the nurse and said, "may we talk to our son privately."

"Absolutely," she said, placing her hands together and walking out with a pleasant smile idle on her face.

As soon as the door closed behind her, Jeff knew he was in for it.

"Does this have anything to do with the fight the other day?" His dad's face was a mixture of concern and anger.

"Yes," Jeff croaked out through his sore voice.

"You sound terrible," his mother gasped, tears welling in her eyes. "You tell us the truth, Jeffery Braen. If you lie to us one more time so help me God, Jeff, so help me God. I will make your life a living hell and you'll be counting down the days till you're eighteen."

"I'd listen to your mom," his dad chimed in.

He had never seen his mother so intense before. Her eyes were beaming lasers at him as she stood next to the table Jeff was lying on — her arms folded tightly.

"I witnessed that murder the other day," he began, telling his parents his best version of the truth he could. As much as he wanted to be completely honest, some details — Marc, the party, and giving Mal Vicodin — had to stay a secret. He did, however, let his mom know he took two for the pain, that way she wouldn't question him when she went for a pill later.

Both his parents harbored incredulous looks on their faces, that then devolved into empathy.

"Thank you for being honest," his mom said, unfolding her arms and rubbing his shoulder. "You look like shit, and the healing will be punishment enough."

"But," his dad added. "If you're ever in danger again call us. We can help; and we don't ever want you to feel like you can't come to us."

"Exactly. We love you and want you to be safe."

By that point, Jeff had already cried while reliving the trauma of taking Adrian's life, and he was now bawling as his parents simply were glad he was alive.

"I love you guys," he said, finally taking the ice pack off, hoping it had done some healing.

The man in the coat stepped into the room. "Sorry to interrupt," he said, doing a curt nod. "I'm a detective and I just need to ask Jeff a few questions, then I'll be out of your way."

"Of course," Jeff's mom said, planting a quick kiss on his right cheek before backing out. His father followed suit, and then Jeff was alone in the room with the detective.

"Jeffery, is it?" The detective flipped out a small notepad. The outside was tattered, the brown leather torn in the edges, flakes coming off from wear and tear, but when he flipped it open, the pages were a pristine white.

"Jeff is fine," he answered, feeling his heart racing. After everything he learned about police violence, he found himself afraid.

"I'm detective Seymour," he said, taking a seat on the stool next to Jeff. Once he sat down, Jeff was able to get a better look at him. His face was very narrow, all coming to a point at the tip of his skinny nose. Cheekbones seemed to be the main feature of Seymour's face, seeing as both sides of his face cratered in to accentuate them. Thin, almost pale, lips pursed together underneath his nose, and below that was a very mild cleft chin. He looked sickly with how pale his skin was coupled with the dark circles under his eyes.

Jeff took note of a scar that stretched from his right eyebrow across to his ear. It looked like he had been attacked with a knife and escaped with his life. Seymour's black hair was short and neat, gelled down to the side with not a single hair standing out of place.

"I need to ask you a few questions about what happened." With a quick motion of his right hand, Seymour reached into his coat, pulling out a pen. With a click, he had the tip against the paper and was ready to write. "Do you have any idea why Adrian would have wanted to hurt you?"

"Yes." Jeff's voice was low, and he didn't look up to make eye contact. His hands were clasped together in his lap, his focus on them, on the blood stains that were still visible on his bare skin.

"Why would he have wanted to hurt you?"

"I…." He paused, knowing he would have to relive this horror over and over again every time he had to tell it to someone new. "I witnessed him kill a kid on the first day of school."

"And you didn't report it?" The detective scribbled notes into his pad.

"He threatened to kill me," Jeff said in a defensive tone, his hands tightening in his lap.

"Then what?"

"After he told me he'd kill me? I kept my mouth shut. I didn't tell anyone. But he found me in first period today, started texting me. I don't even know how he got my number. You can read the texts though, he was threatening to kill my friend if I didn't come outside to talk to him."

"And while all of this was happening, you didn't think that you should come forward and tell someone?"

"Who would I have told?"

"Your parents, teachers, security, the police, anyone." The detective placed the pen flat on the pad and sighed. "Did you go into that bathroom with the intent to kill Adrian?"

"No!" Jeff barked, crossing his arms. "That psycho threw me into the bathroom, talking about some detective questioning him, and then he tried to kill me." Jeff disdainfully rolled his eyes. "How about instead of questioning me, you guys figure out how he was able to sneak a knife and chair into this so called safe school, because I don't feel safe anymore."

"That was my next question. So, the knife was Adrian's?"

"Yes." Jeff suddenly becoming aware of the knife that he had brought, that Adrian kicked under the stall. If the universe was willing to shine just a little bit of luck on him, he prayed that it did so by having the knife slide behind the toilet, and out of plain sight. "He came at me with it and I finally got it and had to kill him. He was choking me to death."

"I can see the handprints," Seymour said, narrowing his eyes and detailing over Jeff's neck as if to make sure they were real.

"Take a picture it'll last longer," Jeff said sarcastically.

Seymour flipped his note pad closed and glared at Jeff, surveying him up and down. "See you around," he said, standing up and exiting the room.

After that encounter, the day began to blur by at the thought of someone finding the knife. Replaying the memory over and over again in his mind, Jeff did not remember ever going by the stalls, and with that thought he prayed that if the detective searched the bathroom he would ignore the stalls. The closing maintenance team might find it, sure, but by then everything would have been cleaned up, seeing as the school was already back in session the day after the freshman was killed. Maybe the universe would start to show some favor on Jeff and he could relax knowing he'd be okay. At the very least, he had to act okay for his parent's sake.

Eventually, the nurse came back in and handed him another ice pack, letting him know he should apply one for twenty minutes, once an hour for the first day, explaining it should help keep the swelling down, and also assist with redness and pain. Jeff thanked her and was finally allowed to leave the school.

When he stepped off of the nurse's table, his knees ached and caused him to limp slightly, but nothing too bad. With each step he grew more and more used to the dull ache and was able to walk without the limp. He had never realized how oblivious he was to his nose before that moment because with each breath he was reminded of the injury. And with every swallow his throat would tighten, causing pain. Although he felt like it was what he deserved considering what had happened.

The car ride home was silent. Jeff sat in the backseat gazing at the trees, shifting his focus from a single car to the landscape, the vehicles melting into blurs. His breath fogged the window and he leaned his forehead against it. Closing his eyes, Jeff saw the knife enter Adrian's throat and twist. His eyes shot open and he let out a heavy sigh.

Once they were home his mom made him a sandwich before giving him a Vicodin. After he ate Jeff went into his room, stripping off his blood-soaked clothes. With little energy, Jeff entered a steaming shower and stood motionless in the middle, the scalding hot water pelting his skin. His head was bowed down as he watched the blood dilute into a pinkish color as it spiraled down the drain. Jeff felt numb watching.

Tilting his face forward, he felt the water wash over his head, drowning everything else out. He stood with his head hunched under the showerhead for minutes, not wanting to emerge and deal with reality, but he knew he needed to. Jeff took a step back, letting the water shoot onto his chest, realizing that his hands and forearms were still bloody. Reaching to the shelf along his shower wall, he grabbed his bar soap and lubed it up in the water, making sure there were visible bubbles on it before beginning to scrub his skin roughly.

As the soap soaked into his skin and helped remove the blood, the water continued with its pink hue. Jeff closed his eyes and a quick flash of Adrian's bloodshot eyes over him caused him to open them back up. He needed the blood off.

The hot water did relax his muscles which was the only enjoyable part of the shower. Once he finally scrubbed the stains off his skin, Jeff exited, grabbing his sky-blue towel off the towel rack to his right. Jeff did a quick wipe down of his body before wrapping the towel around his waist and stepping out.

The bathroom mirror was covered in steam, making it impossible for Jeff to see anything but a blur. He wiped the mirror with his hand and took a detailed look at himself. Compared to earlier in the day when he had seen himself in the mirror after it all happened, Jeff looked much better. Sure, his eye was still swollen, but not nearly as bad as it was earlier. The bridge of his nose did have a gash on it, which Jeff rubbed antibiotic pain-relieving cream on. The bruises on his neck were still red, but they did not seem to be getting anymore puffy than they were. It was manageable.

He was lucky to be able to leave the encounter with such non-life-threatening injuries.

Because of the hot water, his skin was a bright red, as if he had been sunburned. He chuckled seeing it, knowing that if he had turned the hot nozzle any higher he could have caused some burning to his skin.

Jeff changed into grey sweatpants and a burgundy hoodie. Trudging from the bathroom to his bed, he lied down staring straight ahead at the popcorn spackled ceiling. Without even realizing it, his vision began to blur before he felt a tear roll down the side of his face. Jeff tried to breathe in, but his chest was heavy and before he knew it, he was folded in on himself weeping.

With each sob his body shook as he clung to himself for security. No matter how tightly he wrapped his arms around himself, his body still felt like an empty shell. Each finger gripped into his back as he quaked again, tears and snot running down his face. He never wanted to kill someone, and now there was no going back. Sixteen. For the rest of his life he would always have the images branded into his mind. But somewhere deep down, he knew he could never run from the fact that he chose to stab Adrian in the neck, chose to twist the blade deeper into his throat, and he was not sure if he was ready to face what that meant for him. The only person he knew who might understand what he was going through was Marc.

[Jeff 12:45 pm]: Can you come over tonight around 10? I'll shut off the guard lights and you can sneak in my window. I really need you.

[Marc 12:55 pm]: Yeah, of course. I'll be there right at 10 on the dot.

[Mal 2:55 pm]: Hey I hope you're feeling better! Something happened again at school but they're being really hush hush about it all idk but I figured since you didn't come back you went home sick. I have your backpack I can drop it off if you need?

Jeff read the text and sighed realizing that he had not told Mal about what happened. Everything was so hectic and after he cried and texted Marc, his body had given out and he slept. Anxiety crawled across his body and sat on his chest, leaving him unsure of what to do. He didn't want to text her what happened, it felt too serious for a text, but he also did not want to worry her. His mom had told him when he got home that the school had to suspend him for the following week. It was a blessing they did not expel him, Jeff knew that, but he also knew there would be no way of hiding what happened. In that moment though, hiding it seemed like the less stressful option.

[Jeff 3:30 pm]: yeah im not feeling well at all. im hoping that ill feel better by sunday and then I can stop off and get the backpack you dont need to come here. I dont want to get you sick lol but thanks for checking in!

Guilt took over the anxiety as he clicked the send button. Mal did not need to see him beat up like that. Hopefully by Sunday he would be even more healed and be able to calmly tell the story without breaking down. Doubtful about the last sentiment, Jeff still was holding out that his cuts would be much less gruesome.

[Mal 3:32 pm]: Yeah do not get me sick on the first week back lol what bad luck! But of course hope you feel better and get a bunch of sleep. Text me if you need anything <3

[Jeff 3:33 pm]: <33

Jeff made sure the security lights were off after his parents went to bed. The only nice thing about his parents living in suburbia but working in the city was that they went to bed before ten every night due to morning traffic. He sat on the edge of his bed, checking the time on his phone. Five more minutes and Marc should be there. He timed it so that he would be done with the ice pack right at the time Marc was coming over.

As the time hit and Jeff lowered the ice pack, there was a tapping from his bedroom window and he could see Marc's grin being illuminated by his lights. But as Jeff trudged to the window, Marc's smirk dissolved in on itself as he got a better look at him. As he began to open the window, he could see that Marc was about to start asking what happened. Jeff held up his finger to tell Marc to be quiet as he crawled through the window. Once it was closed behind him and the cold air ceased to infiltrate his room, Marc wrapped his arms around him gently, and Jeff felt his muscles relax in the embrace.

"What happened?" Marc asked quietly, pulling back as he peered over the injuries. "Do you need me to hurt anyone?"

"No," Jeff said, feeling his throat tighten. "No." He began to cry and tilted his head to rest on Marc's shoulder. "Can we just cuddle for a little."

"Yeah, whatever you need." Marc lightly placed his hand on Jeff's hip as they stepped over to the bed.

Jeff lied down first, curling his legs up so Marc could fit in. As Marc climbed in next to him, he felt the warmth of Marc's body against his back. He let out a heavy sigh as he relaxed himself, feeling Marc's arm softly wrap around his chest, keeping him securely close. Marc's hand gripped around Jeff's own as they lied together. Jeff rubbed his thumb in a circular motion on Marc's as they stayed silent, the sound of the outside wind mixed with Marc's breathing the only noise.

"I killed someone," Jeff choked out, still not entirely sure he'd ever become accustomed to admitting that fact.

"What happened?" Marc asked, his grip tightening slightly around Jeff's hand as he asked.

"I got grounded after the party." He let out a small chuckle, taking his right arm and rubbing his eyes. "That's why I haven't texted. My parents took my phone away." Jeff wasn't even entirely sure why he was telling Marc that. He knew it had nothing to do with what happened, but somewhere inside himself he felt like he needed to let Marc know, let him know he wasn't ignoring him or trying to distance himself.

He didn't want Marc mad at him.

"And here I thought you were avoiding me after all that," Marc said, a hint of annoyance in his voice.

"Not at all," Jeff said, turning his body so he was facing Marc, their noses only a few inches away. Jeff made sure not to put too much pressure on his cheek by sliding his hand underneath his head as a support. "Besides texting works both ways."

"So, what happened?" Marc ignored his comment, making a nod to his face and neck.

"That kid Adrian tried to kill me," Jeff said, not making eye contact. "I really thought I was going to die. He was relentless. I told him I wouldn't tell anyone," he said, feeling tears fall. "I flicked out my knife once he came close enough and then he just attacked me. I was on the floor so quick, Marc."

"I can see," Marc said, sighing. "Your face looks banged up."

"The swelling is going down," he said, realizing the ice pack had actually worked a bit after the twelfth time putting it on. "It was worse before. Plus, the nurse set my nose and my mom gave me a Vicodin so I'm feeling okay right now."

"That's good. Ice is your best friend after a face injury." Marc ran his fingers softly through Jeff hair, scooting his body closer. "How did you kill him?" There was a twinkle in Marc's eye that Jeff saw for a second but decided to ignore commenting on.

"Well he knocked my knife out and when I was on the floor I kicked him in the shin." Jeff felt a twinge of pride remembering how he was able to defend himself.

"Good spot," Marc commented, watching Jeff intently. "Fights are tough, you need to go in ready for anything. That was a good call kicking him, especially in the shin, that hurts."

"I was just trying to get out of the bathroom alive," Jeff said, not wanting to seem like he knew what he was doing, because he didn't. He really did just want to survive the attack. "Anyways, he tripped me as I tried to get the knife, hence the nose and face, and then he got on top of me with my arms pinned to my side and he started choking me. I was able to get out and grab the knife and then…" Jeff paused reliving the knife plunging into Adrian's throat over and over again in his mind.

"And then?" Marc said, waiting for him to continue.

"And then," he said, taking a deep breath. "I stabbed him in the throat."

"Just once? And you got a clean enough hit to kill him?" That twinkle was back in Marc's eye. "That's impressive."

"No, it's not," Jeff snapped. "It's not impressive, it's murder. I killed someone. I... I don't think...I don't," Jeff began to lose his breath as he got worked up, not even able to finish his thought. "I twisted the knife!" He barked out, immediately slamming his jaw closed, an audible click of his teeth filling the silence.

Jeff watched Marc as he processed the information, his eyes crinkled in thought. Jeff did not know what to make of it all until his lip began to curve into a devious grin. Without warning, Marc pressed forward and planted a quick peck on Jeff's lips.

"You're so cute," Marc said, half laughing.

Jeff was not amused. "It's not funny or cute."

"Jeff, babe, you're freaking out over nothing. You realize that, right?"

"How is that nothing?" He was astounded at how little any of it phased Marc. It was as if it was all just some sort of game and he was congratulating him on winning. Jeff pursed lips in annoyance, waiting for a reply.

"I just mean it was self-defense," Marc said, sitting up and resting his head against the bedpost; Jeff followed suit. "And honestly when you're in the moment, the adrenaline's flowing, a simple twist of the wrist becomes second nature. You don't even think, you just do, and you live. You're alive."

Jeff paused before answering because Marc did get it after all. In the moment when Jeff twisted the knife he did not think about it, it was second nature. Maybe Marc was right, and he wasn't some killer who could have stopped it, maybe his body took over and did the thinking for him. Jeff could feel his lips starting to twinge into a smirk, but he forced it back.

"I didn't think of it like that," he admitted, nodding. "It did feel like second nature, Marc. I can see it so vividly in my head, the blade slicing into his throat and I can see my hand… perfectly. But, it's not as if I'm in control because I can see it and feel it but before I can think my hand just shifts and I watch the blade twist in, ripping the gash open deeper and there's so much blood and I…" Jeff tried to catch his breath, feeling himself getting dizzy. "I can't get that out of my head."

"It'll leave," Marc said, "just like any memory. You'll remember it from time to time, maybe bring it up, but it won't be in the forefront of your mind forever, okay?"

"I don't know."

"Trust me." Marc reached out, lacing his fingers with Jeff's. "Sometimes you just need to get out and see a change, you know?"

"I just want alcohol," Jeff said, really wanting to go numb to it all. He knew alcohol had that effect. "Can you get me some?"

"How about this? I come over tomorrow with some alcohol and take you somewhere that will get your mind off it all."

Jeff thought it over. His parents had said that something had happened involving the insurance company they both worked for, so they would be staying for over time the next day and would not be home until after ten. Then they would need to leave the following weekend to go into a work conference. Once a year his parents leave to go to a conference and Jeff was worried they would cancel it this year due to him.

"Okay," Jeff said, half smiling. "I could use a distraction and my parents are going to be working overtime tomorrow so as long as I'm home by ten I can go to sleep and they won't even know I drank or snuck out."

"Now I see how you never get caught sneaking out," Marc said, raising his eyebrows. "You think it all out."

"Damn right I do." Now it was Jeff leaning in to kiss.

Marc headed out after that, saying that if he was going to get alcohol he would need to go buy some before all the stores closed. Jeff gave him a goodbye kiss, waiting for five minutes after he left before turning back on the security lights. Jeff eventually fell asleep but was awaken constantly throughout the night. Whether he had a dream or not, his body would not lie still and sleep. He kept tossing and turning, wishing his body would just give in.

Eventually it did.

CHAPTER 13

Marc showed up at his house around noon. Jeff answered the door, already showered and dressed, expecting to leave right away. Jeff had put on a turtle neck in an attempt to hide the bruises on his neck. A black eye in public isn't too bad, but choke marks coupled with that seem suspicious, and disturbing. Marc held up a bottle of rum, accompanied with a toothy grin on his face. Jeff gestured him in, giving him a quick kiss before closing the door. Marc went and sat on the green sofa in the living room, placing the glass on the wooden coffee table in the middle on the room.

"Cups or chugging?" Marc asked, twisting off the cap.

Jeff sat next to him. "Swig. I don't want to have to come home and do the dishes later."

"Swigging it is." Marc grappled the neck of the bottle, handing it to Jeff. "You do the honors, seeing as you're the one who needs it the most."

Jeff grabbed it, taking a quick whiff of the inside, coughing. The smell was strong, and he looked down at the bottle, inspecting it.

"Why the 151?" Jeff asked.

"Don't worry about it," Marc said, "it's just the name."

He sighed, tipping his head back and placing the cold tip of the bottle against his lips, tilting it forward and letting the burning alcohol fill his mouth. Jeff was not expecting it to be that strong. Yanking the bottle away, he wiped his chin as some of it dribbled down from his mouth. With an audible gulp, he heaved as his chest felt like it was on fire.

"Holy shit," he said, gasping. "That was strong."

"I know," Marc said, taking a quick shot. "It'll help you in the long run with everything."

"I don't doubt that."

Jeff took another quick gulp of the rum, trying his best not to cough again. He was able to keep his lungs in check, but it coated the back of his throat and made his stomach feel hot. Placing the drink down, he turned to face Marc, smiling.

"So, where are we going to go?" Jeff was excited to see where Marc was going to take him.

"It's a surprise," Marc said slyly.

"I think I've had enough surprises for a lifetime," Jeff said. "Come one, where is it?"

"I'll only give you one clue. I'm taking you there to show you the fun side of Prop 485."

"What the hell does that mean?" Jeff deadpanned, crossing his arms. "How is there even a fun side to the prop, Marc?"

"Just trust me. Besides, I need to go there for some business, too." Marc shrugged, as if none of it mattered, as if saying some vague explanation would pacify Jeff.

"I'm not going then," Jeff stated.

Marc's smirk turned sour as his lips straightened together, eyes narrowing on Jeff. "Are you kidding me?"

"I'm not going to go somewhere I don't know."

"But you're going with me? Do you not trust me?" Marc's voice was cold as he spoke, anger filling his every word. "I show up at the drop of a hat for you at school, take you to a party, come over at night like some booty call and never once complain. I never once second thought going anywhere with you. I mean what the fuck else do I have to do to get your trust? I canceled plans to come over this morning because I care about you."

"I never asked you to cancel plans," Jeff said, feeling guilty but also too prideful to admit he could be wrong.

Marc's eyebrows shot up in surprise at Jeff's comment and the initial hurt that Jeff could see on Marc's face was replaced with rage. His eyes narrowed in as he stood up and started pacing. Seeing Marc that upset was enough to make Jeff admit that maybe he was wrong about the way he handled things.

"I'm sorry," Jeff said, "I just didn't like the sound of the way you described it."

"It's vague so that it stays a surprise. I'm just going to go."

"No!" Jeff shouted, standing up and striding over to Marc, grabbing his hands and holding them. "I'm sorry, okay? I barely got any sleep and I'm just tired, okay?"

"Don't take it out on me."

"I know, I know. I was wrong, and I do trust you. I really do. I just don't trust…." Jeff thought how to formulate what he meant. "I just don't trust the world? If that makes sense."

"It does," Marc said, looking at Jeff in the eyes. "Just don't take it out on me next time."

"I won't," Jeff said, leaning forward to kiss Marc.

"You think that's going to make it all better?" Marc teased, a smile back on his face.

"It couldn't hurt to try."

Marc put his hands on Jeff's hips, placing their foreheads together. "You're right."

They backed up onto the couch, making sure to be as gentle as possible. Of course, Jeff's nose would hit against Marc's as they shifted their lips and it would cause a quick pain, but that didn't matter. As Jeff sat, straddling Marc on the couch, his arms wrapped around his neck, his head leaning down to kiss. It was then when Jeff began to feel the effects of the rum as his body relaxed and the pain slowed down to an almost unnoticeable ache.

"As much," Marc said in between kissing, "as I want…to keep doing…this."

Jeff leaned close to Marc's ear and whispered, "Yeah?"

"We have to get going."

Marc placed his hands under Jeff's chest and pushed him off, plopping Jeff down on the couch next to him. A smorgasbord of emotions were erupting inside Jeff as he watched Marc screw the cap back on the bottle, flash him an award-winning smile, and stand up. For one he was horny, but also somewhere deeper it was more than just the physical aspect, and Jeff wasn't ready to put a word for it yet. Anxiety was also one of the bubbling emotions trying to take over as he thought about not knowing where they were going, and not knowing what the hell "the fun side of Prop 485" even meant. And maybe it was the alcohol that was jumbling it all up, but when it came time to leave and the two of them walked out of the house, Jeff's legs felt as if he was walking on a conveyor belt. He turned to Marc and smiled, hoping the rest of the day would go smoothly.

The scenery changed from suburbia to the city and Jeff watched, block by block, as the perfect two-story houses with green front yards became apartments with no yards at all, and soon they were in what looked like a business district. Large plain white square buildings were everywhere and each with giant parking lots in the front and nothing else but forest; Jeff had no idea where he was.

"We almost there?" he asked.

Marc simply gave him a side-eye glace and kept humming along to the radio. Jeff was getting more and more anxious and as much as he liked Marc, he still found it annoying that he would not tell him where they were going. At that point, Jeff really just wanted to understand why Marc couldn't just tell him how close they were. It was really starting—

"And we're here," Marc said, parking the car in front of what looked like an abandoned factory. Jeff furrowed his brow and looked around. The parking lot was almost full, and he could see that there was a single door leading in with a man standing in front of it. A big man, who looked like he could snap Jeff in half without breaking a sweat.

"Where is here?"

"You'll see." Marc's eyes sparkled.

"Marc," Jeff said, glaring. "Can't you just tell me now? I mean, honestly, we're already here."

Marc reached back and grabbed the bottle, handing it to Jeff. "Take another swig and relax. It's like you don't even know what a surprise is."

Marc got out of the car and shut the door with a little more force than usual. Jeff closed his eyes and took a deep breath, trying his best to convince himself that everything would be okay, that Marc would not take him anywhere unsafe. He unscrewed the lid and could smell the sweetness of the rum fill his nose; without thinking he leaned his head back and swallowed.

You're okay, he kept telling himself over and over in his head, hoping that it would eventually stick. His stomach burned as he let out a belch, wishing he hadn't. Opening up the car door, the cold air attacked him, pricking his bare skin as his breath gained visibility.

The already chill air accompanied by the wind made Jeff want to rush inside of the building, even though he had no idea what was on the other side. It felt like they were in the middle of nowhere as Jeff pivoted and took in their surroundings. Trees were the main aesthetic with a small shed at the end of the building right on the skirts of the tree line.

"You done staring off into space?" Marc's voice gripped Jeff from his mind and brought him back to reality. "Come on."

As they walked towards the entrance, Jeff could hear music coming from inside. *Is it a party?* he thought. The bouncer stood with his arms crossed and Jeff was not sure how the bouncer was even able to bend his arms because they were so enormous. The man's mouth stayed in a straight line, only nodding to the both of them as they walked in. Jeff could feel his heart drumming in his chest.

As they stepped in, Jeff gazed on a crowd of people in the middle bobbing to the music. There were spotlights all above them as if they were on stage and by the far end of the room he could see what looked like a boxing ring of sorts. It had red ropes surrounding the perimeter, along with a wooden stool in each corner. Directly in front of them as they walked in was a bar and Jeff hoped they did not card.

"Marc!" A voice shot out from the middle of the crowd and Jeff watched as Alena maneuvered through people to get to them. Sighing, Jeff rolled his eyes quickly before anyone saw. With a quick one over, he was almost positive she had new tattoos. "Hey! I was beginning to think you weren't going to make it."

"I have money on this. Shit, one of my fighters is going tonight." Marc grabbed her and pulled her in for a hug, but all Jeff could focus on was the word "fighters."

What the hell did that mean?

"We're a little late because my devilishly younger boyfriend over here had his first kill." Jeff winced at the reminder, but Alena clapped her hands in delight and pulled him in for a hug.

"They grow up so fast," Alena said as she released him; he felt extremely uncomfortable.

"Can you watch him for a second?" Marc asked, and Jeff wanted to shout no, but instead he stood awkwardly with his hands shoved deep into his pockets.

"Of course." Alena smiled and grabbed Jeff by his arm. "Let's get you a drink while your man takes care of some business."

He followed her to the bar and was surprised to find two stools vacant. They sat down, and she yelled something to the bartender while Jeff tried to see if he could find Marc in the mass. As he looked around he saw some of the crowd members pulling out money and handing it to specific people dressed in lime green shirts with the word "handler" written on them.

"What's going on?" Jeff asked just as a cup filled to the brim with some blue liquid was placed in front of him.

"What do you mean?" Alena sipped on her drink and Jeff followed, not entirely sure what he was consuming but thankful for the alcohol. The fact that he was stuck with Alena, well, alcohol was a necessity.

"Like what is this place?" Jeff gestured around them.

"Marc didn't tell you?"

"Tell me what?" Jeff grabbed the cup and started to drink it faster, wanting to calm his nerves.

"You're in for a fucked-up surprise." Alena laughed and shook her head. "Hope you're not squeamish."

"Wha—" Jeff got cut off as Alena saw someone she knew and hopped off of the seat, barreling through the pit of bodies, leaving him alone.

Jeff shook his leg nervously on the footrest in front of him and twirled his straw around in the cup. The alcohol was starting to have its effect on him as his legs felt as if they weighed less and his face had a fun tingly feel to it. He palmed his face and smirked as he took another sip; maybe tonight would not be so bad after all, at least if he stayed semi-drunk the entire evening.

A girl snagged the chair next to him and nodded; Jeff smiled back and took the last big gulp of his drink.

"Slow down," the girl said. "Or don't now that I see your face."

Jeff simply raised an eyebrow and stuck out his hand, introducing himself. "Jeff."

"Gabbie." She was beautiful, and he could not help but gawk. The neon bar sign reflected off her naturally tan skin and filled a purple ring around her electrifying golden-brown eyes. Dark auburn hair flowed down her shoulders like a waterfall; she was gorgeous.

"What is this place?" Jeff asked, hoping that she could give him some insight as to where the hell he was.

"Bum fights." She said it as if she was commenting on the weather.

"I'm sorry, what?" Jeff had heard about these. People find homeless guys on the streets and pay them to fight till the death while others bet on the winner. There are trainers who basically own the person and they get the majority of the money, only cutting a small percentage with their fighter. That way the fighter has to keep coming back in hopes of winning more money. Jeff had seen a documentary on it and was disturbed by it, and the fact that Marc felt like this was somewhere to take him.

Gabbie must have seen his facial expression because she covered her mouth and giggled. "You didn't know that's what this was?" She let out a full-blown laugh. "Where the hell did you think you were?"

"I honestly don't know because my boyfriend said it was a surprise and took me here." Jeff wished he had another drink because the buzz he had was not enough to deal with the information.

"Romantic." Gabbie ordered a drink and turned back to Jeff. "Who's your boyfriend? Maybe I know him."

Jeff doubted that, but he figured he would entertain the thought. At least it gave him something to distract from the fact that he was in a bum fighting arena. "His name is Marc."

"Marc? As in Marc Salguero?"

"Yes?" Jeff was not expecting her to know him, in fact, it made him worried what she might say next.

"He's one of the best trainers! His bums always win." He was correct in dreading what she was going to say.

Best trainer? Jeff could feel his head spinning trying to understand everything that was being revealed. Two days ago, his life was semi-normal; he was not a murderer and he was oblivious to the fact that his boyfriend trained homeless people to fight to the death.

Maybe he would need something stronger than alcohol to get through the night.

"Ladies and Gentlemen!" A man shouted from the ring. The lights dimmed, and a spotlight shined directly on him. He had long hair that was slicked back into a ponytail and a thick beard that masked his features. "The fight is about to begin! We have two great fighters tonight. Marc and Trina know where to find the bat shit craziest bums out there and train them well. If you all will gather around the arena we will begin shortly. Any last bets that need to be placed have to happen before the fight starts. Find anyone with a green shirt and let them know who you think is going to win. Are we ready for some fucking blood!?"

The crowd cheered, and Jeff sank further into his seat. He turned around quickly and asked the bartender for another one of the drinks he had earlier. Nodding, the bartender started pouring a variety of different bottles into the cup and before Jeff knew it he had another vibrant blue beverage in front of him. Drinking as much as he could in one large sip, Jeff closed his eyes shut and forced the alcohol down, his muscles feeling looser than before.

The crowd, including Gabbie, all shifted across the room until they were standing on every side of the ring. Most of them were cheering and Jeff could see Marc slipping into the arena through the red ropes, holding his hands up in the air. There was a roar and the room erupted in cheers; Jeff watched as a man stood next to Marc.

The man had on dirty clothes with holes in them and Jeff figured he must be one of the homeless people fighting. Marc took the man's hand and held it high in the air, causing even more shouts from the crowd.

"This is Axel!" Marc yelled as he and his fighter walked to a corner of the ring.

A woman walked into the arena accompanied by a man who was not wearing a shirt, only ripped jeans. She shouted that his name was Patrick.

The announcer came on stage and asked each fighter if they were ready; they both nodded.

"You all know the rules," the announcer yelled. "It's a fight to the death. Whoever wins walks out of here alive with money in their pocket. Are we ready?"

The room cheered and threw up their hands in celebration; Jeff could feel his stomach turning over as he rubbed his sweaty palms on his jeans. He was the only one at the bar, every other person was piling in to see the fight. Jeff could see just fine from where he sat.

The announcer held his hand up in the air, holding a gun. There was a loud bang as the gun fired and Jeff jumped in his seat, covering his ears. As soon as the bullet was shot, the two men rushed in to fight.

Axel was quick, rushing forward at lightning quick speed. Patrick was able to throw his hands up and block as Axel's fists slammed down on Patrick. With his arms up, Patrick was able to block most of the punches, but Jeff saw as some of them landed on Patrick's ribs.

Patrick ducked and was able to roll on the floor. Axel spun around but was met with a quick jab to the jaw, knocking him backwards. Patrick lunged forward and slammed him against the ropes before latching onto his arms and throwing Axel face first onto the arena floor. Jeff winced as he heard the loud pop that accompanied Axel hitting the ground, triggering the memory of himself falling face first. Jeff shuddered and tried to shake it off.

Patrick was on top of him before Jeff was able to register it. Taking Axel's head in his hands, Patrick began to slam his face into the ground. The crowd was screaming in excitement, throwing up their hands and shouting at the fighters – Jeff gawked in awe.

Axel was able to throw Patrick off and get himself back up as he wobbled on his feet, his face covered in deep gashes as blood dripped off his chin. He spit a wad of blood out to his side and cracked his neck. Before Patrick had time to counter, Axel dived forward and tackled Patrick to the ground, pinning him underneath.

In the corner of the arena, Marc was screaming and throwing his hands up in the air. His neck veins were protruding out and his face was beet red. Jeff had never seen him look so angry before, so violent.

Axel's legs held Patrick's arms down to his side as he began to slam his fists down over and over again on Patrick's face. Axel was relentless and did not seem to tire. His fists rained down blow after blow and Jeff could see blood beginning to splatter on his face as he continued to beat Patrick.

Jeff could feel his stomach twisting in knots as he watched the two men fighting. Each time Axel would slam his fists down, Jeff would have flashes of Adrian – spitting out blood as the knife protruded from his neck – and he did not know how much more he could take. His breathing was becoming short as he tried his best to calm his nerves, along with his queasy stomach. *Don't puke*, he kept telling himself.

Patrick was able to jolt one of his legs up and connect it clean with Axel's crotch, which made Axel howl in pain as he fell onto his side. Seizing the opportunity, Patrick pulled himself up by the ropes and stood, trying to catch his balance. His face looked worse than Axel's. If Jeff had to identify him in a line up he would not be able to with how bloodied and swollen his face was. His right eye was completely closed, purple and red with a gash right on his eyebrow. His nose was obviously broken, and Jeff was pretty sure he was missing multiple teeth – although he was not entirely sure if that was because of the fight or due to his life as a homeless man.

Patrick took a step and almost fell, balancing his legs out and taking a deep breath. Axel was rolling over and about to get up, which Patrick noticed and stepped forward. Jeff watched as he took a giant breath and swung his leg forward, connecting his shin with Axel's side, knocking him back onto the ground. The crowd got even louder as Patrick wobbled forward and slammed his foot directly down on Axel's back, smashing his face back into the floor.

Jeff thought Axel was done for and by the looks of Marc's face, he did too. There was something that kept making Jeff watch, even when he was disgusted, he could not look away.

Patrick stepped forward and Jeff was certain this would be the final blow, but then Axel rolled over and kicked his leg out, connecting straight into Patrick's knee with an audible crack. The audience gasped, and Patrick let out a strangled yelp as he crumpled to the ground. His knee had bent in the opposite direction and Jeff could hear the crowd all cheering and yelling for Axel to finish him.

"Whoa!" The announcer stepped out and held up his hands. "That took a turn for the unexpected. It looks like it is about that time." The crowd shouted and threw up their hands in agreement and Jeff could see Marc with a toothy grin in the corner. "Axel," the announcer said, turning and grabbing Axel up by his hand. "You know how this works. It's time for you to put him down."

Put him down? Jeff thought.

Axel nodded, rubbing the blood from his mouth and threw his hands up, baiting the crowd for applause. The announcer then took the gun from the back of his pants and handed it to Axel.

With a smirk, Axel stood over Patrick and pointed the gun at the back of his head. Patrick accepted his fate as his head sunk in defeat. Then there was another loud pop of the gun and Jeff saw Patrick's body crumple in on itself as a pool of blood began to form around him.

Watching as Marc rushed up and grabbed Axel's right arm, holding it up in victory, Jeff wanted nothing more than to get out of the room. He was disgusted with himself for watching, but even more disgusted with Marc.

Pushing the stool out, Jeff walked for the first time after all the alcohol. His legs felt heavy but numb at the same time. He smacked the roof of his mouth with his tongue and tried his best to walk out of the room in a straight line; he failed. Whatever was in those blue drinks must have been strong because Jeff had to steady himself against the bar. Finally, forcing himself, Jeff made it outside and inhaled the air.

There was still cheering coming from inside and Jeff planned to wait outside for Marc. He never wanted to come to one of these again and was livid that Marc thought it would be a good idea for him to come after everything that had happened the previous week.

He felt his phone buzz in his pants and he reached in and grabbed it from his pocket.

Mal [2:00 pm]: I picked up your homework :) hope you're feeling better! Miss you.

Before Jeff could reply he heard something shuffle behind him.

"Jeffery?" A man's voice said. As he went to turn around he felt a sharp pain in the back of his head and he fell face first onto the ground, his vision tunneling out.

Jeff tried to open his eyes, but he felt another burning pain connect with his ribs as he blacked out.

CHAPTER 14

Jeff's eyes cracked open, the back of his skull was throbbing, and his head was bowed down, chin in chest. The first thing he saw were his arms against wooden chair handles, bright yellow nylon rope twisted around his wrists. With an attempt to get out, Jeff tried to kick his legs, realizing that they too were tied down. Squinting, he looked up, trying to get a feel for his surroundings.

A single, bright, light hung above him and as his eyes shifted towards it he winced, pain radiating behind his eyes. Wherever he was it was not big. To his left there were tools hanging on the wall: an electric saw, different sized blades, wrenches, screwdrivers, and even a portable sandpaper machine. A table was underneath it all, a toolbox in the middle with duct tape sitting on top. The walls were wooden, and Jeff saw chips in the paint and holes where he could see light coming in from outside. *The shed,* he thought.

A set of knuckles cracked and popped behind him, triggering his skin to crawl. Frozen in his seat, Jeff's eyes shifted from side to side, wondering who was there. He needed to get his arms loose. Another noise filled the space, the sound of a knife being sharpened. Jeff's breathing became hitched as he attempted to wiggle his hands out from under the rope. His body twisted in his seat as he tried, but all that did was cause the nylon to burn his wrist. That didn't matter, it was his only way out.

"Don't even bother," the man's voice said, his words snaking up Jeff's back. "I know how to tie knots correctly. It's called a constrictor knot," he said, and Jeff heard his boots squeak on the cement floor.

"What do you want?" Jeff asked, still moving his wrists from side to side, seeing blood starting to stain the yellow.

"What do I want?" The man laughed, appearing in front of Jeff's face, and Jeff honed in on his hazel eyes, and the darkness that filled them. The man had a charcoal black jacket that buttoned up to his neck, met by black jeans and matching shoes. He must have been planning to hurt someone because he looked like a burglar Jeff would see in movies. All that was missing was the ski mask. An unfortunate looking soul patch found a home under his thin lips. "What I want is for my son back!"

Spit came careening out of the man's mouth and landed on Jeff's face. Automatically he went to wipe it off before remembering his hands were tied down. Jeff closed his eyes and took in a deep breath, trying to assess the situation.

"I can't bring your son back," Jeff said, making eye contact with him. "I don't even know who your son is."

The man did a disgusted laugh and squatted in front of Jeff, wielding a hunting knife. The blade reflected the light from the bulb and made a bright reflection, causing Jeff to squint. As he opened his eyes fully, his vision caught sight of the tip just as his right cheek felt the frigidness of the blade against his skin.

"I knew this generation was fucked up, but do you really have no remorse?" The blade pressed into his skin, a small cut releasing blood down his cheek.

"I don't know what you're talking about!" Jeff shouted, his eyes focused on the knife.

"My son. Adrian!" The man yanked the knife back, twisting on his heels and slamming his hands to his face, dragging them down from his eyes. Jeff saw tears were falling as he rubbed them away. "You killed my son."

Jeff's stomach plummeted into his gut with the realization of who was in front of him. "I never meant to kill him. I swear."

"You can't talk your way out of this," the man scoffed, taking a quick swipe and slashing a gash into Jeff's left forearm; he wailed as blood pooled out of the wound, already sticking into his arm hairs.

"Please," Jeff pleaded, writhing his wrists, ignoring the burning of his raw skin against the rope. "Please don't do this. You don't have to do this! I didn't mean to kill him I swear it wasn't how you think it was I—"

His voice became muffled as Adrian's father reached into his coat, pulled out a rag and shoved it in his mouth, causing Jeff to gag.

Bile rose up and burned his esophagus as he was forced to swallow it without choking. With a quick step, Adrian's dad reached over and grabbed the duct tape off of the counter, tearing a strip off, and slamming it onto Jeff's face to keep his mouth closed.

"Shut up!" He screamed at the top of his lungs. The vein in his neck doubled in size as his face reddened. "You don't get to apologize and move on. That was my son, my baby boy." The sorrow was palpable in the air as the man's words were wretched out of his mouth, voice cracking, eyes welling up. "I watched you at your house yesterday with that guy climbing through your window, and then come back this morning with a bottle."

Jeff's eyes were wide as saucers as he attempted to plead without being able to talk. His words silenced behind the gag, only muffled cries escaping. Warm tears streamed down his face as he slammed his back against the chair, praying it would break.

"Killing him wasn't enough?" Adrian's father stepped forward and pivoted to stand behind Jeff. No matter how hard he exerted himself, Jeff could not get out of the knot, and he no longer was able to see his attacker. The icy edge of the blade met Jeff's throat as he froze in his seat, the sound of his ragged breath pushing through his injured nose all he could hear.

"This is what you decide to do after murdering my son. Go watch homeless men kill each other? What kind of sick animal has so little regard for life?"

Jeff tilted his head back, getting the blade as far away from his windpipe as possible. The knife inched slowly down until it was above his heart, pointed in. Jeff scrunched his eyes close in fear, waiting for the pain to branch through his body before ultimately ceasing.

Instead, a sharp prick started at the bottom of his right arm and dragged upwards, tearing his flesh as it went. Jeff shrieked in agony, eyes burning, as he watched the crimson hot blood start to coat his arm and stain the wood on the chair. The gash began at his already bloody wrist — a zigzag motion that tore the skin apart like paper — until it stopped half way up his forearm.

With little time to process the torture, burning erupted from Jeff's other forearm as Adrian's father slash through more of his flesh. The torment felt never ending as Jeff watched his arms once again be masked with blood — this time his own. His eyes were burning as tears blurred his vision. Light headed, Jeff's eyes vibrated in his skull, rolling back from the stinging that found permanent residents in his arms.

"Oh, no, no, no." A slap connected against his already bruised cheek, sending his eyes shooting open. "You don't get to pass out. You're going to feel every slice I make."

Jeff was wailing as tears flooded down his face, his nose full of snot, blocking him from breathing in. There was a burning in his lungs as he began to hyperventilate, the soaked cloth in his mouth pushing against the back of his throat, causing him to dry heave. He wanted to scream for help, tell the guy to stop it or finish it, at that point Jeff needed it to end.

Adrian's father must have realized that he was losing oxygen because Jeff felt the tape rip off of his skin, barely registering the sensation through all the other wounds. With his tongue pushing out, Jeff was able to spit the rag out and inhale a lungful of air.

"Please," Jeff coughed out, shaking his head back and forth. "Stop, please!" Begging was all he could do as he watched his assailant cock his head and narrow his eyes.

"I see my son did some damage of his own," he said, admiring the cuts and bruises along Jeff's face. "I'm going to leave your face alone, let the last thing my son ever did be permanent on you when you take your last breath."

"It's not what you think, please!" Jeff was bucking in his seat, desperately twisting his wrists, back slamming against the chair. Anything to get out. His ankles were sore from attempting to kick off the chair, and his wrists had stained the yellow completely red at that point.

Everything slowed down in that moment. All the noises ceased to exist as Jeff observed the man simply watching him struggle to get out, knowing that he couldn't. His eyes had a sparkle to them that Jeff noticed in Marc's during the fight, and he had a moment of awareness.

Jeff wasn't going to make it out of the shed alive.

With an acceptance, Jeff glared up at Marc's dad and spit at him. "Your son was a psychotic piece of shit that no one liked or respected. The school nurse thanked me for killing him, for God's sake! No one cared about him." Jeff was not entirely sure where it was all bubbling up from, but the words fell out of his mouth without warning, hot with anger. He wanted it over and he knew what the man's weakness was: Adrian.

"Shut your mouth," he said, stepping forward with the knife pointed out.

"I stabbed him in the neck and twisted the blade. Made sure he was dead before leaving the bathroom. Your great son," Jeff said in a spiteful tone, "died on the piss-soaked floor."

Adrian's dad lifted the knife in the air and was about to swing it down when a banging came from behind them and Jeff felt a gust of frosty air come soaring in. Adrian's dad had a look of shock in his eyes and Jeff watched in anxiety ridden fear not knowing if someone would save him.

"What the hell?" A girl's voice said.

"This doesn't concern you." Adrian's dad kept the knife at bay.

"Like hell it doesn't. The cops just raided the arena, everyone's running."

"Shit," Adrian's dad looked down at Jeff and snarled.

Jeff could hear footsteps behind the chair and tilted his head back, trying to see who had come into the room. As the girl stepped into view, Jeff noticed who she was. Gabbie. She must have registered who he was too because she immediately pulled a sable handgun out from her jacket and pointed it at Adrian's dad.

"Get back," she said, stepping forward, not even hesitating.

"What the —" Adrian's dad was cut up as she took the butt of the gun and smashed it into the side of his face. He crumpled to the floor, dropping the knife.

Gabbie kept the gun aimed at him as she picked up the knife, turning around quickly to cut his right arm out of the rope. Once it was out, she handed Jeff the handle and turned back to aiming her gun at Adrian's father. Jeff rotated his wrist, the bloody raw skin rubbing together made holding the blade difficult. Placing the tip against the rope, he cut until the nylon fell free, moving onto his legs.

The gashes in his arms were bloodied and sticky, and he needed to get to a hospital soon. Jeff wobbly stood up, leering down at Adrian's dad who was holding his hands to his temple, red dripping between his fingers and down the side of his face. Jeff wished he could say he felt sorry for the man, but his son was an aggressive killer and it looked like the apple did not fall far from the tree.

"Hey," Gabbie said, gesturing with her arm to the knife. "Finish him."

"What?" Jeff said.

"Dude, he's going to keep coming for you if he's going through all this trouble to make you suffer. Most people just shoot someone and move on." Her eyes widened as she shifted her gaze to the man on the floor again. "You need to end this."

Jeff felt in a trance as he knelt down, unsure if he could kill another person. Adrian's dad pushed himself against the shed wall, still holding his hand to his head. Jeff's heart pounded in his chest as he contemplated what to do.

"You need to hurry," Gabbie said, checking over her shoulder. Jeff could hear people shouting in the distance. "Sometimes it's just the way it goes. It sucks but life is a gutter. Now finish him so we can get out of here and I can get you help. You're not going to last much longer if you don't."

Jeff's vision was tunneling as she finished her sentence, his eyes honing in on his arms, noticing hot fresh blood was still seeping out of the cuts. *She's right,* he thought, standing up, Jeff stepped in front of Adrian's father.

Squatting, Jeff leaned forward, knife pointed out, plunging it directly into the dad's abdomen. Jeff slowly pushed the blade in as he felt it puncture and tear through his flesh. Adrian's father gasped, his eyes widening as the hilt of the blade connected with his skin. Jeff's eyelids were half hanging, his breathing slowed as he leaned his face forward, gripping the back of Adrian's father's neck and pulling him close. With the same motion, Jeff slid the knife out and then stabbed it back into his gut, keeping his shaking hand latched onto the man's neck. Jeff took the blade and stabbed him again, and again, and again, seeing blood begin to drip out of his mouth.

"You good?" Gabbie asked, eyes shifting to the wooden door leading in.

Jeff snapped out of it, taking a step back, and dropping the blade on the concrete floor. The man's chin hung in his chest, long red spit dripped out of his lifeless lips, staining his jacket. His stomach was a combination of torn fabric, meaty flesh, and the metallic smell of his life leaving him.

Stumbling back, Jeff held his hands up in front of his eyes, watching them shake uncontrollably. Without being able to stop it, his eyelids rapidly fluttered in shock and confusion as his world slowed. Jeff spun his head to his right, then to his left, a queasy feeling washing over his body. His eyes began to roll back as he stumbled, hitting his lower back against the tool table.

"Jeff," Gabbie said, gripping his shoulders and shaking him. "You need to get a hold of yourself."

Voices came closer to the shed.

"Go," Jeff said, pointing to the door, which was facing the forest. "Run." His legs buckled underneath him as he sank to the ground. "I can't…. I can't run, I can't…." Jeff started crying as he sat — directly across from the body of another life he took – slumped over on himself, almost mirroring Adrian's father.

"I," Gabbie said looking around frantically and then back down at Jeff. "Okay. But don't tell them anything. Just say you came to check it out and before you got in this guy took you."

"Why?"

"They'll arrest Marc," she hissed, crouching down and whispering. "Trust me on this, even if he is your boyfriend, don't cross Marc."

Was that a warning? Was she actually warning him about Marc? Jeff's entire universe had been imploding around him but that added detail in some way didn't change anything because he knew it all along. There was something off about Marc, and he didn't want to be on the receiving end of it.

"Okay," Jeff said, half nodding. "Go."

"Stay alive."

And with that she bolted out the door, leaving an icy breeze against his skin. Or maybe that was the blood loss, he couldn't be sure. His head was resting against the table, waiting for death, waiting for help, it didn't matter. Death seemed like the easiest way out. He would never have to live with himself knowing he killed again. Maybe that was what he wanted. For it all to end.

Jeff closed his eyes, his fingers numb. A chill crept down his spine and he was certain that was a sign he was close. He never imagined his life would be snuffed out at sixteen, five days into his junior year of high school, but like Gabbie said, "life is a gutter."

"We need a medic!" A voice shook Jeff from his thoughts, his eyes barely opening. "Jesus Christ, look at this."

"I hate this law," another voice commented.

Jeff's head tilted back as he started to float. They were too late, he was already gone; he was levitating. Did that mean he was going to heav— his foot hit against something hard and his body became freezing as he felt wind nip at his face.

And with that final sensation, Jeff blacked out.

CHAPTER 15

Beeping came from above him, and Jeff could hear some adjusting themselves in what sounded like a cushioned chair, to his left. He didn't bother to open his eyes, he didn't want to be awake. There was something clamped to his left index finger that he wanted to shake off but refrained.

Beep.

No pain erupted from his arms or seared through his skull. Instead he found himself engulfed in a fluffy pillow, arms by his side. *The hospital,* he thought. There was a part of him that wanted to live like this for the rest of his life, comatose. Even though he knew he couldn't, the idea of existing without having to actually exist was appealing.

That was until he heard a muffled voice shouting from most likely a room or two down.

"How dare you ask me if I tried to drown my daughter!" Jeff could not see her, but by the infuriated tone, he had a feeling he knew what the woman looked like. "This is a hospital for God's sake! I came here to get help not be accused of trying to kill my own child."

Another calming voice interjected, and he had to use all his energy to focus on it. "I understand your frustration, ma'am. Unfortunately, these questions are now routine when anyone comes in."

"You think I'd kill my daughter!?"

"No, ma'am." Jeff heard a bang and then, "security!"

"Jesus," a familiar voice said to his left. Gabbie.

Jeff waited to see if anyone commented back. When silence was her only companion, he peeked through nearly closed eyes. Gabbie was sitting on a light brown wooden chair with a blue cushion, her legs dangling over the arm rests. Her head was tilted back, and her hair hung behind it over the jacket that was hanging on the back of her throne.

"What just happened?" Jeff commented, his voice coming out far croakier than he expected.

"Oh, my God," she said, bolting up from the chair, immediately by his side. "Holy shit, dude, I thought you were dead."

"Still breathing."

"Like a champ." Gabbie fixed eyes with him and smirked, half laughing.

"What?" he asked, somehow feeling better with Gabbie by his side. Maybe it was because she just met him and didn't know anything about his past, or because she saved his life and came back for him, but whatever it was, Jeff felt calm.

"You're so high right now." She busted up laughing, and Jeff couldn't help but grin from ear to ear. "I don't know what they have you on, but you should see your face right now. It's strangely comforting."

"Is that why I don't feel like I just got tortured?" He joked, peering down at his arms. White gauze covered his forearms and wrists, with no visible blood leaking through. "But wait," Jeff tilted his head and glanced up into Gabbie's eyes. "How is it comforting?"

"Well, I mean, you were just on the brink of death, and look," she said waving her hand over him. "You have visible proof of it and yet," she paused, looking up, and Jeff could see a sparkle in her eye as she thought it over. "I don't know." She smiled, nodding her head and looking directly into his eyes. "You should be in so much pain but you're not, because of medicine, drugs. It's just incredible to think about how everything is literally just our brain's perception of it. And with a small change, it's all different."

Jeff felt mesmerized as he listened to her voice, smirking. "I never thought of it that way," he said, feeling his cheeks flush. "It's a cool way to look at things."

"It's the truth," she stated, turning around and reaching for the chair. As she did, Jeff saw a single tattoo on her neck, dreading the idea that she also reveled in killing. He could not make out what it was before she planted the chair next to the bed and sat down eye level with him. "Science is fact. And the fact is we're nothing more than atoms that are lumped together."

"Yeah," Jeff said, "but, I mean, we're people. Atoms make up everything but we're still living, breathing, unique individuals."

"Oh, totally," she agreed. "I just think when you break it down it makes life less daunting, I guess. If you can explain the situation in just atoms and neurons, it almost absolves you of everything."

"Sure, in a sense, but also you can't use that to justify everything."

"Why not?" There was a mischievous look in her eyes as she waited for him to counter. She was enjoying this, going back and forth. And he could see why. Talking about it, with her, somehow was easing his mind to the fact of what happened.

"Because," he said, mulling it over. "Because if we do that, and we no longer take responsibility for our actions, there's no humanity. At that point we're just…we're just machines."

"I never thought of it that way," she said, winking. "It's fun to look at things in different perspectives."

"I guess it is," Jeff admitted, sighing. "It still doesn't change what I did."

"No, it doesn't. But it might be able to help you cope with it, somehow move forward? Besides, he was going to kill you. Even if it wasn't legal, it would still be okay because it was self-defense."

"Was it?" he said, reliving the knife going in and out, multiple times. The iron scent of blood stained the inside of his nose, and knowing that he didn't stop until Gabbie interrupted him made him wonder if it really was self-defense.

"It was," she said seriously. "You were half dead when you stabbed him. Adrenaline and anger were probably all that were firing off in those neurons up there." She did a sympathetic shrug. "It's understandable."

"I just don't feel okay. It's, like, deep down I know it was self-defense, I know it. But when I close my eyes all I can see is the blade just going in and out, and the blood. I don't think I can look at it as logically as you."

"No shit," she chuckled. "Whether self-defense or not you still have to live with it. I don't know what to tell you to help with your mind replaying it because that's what brains do — make you relive the most awful memories and never let you forget."

Jeff's eyes started to get watery as he lied in the hospital room, Gabbie by his side. He felt a warmth fill his palm as she reached over and grabbed his hand, giving it a light squeeze. Her thumb gently rubbed up and down against his fingers, calming him.

"You're going to be okay, Jeff."

"Am I?" His mind had been so focused on Adrian's father's corpse, that Gabbie's comment about Marc almost slipped by. "You told me not to cross Marc. Why?"

The warmth left his hand as she pulled hers away, sighing. "I've just seen him when he's upset, and I didn't want you saying anything to the cops that could get him in trouble."

"What's he like when he's upset?" He unconsciously held his breath as he waited for her explanation. During the party when Marc put his finger down for stabbing someone, Jeff was alarmed, not to mention the people he hung around with made him feel unsafe. If they nonchalantly can admit to mass murder with no remorse or even a slight hint of guilt, then they were to be feared.

"I don't want to—"

"Tell me."

Jeff needed to know. Even if Marc was Gabbie's friend, she did not seem like the type from the party. She didn't glorify him killing Adrian's father, but helped him and came to check on him to make sure he was okay. Marc was nowhere to be found, not to mention the more he learned about the world and people around him, the more he wanted to be informed for his own safety.

If Marc was dangerous, and there was even a chance that he could turn violent on Jeff, he had a right to know.

"I've heard stories." Gabbie's fingernails clicked together as she fiddled with her hands in her lap, seemingly nervous. "And I've seen things."

"Just tell me," Jeff deadpanned. "I'm hopped up on drugs, now is as good a time as ever."

Gabbie's eyes shifted side to side as she sighed, her two front teeth gnawed at her lower lip. As she sat forward a picture came into view on the wall by the door leading to the ghostly white hallway. A butterfly was in the air, a light blue background — a vibrant red flower in the middle of the painting — and a small trail of dashes did loops from behind the bug, detailing its winding path.

Is that supposed to be calming for patients? Jeff thought.

"Okay." Gabbie's voice brought his focus back to her where he could see her eyes were full of concern. "I've heard that the last guy he dated broke up with him because he was getting abusive."

"Abusive how?" Memories of Marc in the car grabbing him and making him say he was in charge came flooding into Jeff's mind.

191

Even the way he would show up unannounced at Jeff's house and always push certain subjects.

"I heard, and it could be totally wrong, you know? Sometimes people exaggerate."

"Gabbie."

"I heard his boyfriend was pretty innocent, not really a fight back kind of guy. And Marc can get pretty angry and mix alcohol with that and he can get violent."

Marc had gotten snippy after drinking before tricking Jeff into going to the bum fighting. That was the only time Jeff had been around him while under the influence, in fact, Marc didn't drink anything at the party he brought Jeff to. Instead he went and got Jeff high and stayed sober. Suddenly Jeff became aware of how in control Marc always seemed to be around him, never letting his guard down. Even when Alena called him that day he walked into the other room.

Did Jeff even know the real Marc?

"What happened?"

"The kid broke up with him and he lost it, got drunk, showed up at his house and stabbed him to death. The police couldn't rule it as a breaking and entering because he had convinced the kid to give him a key, even filmed the moment of him receiving the key to show the cops. Plus, I've seen him after one of his fighters loses, and it's bloody."

Whatever Jeff was on was not strong enough to numb him from his stomach closing in on itself as dread filled his toes and rose to his eyes.

"But it's just rumors," she quickly added, raising a half smile. "Maybe it's not true?"

"He shows up at my house unannounced."

"Jeff, I —"

"Thank you for telling me," he said, feeling his eyes beginning to well up. "Can you give me a second?"

"Sure," she said, standing up and walking out.

Rumors or not, there was a pulling at his chest that had him wishing he never gave Marc his number, never started dating, never cared. The need to know the truth was bubbling up inside Jeff as he thought it over. He had seen Marc at the arena, seen the aggression in his eyes. Dating was supposed to be fun, at least that's what he assumed, but the deeper their relationship went the more work it was just to convince himself he was okay in it.

Warm tears rolled down his cheek as Jeff silently lied in the bed, unsure of what he would do. Breaking up would be the appropriate option in any other circumstance, but after that story, it was dropping down on his list. He felt like he was in a trap. No matter what happened, it was either breakup or stay in the relationship.

Jeff needed to have a talk with Marc.

"Jeffery Braen," a similar snarky voice jutted him from his thoughts. "When I heard they had raided a bum fighting arena and snagged someone I got excited." Detective Seymour stood, hands shoved in his pockets, leaning against the doorframe of the room. "Then, I hear it's some high schooler and low and behold it's you."

He strode forward, swinging the door shut behind him. Jeff's eyes darted to the window with the view of the hallway; Gabbie was nowhere to be seen. There was no point in lifting his arms to wipe away the tears. No shame in crying when life continually kicks you down.

"And boy was I even happier to hear you were seventeen. No parents getting called when there are situations like this," he said, raising his right eyebrow high as he scoped Jeff out. "You're lucky the law protects minors because I'm sure your parents would love to know where you are."

"Is there a reason you're here?" Sure, he knew that being attacked and killing someone when underage protects you under law if you end up in the hospital. Just like a girl getting an abortion when underage. It was more for the safety of the child rather than shielding the parents from the truth. But what he did not understand was why this detective seemed to have it out for him. It was apparent that he was dying when the paramedics took him, the bandages were still fresh on his skin.

"To do my job." Seymour sat down, making sure his shining silver pistol was visible in his holster as he unbuttoned his coat. "So, want to explain to me why you were at a homeless fighting ring, murdering the father of the kid you murdered *yesterday.*"

"I didn't murder anyone," Jeff stated. "Each time was self-defense. I'm not a killer."

"And yet you've killed. Multiple times." The detective had a toothy grin as he reached into his pocket, pulling out the same notepad. "And within a twenty-four-hour period. Seems an awful lot like a killer."

"I didn't go out and want to kill." His voice cracked. "Both times I almost died!"

"So, why were you there, then?" Seymour's eyes crinkled in the corners as he narrowed his sights on Jeff. "Why were you at that bum fighting arena the day after killing a classmate?"

"It wasn't like that," Jeff said, about to blurt out that Marc had taken him without him knowing, but caught himself before, remembering the warning, the story. "I just…. I heard about it and I didn't believe it was real."

"That's why you were there?" A condescending tone found home in Seymour's voice.

"Yes."

"To see if it was real?"

"Yes. Is that hard to believe?"

"In my line of work," Seymour said, leaning forward, muttering. "Yeah, it is hard to believe."

"Well, that's the truth," Jeff lied.

"It's peculiar to me that Adrian's father was also there."

"I showed up and before I could even walk inside, I was hit over the head and woke up tied to that chair in that God-awful shed." Seymour scribbled notes as Jeff spoke, not even being respectful enough to listen or care about what happened. Sure, he escaped alive, but that didn't make his trauma any less, make the horrors he went through invalid.

"How did you escape?"

"I was able to loosen the knot enough to get my hands out." The lies were flowing like water as he attempted to work through the truth without actually explaining the truth. No mention of Gabbie or Marc made it more difficult for him to come up with realistic ways of Jeff getting out, but he needed to.

"Interesting," Seymour said, closing his notebook. "I saw the body. You stabbed him over and over again. Seemed a little more than just trying to get out alive."

"My arms were torn open and bleeding, my wrists were raw flesh and I was on the brink of dying. He had tortured me. So yeah, I stabbed him more than once, big deal." Anger filled his bones as he watched the Detective staring at him with disbelieving eyes. Jeff had never had an adult not believe him. And sure, he was technically telling a lie, but the truth remained — after being tortured and almost killed he then stabbed Adrian's dad. But it was never intentional, and he did not ever want to kill again.

"I have a theory," Seymour said, standing up, towering in front of Jeff. "You killed Adrian. Went to the arena to celebrate and saw his dad there. Or maybe his dad did show up to kill you, I don't know. But I don't think you were tortured."

"I was tho—"

"No," he said, reaching forward and latching his hand around Jeff's wrist; he grinded his teeth together in agony as the detective's hand squeezed around his left wrist. After a few seconds he let go, smirking. "I think the dad confronted you and you didn't like that. He was ruining your day, turning your celebration sour."

Jeff tried to interject but the detective continued on.

"I think you took him into that shed and stabbed him to death, then took the rope and made it look like you were struggling. Even cut your own arms to really commit."

"That's insane!" Jeff shouted, his cheeks flushing red.

"The rope was cut," Seymour said. "You said you slipped out of it."

"I did."

"Just admit it," Seymour said, shrugging his shoulders. "It's legal, right? Why are you so adamant about playing the victim?"

"I'm not playing anything," Jeff said, looking down and seeing red seeping into the bandage where Seymour grabbed.

"Neither am I." Seymour glared, shoving his notebook back into his coat pocket. "I expect —"

The door swung open and Gabbie barreled into the room. "Jeff, baby," she said, rushing over to the bed and leaning forward, planting a kiss on his lips. Jeff was taken aback, his eyes widened as her lips touched his, and wow were they soft. His eyes fluttered closed in that moment and he couldn't help but grin as she pulled her face away.

"Hey," Jeff croaked, trying his best to not seem surprised.

"Why is your wrist bleeding?" She said, immediately turning to Seymour. "Did you do this?" Her voice changed from caring to the tone he hears when his mom does not get the correct deal at the grocery store. "Did you do this to my boyfriend? I know how easy it is to get away with police brutality but if you don't get the fuck out of this room I'm filing a lawsuit and getting your ass fired. I know people high up and don't think I won't go up against you."

With a dismissive glance, he rolled his eyes. "I'll see you around, Jeff," Seymour said, his voice slithering out, not even looking at Gabbie.

"Wow," Jeff said once Seymour was out of the room. "That was...unexpected."

"Let's not tell Marc," Gabbie said, winking.

"Yeah, hell no."

"Speaking of," she said, not sitting down, her arms crossed. "I had texted him after I got out of the shed letting him know that you got taken away with paramedics and that I'd go check on you."

"So, he knows I'm here?" Gabbie shook her head yes. He looked up at the ceiling, a feeling of defeat taking over. Marc knew where he was, he always did, even when Jeff was unaware. He had this moment of relaxation with Gabbie in the room, thinking no one knew. They were in a bubble together, both having experienced the horrors, and that popped the moment he found out Marc knew. It was only a matter of time before he showed up, putting on a worried act, even though he was the reason Jeff was in the predicament in the first place.

"He said he'll pick you up when you're released later on today," she said, no longer making eye contact with him. "He just can't come right now because of the detective and stuff."

"Sure," Jeff said, rolling his eyes. "Thanks for everything, but you don't have to stay. I'm fine. I'll be fine."

"Jeff."

"I want to be alone," he said, staring off. "Thanks again."

"Okay," she said, looking down. "I'm going to write down my number. Text me whenever, okay?"

"Okay."

After signing paperwork and receiving a prescription for painkillers, the hospital let Jeff leave. They did not make sure he was safe, ask if he had a way home, or even remotely seem interested in helping him. Maybe it was because of the reason he had come in, but something seemed as though they did not actually care about his well-being. No one in the hospital really did. The nurses were rude, dismissive, coming in to write down his vitals and leaving. One even ignored him completely when he asked her if he would be released.

His wrists had been stitched up and the doctors had cleaned his wounds with a new form of medicine that helps regrow skin cells at a rapid rate. His wrists and arms would still be in pain, and still need time to heal, but it would not be too long. Modern medicine did have some new improvements since Prop 485, seeing as people were being injured much more than usual. Until they were fully healed, however, Jeff would have to refrain from wearing anything that showed his arms. Easy enough since it was frigid out but hiding his wrists would be a little more difficult. He decided to fake being sick, so he could stay in bed, rub more of the cream on his cuts, and be able to go back to school the next week.

As long as his parents did not see he would be fine.

The sun was setting as he stepped out of the hospital. His clothes had been swapped out for baggy coral green sweatpants and a navy-blue zip up. The parking lot was completely full and there were ambulances parked along the curb, ready to leave at any minute. Instinctively he reached for his phone but became aware he did not have it, nor could he remember having it since the encounter.

"Shit," he hissed, discerning Adrian's father must have ditched it. Sighing with a roll of his eyes, Jeff pivoted on his heel about to trudge back inside and ask to use their telephone. If he had to bet, they would most likely glare at him and refuse, but he needed to at least try.

"Jeff," Marc said, jogging up beside him and blocking his way to the sliding glass doors. "Are you okay? I was so worried!"

"Were you," Jeff said spitefully. No matter how much he understood he needed to play it cool and not upset Marc, his emotions took over. "I almost died, again! And this time, while I was being cut up and thinking I'd never breathe again, you were in the building next door, training bums to fight and kill each other." Scoffing, he turned around and started walking down the sidewalk away from the hospital and away from Marc.

"I'm sorry, okay? I didn't know where you were and then the cops came and—"

"And what?" Jeff spun around, his eyes narrowed in on Marc's. "You ran, left without me. Gabbie saved my life and made sure I was okay while you were collecting your money and doing whatever the hell else it is you do because I don't know anymore."

"That's not true!" Marc barked, stomping forward until he was breathing in Jeff's air. "I looked for you, I hid and tried to find you while the cops raided the place. I figured you had bolted and then Gabbie texted me and I felt sick."

"So, did I. I felt sick when I was tricked into going to a fighting arena!"

"I didn't trick you, I just — can you stop for a second and listen to me."

"No."

"So, what? You're going to walk home? Because that's safe."

"It might be safer than driving with you." The comment came out before Jeff had time to think it over and by the look on Marc's face, it cut deep: his mouth straightened into a line, eyes widening, and there was a hurt in them that made Jeff second guess saying it.

"If you don't want to be with me," Marc said, his voice cold and distant, "just say so. You act happy one moment and then mad the next and I don't get it."

"I don't want to —" Jeff stopped mid-sentence and took a deep breath, trying his best to come up with a way to explain how he felt. Because even though he had been questioning their relationship, especially after what Gabbie had told him, he also had seen Marc be good, kind. There was an emotional level to Marc that was rare, but Jeff had seen it before and had continued to be on the receiving end of it. And because of that, he felt semi-wrong for judging Marc based on rumors, but he also needed to know the truth, needed to have a discussion with Marc and be open about everything. They both did. If their relationship was going to last, and they were going to try and make it work, Jeff needed open communication. It was the one part of the relationship he felt was missing at that point.

"I can't be with someone who isn't going to stay," Marc said, looking down and kicking his heel against the floor. "I want to be with you."

"I like you, Marc, I really do." Jeff sighed, the pain in his arms was beginning to radiate as they stood on the sidewalk. His lips were chapped, and he could taste a hint of blood in his mouth. "I just don't feel like you're being honest with me."

"I am. I'm being honest!"

"I want to believe you," Jeff said, his eyes burning against the wind as it nipped at his face. "I really do."

"Okay," Marc said, bobbing his head up and down, swiping his hand through his hair. "Okay, how 'bout this? You have a prescription, right?"

"How do you know?" His stomach tightened at the thought of Marc knowing everything already.

"You're pretty banged up and hospitals are basically just drug dealers at this point. I put two and two together."

"Oh." Jeff felt bad at how tense he had gotten. His distrust for Marc was growing with each passing moment and they needed to fix it if they were going to work.

"So, here's what I'm thinking. I drive you to get it filled and then we go back to my place and talk. Talk about whatever. I will be honest, and it will be good for us because I don't want my boyfriend to not trust me. I feel like shit when I look at your face and see how much pain you're in from the past few days and know that when you look at me I'm not taking away any burden but I'm adding to it. I don't want to add to your pain."

"I don't—"

"Please." Marc's eyes were pleading, his lips pouted up, and in any other situation Jeff would find it cute. But in that moment, he simply felt melancholy.

"Okay, fine. But I need to be home by ten, remember?"

"That's fine." Marc's mouth morphed upwards into a genuine smile, his eyes sparkling. "We can talk and then I'll take you home. Promise."

"Okay." Jeff did a half grin, trying to force himself to be positive. Maybe the talk would be good for the two of them, maybe it would clarify the mixture of emotions that were currently flooding through his entire body. Or maybe it would force him to make the decision to leave. Only time would tell, but in that moment, Jeff simply wanted to get inside of a car and turn the heater on.

CHAPTER 16

The pharmacy was not far from the hospital, which meant that it too was not in the best area. Most of the businesses were closed down along the street. Some had cardboard posters blaming the Prop, others were vacant and dark, an occasional wood board in place for broken windows. The weather was overcast out and the gloomy vibes from nature matched the feeling inside Jeff. He leaned his forehead against the window of Marc's car, eyes heavy. His arms were beginning to sting more than they had earlier, along with a throbbing headache that nestled deep in the back of his skull. Silence had been their only companion as Marc drove.

Jeff sighed, feeling his throat tighten around the words he needed to say. "I don't understand."

"Understand what?" Marc asked, turning his gaze from the road to Jeff, shifting his eyes back after a few seconds.

"You. I don't understand you, Marc. You're so in control, calm all the time, and I don't get it. You admit to stabbing people to death, train people to fight to the death, have a foster sister I never knew about, and you never seem to care about anything. Yet, you somehow care about me and want to make this right? It doesn't make sense to me."

Marc didn't say anything right away. Instead he cocked his head to the side and tightened his grip on the wheel. "To me it sounds like it's just the more you find out about me the more you don't like me."

"No, it's that —"

"No." Marc barked out, cutting Jeff off. "You brought up your opinion and now I get to tell you mine." With a cool ease he glided his hands across and rested it on the back of Jeff's seat. "I didn't tell you about my foster sister because it never came up because it's almost always about you. And I get it, you're a teenager and the world revolves around you, but here's the thing Jeff," he said, the sound of his hand tightening on the chair's leather filled Jeff's ears. "While you've been sheltered and protected and cared for, there is a good portion, if not the majority of people, who don't have that upbringing, aren't afforded the privilege. I'm one of those people. So instead of saying you don't understand me, understand that you're just ignorant to life."

"I'm not ignorant," Jeff countered, his cheeks flushing with anger. "And I'm not talking about where you came from, I'm talking about now, the present, your actions *now*, not the luxuries of life that you missed out on."

"Yeah, but you're saying you don't understand how I'm calm about it all and still loving to you, which in itself does not make sense because they're not connected at all. But here's the thing, Jeff, people grow accustomed to the upbringing they had. Which is why you can't seem to wrap your head around the fact that I've killed and am okay simply because you're not okay with yourself killing."

"I just…" Jeff trailed off, realizing maybe he didn't have a point. He wanted to bring up what Gabbie had told him about Marc's ex, but he also didn't want Marc to know he knew more than he was letting on. With a nod of his head, he turned back to the window, watching a swarm of crows sitting on the telephone wires. "I guess you're right." His breath fogged up against the glass, blurring his vision of the black birds. "I have been privileged and, you're right, I'm not used to killing or seeing people killed or being around people who murder. It's scary to me."

"Life's scary," Marc commented as he pulled into the parking lot.

The pharmacy was a large grey bricked building. The lot was empty except for one other forest green car sitting idle across from where they parked. Marc turned the key and the engine ceased, reverting them back to silence. The sound of their breathing filled the small space between the two of them as Marc reached over and opened the glove box, yanking out a black pistol.

"What the hell?" Jeff said, backing up into his seat and as far away from the gun as possible.

"Protection," Marc said, slamming the glove box shut. "It's kill or be killed, you need to understand that."

"We're just going into the pharmacy."

"Are you that naive to the world?" Marc scoffed, furrowing his brow. "I mean, honestly, no one goes out without protection. If anything, you should be happy I was smart enough to carry along a weapon in case something happens."

"It doesn't have to be kill or be killed though," Jeff said, gripping the latch on the car door and opening it, the cool air tightening his skin and stinging his face. Wincing, he stepped out and shut the door, seeing a plethora of graffiti along the back of the pharmacy. Most of it was names, but there were pictures also. One depicted a gun with an equal sign next to a noose and the words "The New Form of Lynching." Jeff didn't know what that meant, and before he could look it up, Marc was out of the car interrupting his thoughts.

"It does." With a swift swipe, he tucked the gun into the back of his pants, pulling down his grey jacket to cover any indication of it. "It's always been kill or be killed, Jeff. Take a look in a history book, watch the news. Humans have some innate sense of violence in them, always have. Genocide happened long before this Prop came into law, and people always get away with it. America United just decided to lose the facade and let the people live out their true selves."

"I disagree," Jeff said, starting to walk towards the sidewalk. The parking lot was located behind the pharmacy, forcing them to walk together. "So, what then? Everyone's evil and the sooner I accept that the better off I'll be?"

"I'm just a realist, okay."

"I think you're just numb to it all."

"Maybe," Marc said, smirking. "Which means soon you will be too."

Before Jeff could comment back, a homeless man staggered by, a ratted tin cup in hand. He had an untrimmed beard that covered his mouth and knotted together under his chin. His eyes were bloodshot, and Jeff could see track marks on the inside of his arms. The only clothes he had were a torn-up shirt and baggy cargo pants that dragged on the sidewalk. They made eye contact for a second, but the man's eyes shifted to meet Marc's gaze and Jeff watched as his face dropped as a look of terror took over.

"Well, well, if it isn't Julian." Marc said, flashing a toothy grin. "How you been?"

"I'm...I'm good, yeah, yeah, I'm good." The man scratched at his arms and looked down, continually nodding his head. Jeff saw that his fingernails were covered in dirt as he picked at his arm.

"That's good." Marc turned to Jeff, placing his hands on his shoulder. "This is my boyfriend, Jeff." Pointing to the man, Marc said, "Jeff, this is Julian."

"Hi," Jeff said awkwardly, wanting to go inside and get his pain killers, and not have to deal with whatever was evolving in front of him.

"Hey," Julian said, still bobbing his head up and down. "Marc, man, I.... man I—"

"Where you been?" There was a tone to Marc's voice that sent a chill down Jeff's spine. His eyes were narrowed in on Julian as he waited for a reply, tapping his foot. "I haven't seen you in a quick minute." Laughing, Marc swiped his hand down his mouth. "Thought you died on me."

"Nah, no, I just needed to — well you know, man." His voice was quaking as he talked, still not making eye contact with Marc.

"I actually don't."

"I just needed to get away, stop, but I — life is crazy, right!"

"Jeff," Marc said, still grinning. "I have to talk to my friend really quick. You go inside and get your prescription and I'll be out here talking."

Jeff's eyes shifted back and forth from Marc to Julian, seeing the complete contrast of the two. Marc was well groomed, standing proudly on the street with a million dollar smile while Julian appeared to be caving in on himself, fearful. There was a tugging at Jeff's stomach along with a ball forming in his throat, but he swallowed it down, nodding and turning away, walking towards the front of the pharmacy. Something inside him screamed to not go in, to not leave that man with Marc, but he convinced himself that nothing would happen, that he would be done before anything *could* happen.

As he made it to the front sliding glass doors, Jeff turned around and saw Marc putting his arm around Julian's shoulder, still smiling from ear to ear. It all felt off, and he wasn't sure what he should do about it. It probably was nothing, just his paranoid mind making him see the worst in everything, especially after the last few days. He needed to trust Marc if it was going to work, and part of that was trusting his word. Talking was what he said they were doing, and Jeff needed to believe that. Physically shaking off the feeling of guilt and anxiety, he stepped forward and entered into the pharmacy, instantly feeling the heat from inside engulf his body.

He let out a sigh, walking down the aisles to the lone cashier standing at the opposite end, shielded behind bullet proof glass. With a quick pace, he made it to the window and did a closed mouth smile, reaching into the sweat pants pocket from the hospital for his prescription. They had informed him before he left that it had already been called in and all he needed to do was hand the paper over. His hand closed around a paper and he slid it under the glass.

"I'm here for my prescription," he said. "Jeffery Braen."

The woman behind the counter had short pink hair that was spiked up, her eyes a beautiful cocoa brown. "This is some number," she said, sliding the paper back.

Jeff looked down and felt his cheeks heat up at the realization that he had slid Gabbie's number instead of the prescription. "Oh, shit, sorry," he said, his hands fumbling to grab the paper. "I just got released from the hospital, my bad."

"Mhm," she said, eyeing him up and down. "I can tell," she chuckled.

"That bad?" Jeff felt around his pocket for the prescription. He took out the paper and handed the indecipherable doctor's handwriting to her. "Here you go."

"Not really," she said, taking the paper and typing away at her computer. "I've seen much worse, to be honest. Part of the job, though. We're the closest pharmacy. Most places closed down or couldn't keep up with the supply. It was like Black Friday for us, though," she laughed, turning around and walking over to the wall of already stapled white paper bags. "We had to hire more people just to keep up with it and then it died down eventually. Now it's just me and some other guy who does the nightshift."

"Oh, wow," he said, not even thinking about how pharmacies would have been affected. "That's insane."

"The world is insane," she said, handing the bag over. "The instructions are on the pill bottle."

"Thanks." Jeff grabbed onto the bag and pivoted on his heels, ready to head back out into the cold.

"Be safe, kid," the woman said.

"I will. Thanks again." And with that, Jeff waltzed out of the store, turning down the sidewalk to be met by no one. Marc and Julian were nowhere to be found and Jeff's stomach suddenly started playing twister inside him. "Shit." His heart started to race as he whipped his head back from side to side, seeing if maybe he would be able to see them somewhere else.

No one.

He couldn't very much well just stand in the middle of the sidewalk, especially not in that area, so he started down the street towards the parking lot, hoping maybe Marc and Julian were waiting for him there. But a gut feeling told him that that wasn't the case. With a tight clutch on the bag of prescriptions, Jeff sped up his pace, a distant sound of shoes clashing against concrete picked up volume behind him.

"Jeff!" Marc's voice cut through the tension. Turning around, Jeff saw him jogging up the sidewalk, hair disheveled and no jacket on. "Where are you going?"

"To the car," Jeff said, standing and waiting for Marc to catch up to him. "Where were you?"

"Oh, that, I just had to talk to Julian." He slowed down and stopped in front of Jeff, a genuine smile beaming on his face. "I hadn't seen him in forever, just had to catch up."

Jeff eyed Marc up and down, trying to see if there was anything visible that would say otherwise. There were no blood stains on his clothes, no bruises or cuts, nothing that would indicate he did anything other than talk. Except, of course, for the missing jacket, which was strange seeing as the temperature was already dropping as the sun careened across the sky towards the west.

"Where's your jacket?" Jeff kept eye contact with Marc.

"Did you not see what Julian was wearing?" Marc headed forward, rubbing his hands on his arms. "He was an old friend. I couldn't leave him out there with no coat or anything, so I gave him mine."

"That was nice of you." The feeling of worry passed, and Jeff felt himself wanting to chuckle because he had been so paranoid. Marc wasn't evil, or a cold-blooded killer, he was just living, like Jeff. And with that, he felt like he was beginning to understand Marc a little better. But they still had talking to do, and Marc had promised the truth. They just needed to get back to his apartment safely and then they would be able to lay it all out on the table, be honest, grow together.

"I'm a nice guy," Marc laughed, winking. "Now let's get you back to my place and drugged up."

"That sounds like the best idea. My arms are really starting to burn now that the pain killers from the hospital are wearing off."

"My poor baby."

"Shut up."

"Make me," Marc teased, biting his lower lip.

"Are you flirting with me," Jeff said, flirting right back.

"It's hard not to when your boyfriend is so damn cute." Marc unlocked the car and sped around to the passenger side door, opening it for Jeff.

"Wow, what a gentleman."

The door closed, and Jeff let out a massive sigh of relief, his shoulders loosening up and his body relaxing into the leather seat. Marc got in and sat down, pushing the start button and switching on the heat.

"Let's let the car heat up for a second," Marc said, putting his hands up to the vents. "I'm freezing."

They made it to Marc's house without any issues. Marc, however, did give Jeff a kiss at every red light they hit, and as much as he hated to admit it, Jeff had a heartfelt smile across his face the entire car ride, secretly hoping they'd hit more red lights as they went.

Once they were inside, Marc made him a sandwich, making sure that Jeff had something in his stomach before taking the painkillers. It was a small gesture, but it made Jeff feel cared for. After he ate, they sat together on the couch, Marc's hands clamped together. He didn't make eye contact, just looked down at his intertwined fingers, his index finger rapidly tapping.

"Okay," Marc said, looking up. "I'm going to be completely honest with you."

"That's all I want." Jeff smiled, feeling the pain subsiding by the minute.

"I'm just going to tell you about my life and everything that's lead up to now, okay? I've never told anyone this before."

"Hey," he said, placing his hand over Marc's. "I'm glad you feel comfortable enough to tell me."

"Yeah."

"Just start whenever you're ready."

"Okay."

CHAPTER 17

His mom was lying, face first, in a puddle of her own blood. The initial gunshot had him terrified as he watched his father crumple in on himself, then his mother. The pistol hit the wooden floor with a loud bang, an aftershock to the violence. Marc's legs were numb, his throat was dry, burning when he swallowed. Inching forward, he left his toy car on the floor, the wood creaking as he stepped forward.

"Mommy," he said, seeing her hair knotted together, a gaping exit wound on the side of her head, matted hair covered in blood and brain matter. "Mommy!" Marc started wailing, screaming at the top of his lungs.

His dad lied completely still, the news still on in the background. The anchor explaining what it all meant, explaining that President Hughes would let the law go into effect immediately, not waiting until January like previously speculated. Another gunshot rang out from outside causing Marc to cower against the hallway wall, sliding down until he was folded in on himself, avoiding the pool of blood as it got bigger. Breathing was difficult, his lungs burned along with his eyes. Tears streamed down his face, snot filling his mouth as he cried.

The metallic smell of the blood mixed with the gunpowder spread through the room like a virus. Marc rocked himself back and forth, arms wrapped around his legs, shoved into his chest. Something dripped onto his head, sticking into his hair. With a scared swipe of his hand, he felt something warm and wet against the tip of his fingers. Slowly, fearfully, he placed his hand in front of his face, seeing a vibrant red dripping down his hands.

With a sudden jump of terror, Marc stood up and turned around, blood and brain matter splattered across the wall, across their family photo. His breathing hitched in his throat as he stepped back, eyes as wide as they could possibly open. His foot knocked against the gun and he felt his sock land in a hot pool of his mother's blood. Vomit came barreling up, burning his esophagus as he threw up, hunched over.

Another gunshot.

Marc felt dizzy, his eyes tunneling out. Before he knew what was happening to him, his face tingled, and his vision blurred as the wooden floor came closer and closer until he was passed out, lying in a mixture of vomit and blood.

When he woke up he didn't know what time it was, but the blood was cold, and the stench of throw up filled his nostrils, causing him to gag. His arms were weak as he tried to push himself up, fingers slipping in the red liquid. Nothing felt real. He was able to stand up, legs wobbling, as he looked back at the lifeless corpses of his parents.

His knees shook with each step he took, fingers sticking together. Red stained the front of his pajamas; small chunks of bone and brain were sticking to his flannel. He needed to get his cellphone from his room. His parents had said to only use it in emergencies, and he never really thought he would need it, but now it was going to be his saving grace.

Or at least he thought.

Once he made it to his room, he grabbed his phone, sliding the screen open, his sticky fingers barely registering with the touch screen. He was able to dial 911, but no one answered, it didn't even ring. There was simply a recording.

"We're sorry, but your call could not be completed at this time. Please try again later."

Marc wiped his eyes as his tears blurred his vision, hanging up and trying again. The same recording played, over and over again, for hours.

Eventually he gave up, sitting on the carpet, crying. No one was coming to save him, no one was alive to care for him. He was utterly and completely alone.

Eventually he was able to get a hold of the police, but by then his parents had started to decompose, the rancid smell filling every corner of the house, staining the walls with its permanent stench. He wanted to leave and find help, but gunshots rang out more and more, stirring an uneasiness and horror that if he did go outside he would be killed. The only thing he understood was that murder was legal, his parents were dead, and he had no one.

When the police found him, he was paler than ever before, dark circles clouding his eyes. He was malnourished and needed hospital care, but every hospital was overcrowded. An officer said he would take him home and nurse him back to health, make sure he was okay before they figured out what to do with him. The officer's name was Samuel, but he told Marc he could call him Sam. For an officer he had a very round belly that protruded out. He was bald, and his scalp was a completely different shade of white than the rest of his face. It almost looked comical.

The first night was fine. Sam made him tomato soup and a grilled cheese, made sure he was getting the care he needed. It didn't stop Marc from crying himself to sleep that first night, remembering the smell of their bodies, dead and rotting in the room over. When he turned his head to try and sleep, his pillow was wet and cold from the tears. Eventually his body did succumb to sleep, unaware of what waited for him.

Marc sat down at the dining table next to the kitchen, smelling bacon. His eyes were heavy, and his stomach growled as Sam sat down with a plate in front of him, but not one for Marc.

"Can I have some?" Marc asked, his mouth curving upwards ever so slightly.

"I don't know, can you?" Sam said, sticking the fork into a slice of bacon, bringing it to his mouth. He stuck the entire piece in, chewing with his mouth open. "You need to learn manners, boy. It's 'may I' not 'can I.'"

"Sorry," he said, looking down, a pulling at his stomach warning him to leave. But he had nowhere to go, and no one to talk to. Sam hadn't even taken him to the station, he just took him from the house. No one else knew he was there. His heart started to race as he watched the man cut the egg apart and shovel it into his mouth. "May I have some?"

"You can have my leftovers," he said, laughing. "That's if there are leftovers."

"But my stomach's growling."

A second later Sam's hand was across Marc's face, knocking him out of his seat. His vision spotted as he hit the tile, the taste of iron filling his mouth. As he was down on the floor, the smell of lemon scented cleaner was what he focused on. He didn't move, stayed on the floor in fear. Sam leaned down, and Marc cowered in, expecting to get hit again. Instead the man placed the plate in front of him on the floor.

"Here," he said, nudging the plate forward with his foot. "Eat it."

There was half a piece of bacon, running egg yolk, and a crust of the toast left in the middle. Marc gawked up at him, not sure what to do. Sam knelt down, putting his face close to Marc's. The smell of coffee breath destroyed the fresh scent.

"Eat."

His hand gripped the nape of Marc's neck and squeezed, pushing him forward. His nose hit the plate and he shrieked out in pain, but the grip remained.

"I said eat, now fucking eat."

Marc had to position his face to the side and use his tongue to slop the food into his mouth. His face ached, neck sore, and he felt like he might vomit. Not to mention his tears were mixing in on the plate and he just wanted the nightmare to end.

Sam took his hand back and Marc lunged his head back, gasping as tears flooded down his cheeks. His body was shaking as he stayed on all fours, in front of a plate, looking like a broken dog.

"I'm sorry," Sam said, standing up and sitting again at the table. "Come here," he said, patting his lap.

Marc stayed petrified in place.

"Come here." His voice had a sweetness to it. "Listen, I'm just — I hate this law. I fucking hate it. Your parents died because of it, and my job…. just come here."

Marc pushed himself up, steadying his balance against the table. He stepped forward, still shaking, until he was directly in front of Sam.

"Here," he said, holding out his arms. "I'll lift you up."

His insides were knotted, his mind was racing, and his face felt like it was on fire. Nothing felt okay, everything felt aberrant to him. But he still stepped forward and let Sam lift him up onto his lap because even though he had that gut feeling, he also knew if he said no he would most likely be hit again.

Fear drove him.

"I'm sorry," he said again, running his fingers through Marc's hair, sending a chill down his spine. "I didn't mean to take it out on you. You must be so scared, what with your parents, the law, and now me. I didn't want to scare you." He placed his fingers under Marc's chin and tilted his head to look up at him. "I don't want you to be afraid of me. We're going to be living together. We have to get along. Plus, I have to take care of you, right?"

Marc nodded, as he teeth chattered.

"Exactly." Sam took his hand away and placed it on Marc's back, scratching up and down, rubbing circles into it. It actually felt good and the tension in his body did relax as he continued on. "I have to take care of you. So, no more hitting. It was a onetime thing."

"Okay," Marc said, hoping it was true.

"Good. Now how 'bout I make you some food."

"Yes, please."

"This will be fun." With a last tussle of Marc's hair, Sam leaned down and kissed him on the top of his head. Marc froze, his body immediately tightening up.

Sam picked him up and placed him in the chair he had been sitting in before. He sat on his hands so that it wouldn't be visible that they were shaking. The sound of crackling bacon, chattering teeth, and ragged breathing were all Marc could hear. Sam was talking, but it was background noise. He faced forward, his body slowing rocking back and forth, tears falling down his face.

A plate was placed in front of him on the table, this time brimming with food and no indication that Sam was going to hurt him. His hands had gone numb from sitting on them, as he soon found out when he lifted them up and felt the tickling prickle invade both of them.

"Eat your food and then we can watch cartoons and have a sleepover tonight so you're not scared."

Sam had a look on his face that made Marc uneasy as he grinned. Nodding, tears still falling, he picked up his fork and started to eat. He could only stomach a few bites before he felt like he was going to throw up. Sliding the plate away, Sam cocked his head.

"You didn't eat it — you know what, that's fine. It's fine. You ask for food," he said, standing up and snagging the plate off the table, walking over to the kitchen sink. "And then you don't even eat it." He threw the plate into the sink, a loud crashing sound of porcelain smashing made Marc jump in his seat. "But it's fine. Let's just watch cartoons."

Sam walked over to the green striped cotton couch, sitting down and grabbing the remote. Marc didn't move, and Sam didn't seem to mind. Instead he just flicked through channels until he landed on something that had a lot of gun fire in it. Marc took that opportunity to look around and gauge his surroundings.

The walls were ghostly white and plain. There were no pictures hanging anywhere, not even of Sam or family members, which was a stark contrast to the pictures that riddled the walls of Marc's home. A wine bottle cabinet with glass doors was standing tall in the kitchen, next to a door that was open, showing off the laundry room. The hallway to the bedrooms were to Marc's left: his was the first door and Sam's right before the bathroom door which was at the very end. Marc made a note to remind himself not to go to the bathroom at night, so he wouldn't need to walk past Sam's room.

The television clicked off and Sam stood up, walking into the kitchen and opening up a cabinet. Marc could not see what he was grabbing, but he heard pills in a bottle. Next thing he knew Sam was offering him a pain reliever to calm him down. He didn't want it, but he had no choice, and after taking it, he blacked out.

Marc woke up in an unfamiliar bed, with pain he had never experienced before, bruises on his wrists and arms, and a throbbing headache. His mouth tasted foul and was as dry as a desert. When he swallowed, a shooting pain would crackle down his throat. He let out a cough, feeling someone move beside him. Dread seized hold of him as he tried his best to lie perfectly still, feeling himself shaking.

"That was fun."

The abuse continued for a year. Marc's outlook on life was bleak, he barely could respond when spoken to. His eyes, hollowed out memories of the horrors he faced. But luck came in the form of a fire. Sam was a smoker and a drinker. When he drank, the abuse *would be horrible, but on certain nights he would drink too much and not be able to get up from the couch. Marc loved those nights. They were when he got to lock himself in the bathroom and sleep in the tub. Those were his best sleeps.*

That particular night however, Sam had fallen asleep while still holding a lit cigarette and dropped the cigarette, igniting the old couch in flames. Marc smelled smoke and unlocked the bathroom door, peeking out. He could see smoke coming from the living room and the smell of a fire. Rushing out to see what was going on, Marc saw the couch on fire and Sam still blacked out drunk sleeping. His first instinct was to wake up Sam because that was what you were supposed to do in a fire. But then he paused and walked into the kitchen, pulling out the spray on cooking oil.

Sam had used the oil to cook, but one-time Marc had seen him accidentally spray it into the stove flame and it ignited. There was something in the back of his mind that told him no, to just leave and if Sam died he died because of himself. But there was another side of him, a side that was louder, telling him to get revenge. So, Marc stepped up and held the can out in front of him, making sure to aim it above Sam and the flames.

He took a deep breath before slamming his finger down on the can, spraying the oil onto Sam. The flames ignited and engulfed him.

The shrill screams of the man haunted Marc as he watched in muted horror as Sam shot up, covered in flames, shrieking in agony. He rushed forward, tripping over the glass coffee table and fell into it, shattering the glass with his fall. The wailing continued, the stench of burning flesh and hair circulating through the room.

The fire was growing with each passing moment and he needed to get out. Marc rushed to the front door, seeing the keys hanging next to it. The lock was different than he had ever seen before. Only a key could unlock it on both sides, there was no latch to turn. He had learned that the second day when he tried to run out of the apartment, only to realize he was trapped. The windows had bars and the only door leading out was impossible.

He was able to reach the keys and unlock the door, taking one last look at Sam burning. His arms were still flailing but he was no longer screaming. Marc slammed the door shut behind him, locking the door and running out into the night.

The nightmare was finally over.

Or at least that is what he thought as he escaped into the crisp night air. The street was empty as he trudged down it. He had expected to find someone and get help, but no one was out, no one was there to care about him. Nine years old and alone on the streets. Marc suddenly realized that the abuse was over, but now he had nowhere to live.

Eventually he did find someone and ended up in foster care.

He was in foster care for a month before a family took him in, but that month was enough to disturb him to his core. The first week there he was under constant attack from the older boys, and the guards. A few of the boys jumped him and the guards simply turned a blind eye. Another night he heard someone shouting for help and the noises of grunting; he knew what was happening, the sounds were all too familiar, but his apprehensiveness kept him idle in bed, not aiding the boy. After it was done he heard a gurgling noise and found out the next morning the boy was killed, throat slit. Abuse like that plagued every corner of that compound. The boys all slept in a large warehouse type room, bunk beds filling up every inch.

Overcrowding was an issue and Marc was lucky he was even able to sleep on a bunk. A week after he got in, they ran out of beds and boys were being turned out, made to go on the streets and wait. They didn't have to wait too long though because people died in the system, people died all around him. Marc was starting to wonder if it was a curse being alive. Maybe the victims were actually lucky, their suffering was over.

But he did leave, he did find a home with a family, and he met Alena. She was a year younger than him and they bonded immediately. Her parents also died after the law, but she had been staying with the family that took Marc in since it all happened. The family seemed nice on the outside. They had a two-story house with a basement, a backyard that was home to a jungle gym, and a fenced in front yard that Marc was excited to play in. Inside was different, though. The walls were wooden, and there were pictures of President Hughes in each room of the house.

The shades were always drawn, artificial light trumped the sun, and Marc learned quickly that everything he thought was great about the house was a facade. The kids were not allowed in the front yard, nor the backyard, but were to remain in the basement.

Besides Marc and Alena, there were six other foster kids who stayed down in the basement with them. They were not allowed to sleep in the upstairs because the adults had kids of their own, and *they were the ones who were allowed outside, allowed to play. The foster kids were there to damage.*

Maybe that's all kids were in the world for.

John and Lucy were the names of his foster parents. They had two boys — Donald and Eric — who Marc only saw when the foster kids were forced to do chores. Him and Alena got to work together, cleaning the bathrooms, scrubbing the floor, and taking out the trash. If they did anything wrong, one of the parents would discipline them.

The punishments ranged from a backhand, to burning their fingertips on the stove. At night they all lied together, on the concrete floor, sharing blankets to stay warm. Alena and Marc slept together, holding onto each other out of fear.

Some nights John would come down to the basement and take Alena. Marc tried to stop him once. It ended badly. The man dragged him by his hair up the stairs, Marc screaming at the top of his lungs. A dirty wash cloth was shoved in his mouth to keep his silent, the awful taste of cleaning product and dirt consumed his insides. Gagging and choking, Marc was lifted into the air by his pants and thrown, forcefully, against the wall across from the basement. As his body hit the tile, his knees collided hard. His ribs took a kick and he reeled back up, hitting the wall again, the wind expelled out of him. The inside of him burned and ached as John took his leg and kicked him again. Marc blacked out. When he woke up, he was lying face down on the cold concrete, no Alena next to him. He lied in the dark, eyes wide open, waiting for her to be brought back down.

Eventually she was taken back into the basement, shaking and cold. Marc scooted close, putting his arms around her, but she shuddered and pulled away, crying. He understood. He didn't touch her, just let her know he was there. They cried together that night.

The next morning John stomped down the stairs, waking everyone up. He made them stand in a straight line in front of him. Most of them were thin and pale, shaking in fear. Marc's side was purple and swollen, stinging his chest when he breathed.

"It's come to my attention that some of you think this is a free pass," John said, pacing in front of them. "I thought to myself, how can I make them understand that if they don't do what they're told they will be punished. And it dawned on me. Punishment isn't enough." With a swift motion, John pulled a long-barreled pistol from his pants, tapping it against the side of his head.

The kids all stood still, bodies tense. Marc was positive that he was going to be killed. He had attacked the man the night before and this was his final punishment, death. And as visceral as his fear was, he also looked forward to an end to abuse, an end to the torment. John continued talking and Marc closed his eyes in anticipation.

"It's simple. Do your chores and listen to whatever Lucy and I say. One of you doesn't seem to understand that." Marc felt Alena's cold and clammy hand latch onto his, causing him to open his eyes and see John pointing the gun at him. "But I'm going to fix that."

Marc shut his eyes again, closing them as tight as he could, face scrunching up while his hand squeezed onto Alena's.

A gunshot reverberated through the room and deafened Marc, but he didn't fall, didn't feel any burning sensation or anything. There was a loud ringing that remained in his ears as he opened his eyes and looked down at his chest to see if he was shot. Nothing. His vision *was spotty as he turned to his side to see if Alena was okay. She had not been shot.*

Down the row, however, the oldest foster child — a thirteen-year-old boy — was bleeding out. John had shot him in the side of his neck, and it didn't kill him. Instead he was shaking on the ground, his hand clamped to the side of his throat, crimson red pouring out in between his fingers, dripping from the sides of his mouth. The loud pitched sound slowly diminished and was replaced with the sound of the boy choking on his own blood.

The torment continued for years, and years.

It wasn't until Marc was fourteen that there was a change.

Alena was John's favorite and she was subject to the most abuse at his hands, but that did not stop him from hurting others, including Marc. Trust in men was non-existent in his life. He would dream at night about getting revenge, making John and Lucy pay for all they had done to the kids. Vengeance was all that kept him going.

One night when he was pinned to the bed, head smashed to the side, tears falling down his face, he wished the bed would swallow him whole and end the torment. As his head jerked forward and backward, his vision honed in on Eric through the crack of the door, and by the look on the kid's face he was horrified at what he was seeing.

The next day Marc was cleaning the upstairs bathroom when Eric stood, leaning against the doorframe.

"Are you okay?" He seemed to care. Maybe the kids were unaware of all the torture, or turned a blind eye to it, but now Eric

had come face to face with what kind of monster his father was, and it appeared he was disturbed.

Marc didn't talk back; he continued to scrub.

"I had no idea."

"Now you do." Marc stood up, lifting his shirt. Purple welts aligned his rib cage and back, rope marks along with ankles and wrists.

"I'm so sorry."

"Do something. Help us."

"Like what?" His voice cracked. Eric was thirteen and his eyes were wide with anxiety, Marc could see it. If Eric would help him and Alena escape, the horrors could finally cease.

"Tonight. Just sneak down and let us out of the basement. We'll leave and never come back." Marc had to lean against the bathroom sink, his entire body aching as he stood. "Please, I'm begging you."

"I, I don't...." And with that Eric backed away and left, slamming his bedroom door shut.

"What were you saying to my son?" Lucy's voice coiled around Marc as she emerged from the shadows of the hallway, a sinister look on her face. "What did you say to my son!"

It didn't matter what Marc said, he knew that. She was mad, and he was going to be beat. He could see that she was holding a broom as she stepped forward, blocking the door frame.

"Tell me!" Her voice cut into him as she lifted the broomstick, about to start hitting him with it.

"Mom, stop." Eric's voice came from the end of the hallway. "I asked him how old he was. I'm sorry. I won't do it again."

Marc watched as her hands shook, white knuckling the wooden stick. Her face harbored an evil expression as she lowered the broom, swiping a loose strand of hair from her face.

"Don't do it again, sweetie," she said, backing up and slamming the bathroom door.

Marc crumpled onto the floor, hoping that Eric would let them out that night.

Alena and Marc were ready to go the moment the door to the basement was locked. They didn't let anyone else know because trying to escape with seven kids was too obvious. Plus, in the back of his mind, if Eric did come through, he had a plan, and he knew Alena would go along with it. It was something they whispered about at night, and now it might become a reality.

The two of them stayed crouched at the bottom of the rickety staircase, waiting. Time continued to pass and the two of them were beginning to lose faith that Eric would actually help them, but then the sound of a lock turning broke the silence, along with the creaking of the door slowly opening. They held their breath, hoping for Eric, but also aware it could be John.

"Come on." Eric's voice broke the tension and the two of them quickly made it up the stairs where he had the door cracked open and was waving for them to hurry.

Marc peered out, making sure they were alone before letting Alena step out. He made a vow to himself to protect her, and that is what he planned to do. Once they were both outside of the basement, Eric locked the door and turned to them, smiling. A moment came where he felt semi guilty for what he was about to do, but ultimately, he reveled in it.

Before Eric could start back upstairs, Marc took a washcloth that he had been hiding in his pants and shoved it deep in the boy's throat, wrapping his arms around him and placing him in a choke hold. They both slowly lowered to the floor, Marc's grip tightening around his throat, the sound of his feet knocking against the floor was all the noise being made.

"Hold his legs still." Marc pointed to Alena who immediately latched onto his two legs, holding Eric in place.

Marc's arms were shaking as he tightened them even further. Eric's eyes rolled back, and his body went slack. Removing his arms, Marc told Alena to grab the keys from his pocket and unlock the basement door. They weren't going to let everyone know, but they also weren't going to leave them down there defenseless. She did, and then she rushed into the kitchen, finding the twine that the two of them had grown too accustomed to.

They set Eric up in the living room, tying him to a chair. Alena made sure the rope was tight before they made their way up the staircase to the second floor, kitchen knives in hand. Next was Donald. Together they pinned him down on the bed, shoving another cloth in his mouth. Marc then took the handle of the knife and smashed it down on his face, again and again until he was knocked out. *Marc took his arms and Alena had his legs. They lifted the sixteen-year-old down the stairs, attempting to be quiet, knowing if they dragged him down the sounds would wake the parents. Once they were down they tied him to another chair in the living room next to Eric, who was awake at that point. He was struggling to get out and Marc smirked, smashing the handle into his nose, blood pouring down his face.*

Next was John and Lucy.

Alena and Marc slowly opened up their bedroom door, seeing the married couple lying together, sound asleep. They had decided that they would drag the couple down and force them to see their kids, but first they needed to make sure that the two wouldn't be able to run.

John slept on his stomach which made it easy. Alena stood over him, knife in hand. Marc stood over Lucy, and nodded to Alena who smirked, bringing her knife down until it was above John's Achilles tendon. Then with a quick jab, she stabbed the knife into the back of his ankle and he woke up screaming. Lucy popped up and before she had to time to register what was going on, Marc slammed his fists into her face, hearing her nose pop and head hit the bed post.

Alena lifted the knife and stabbed again and again, his legs a bloody mess. John tried to stand up but fell, wailing. He tried to drag himself towards the safe where he kept his gun, but Alena kicked him in the side, multiple times, screaming as she did it.

Marc grabbed a handful of Lucy's hair and yanked her to the ground, her face colliding onto the carpet. He slammed his knee down into her back, taking his free hand and smashing her face into the carpet, rubbing it in, knowing damn well how much carpet burns hurt. She had done this to him plenty of times, now it was his turn to get revenge. Taking the knife in his other hand, Marc looked back at her legs kicking up and stabbed her in the thigh. Her shrieks were being muted by the carpet.

Turning to see if Alena was okay, he watched as she kicked John in the crotch with no looks of stopping. A feeling of pride soared inside him as he watched her exact her revenge. This had been a long time coming and the two of them needed this, wanted this, enjoyed it.

"Let's get them downstairs," Alena said, slamming her foot down on John's back.

"Gladly," Marc said, smirking.

Keeping his grip entangled in Lucy's hair, he stood up and started to drag her along the floor. Her legs kicked out, hitting the nightstand and bed post, a trail of blood staining the beige carpet. Her hands latched onto Marc's wrists and she dug her nails into his skin, piercing his flesh. Wincing, he took his free arm and with all his might rained his fist down directly in the middle of her face. Her talons let go immediately, and so did the kicking of her legs.

Alena had cut both of John's Achilles tendons, making that the point where she gripped, dragging his screaming body out. She was right behind Marc who tossed Lucy down the stairs, hearing her banging against them until she hit the tiles. John had grappled onto the doorframe, making it hard for Alena to yank him on the carpet. Striding towards the two of them, Marc lifted his right leg up and kicked John in the face; he went limp. They threw him down the stairs too, watching as he fell on top of Lucy. Once they were downstairs they set up the parents across from their kids, tied to chairs, gags in mouth. Alena and Marc sat on the couch and waited for everyone to wake up.

The boys were first to wake up and they struggled with all their might, crying, shaking, the same as Marc had done for the last six years. It felt good to watch, to know that for once he was in control, for once he was not on the receiving end. Eventually Lucy woke up, at first groggy but then she also started to writhe in her seat, followed by John. Before they started their revenge, Marc took a moment to take it all in. His mind had never felt surer of anything, his body had never felt like this before, buzzing. He grinned, tilting his head forward and glaring. There was a certain gratification he had never felt before as he watched them, knowing they were trapped and he was dominant.

Alena rose first, shaking Marc from his thoughts. He stood up too, stepping behind Eric. She stood behind Donald, both of them gripping onto the knives.

"You tortured us, raped us, beat us, and broke us," Marc said, sticking the tip of the blade against Eric's neck. Lucy's eyes widened as her screams were muffled. John stayed perfectly still, defeated. "Did you really think you'd get away with it? That we wouldn't grow up? Or were you just planning on killing us once we were too old?" He applied more pressure to the handle and heard Eric let out a cloaked shriek as the tip cut into his skin.

"This is your fault," Alena said, slashing the blade down into Donald's thigh. His mom wailed as her son shook in his chair, vomiting into his gagged mouth, choking. Marc watched with a twisted smile on his face as Donald hacked and bits of throw up dripped from the sides of his lips. Alena yanked the knife out and then aimed it forward, stabbing him directly in his chest. His eyes rolled back as his plain white shirt stained red.

Eric was twisting in his chair. Marc dropped the knife and gripped the sides of his head. With a harsh shift of his hand, he snapped Eric's neck, watching John and Lucy's reaction, feeling a rush course through his veins.

"Nice," Alena said, wiping the knife on the back of Donald's shirt.

Marc picked his up and they stepped to stand in front of the parents, making eye contact and smiling. Alena stood in front of John, and Marc in front of Lucy. They raised their blades at the same time and began to stab the couple in front of them. Anger and pleasure danced together as Marc continued to bring the knife down. The warm blood flying back and landing on his face, on his clothes, his mind. He didn't look away once as the body in front of him began to become unrecognizable. Everything felt at peace as he took control of his life.

They stayed in the house, burying the bodies in the backyard. As long as they figured out a way to pay the bills they should be okay. The lot of children all gathered around them, listening to Marc and

Alena like they were their parents. If they left the house they would all be back in foster care, and the two of them would not be apart. They had formed a bond over their abuse, and their revenge. Nothing would separate them.

None of them could get a job and the end of the month was coming soon. Alena had posted an ad on a website asking if anyone had work for two kids who needed to get out. She said they were willing to work and were not afraid to kill anyone who crossed them. Without that last part the both of them felt that they could be taken advantage of.

A person responded and turned out the be their saving grace. It was a woman named Willa, who gave them shelter, a place to eat, and work. She ran an arena where they were beginning to train homeless people to fight. The framework was set, and she was accumulating quite a following, realizing there could be a business in it. With a smile that would make dentists jealous, she welcomed them into her business, no questions asked.

Alena was made to walk around and collect bets. Marc had a hands-on job, cleaning up the bodies after the fights. And eventually he learned how to train. His life was set, and he enjoyed the violence, so long as he was always in control.

CHAPTER 18

Jeff was lying on his back, covers up to his bruised neck, when he heard the front door open, his parents getting home from work. He had already turned off all the lights in the house, including his room, in hopes his parents would assume he had gone to bed and leave him alone. The pain relievers would help him sleep, but he couldn't have his parents seeing his arms. In the morning he would need to text his mom and let her know he wasn't feeling well, that way he could stay in bed all day without question.

The hallway light turned on, a beam shining into his room from the crack under his door. Without hesitation, he shut his eyes tight, listening to hear if the door would creak open. After a few minutes nothing happened, and he peeked out, seeing that the hallway was dark again. A sigh filled the silence in the room. Jeff took his pillow and flipped it over, lying back down on the freshly cold side, trying to ease his mind to sleep.

That was hard though, seeing as his entire view of Marc had been skewed by learning about his childhood. His heart was heavy with empathy. With each new horror that was described, Jeff had wondered how Marc was not more damaged. Aside from the fighting arena, he was surprisingly well put together for a person who survived such trauma. But most of all, there was a new-found sense of understanding brewing in Jeff. All the traits that he had noticed — the controlling patterns, the closed offness, even his relationship with Alena — were now a clear sum of all the abuse Marc had suffered in his life.

A heaviness lied on his chest as he closed his eyes, trying to sleep. It didn't matter, though, because even if he could fall asleep, his dreams would be riddled with memories of the past couple of days, each time gripping him from his slumber as he would try to catch his breath. It would not be hard to fake being sick in the morning. Dark circles would add to the aesthetic of being ill.

Saturday came and went, and Jeff was able to stay in his bed all day. His mom offered him food, but he denied it, saying he felt like he would throw it up. It was not entirely a lie. He had no appetite and forcing food down really did feel like a cause for vomiting. Instead he lied under his covers, flicking through the channels, texting Marc and Mal. The two conversations were similar and yet completely different, seeing as Mal was in the dark about everything that had happened.

There was no way he would be able to make an excuse to not see her, nor did he want to. He needed to vent, to talk to her, fill her in on what happened. She was his best friend and she would sympathize with him. Not that Marc didn't, but it would be different. Mal had never killed anyone. In a strange way, Jeff wanted her to react with disgust. Not at him, but rather at the fact that he was now a product of the law. For a brief moment, he needed someone to react with horror because it was, on all accounts, horrific. Marc had brushed it off as no big deal, the nurse even said he did a good thing. And as much as he wanted to be okay with what he did, hearing nothing but normalization for his actions made him uneasy and painfully aware of how numb the world truly was.

It didn't matter really. This was the norm, and it was him who was not getting with the times. Maybe desensitization was all he had to look forward to as he grew up. Each new encounter was proof enough that it was, at the very least, part of maturing.

Before leaving, he took a moment to check how he looked in the mirror. Long sleeves kept his gashes out of sight — although at that point after the medicine the doctors rubbed in and all of the antibiotic ointment Jeff had been rubbing, they were almost closed completely. There was no getting around scarring, but at least by the end of the week he wouldn't have to worry about the skin breaking open. Until then, an ace bandage was wrapped around both arms.

His face was another story. The handprints that enwrapped around his throat were more of a greenish hue now. At the bridge of his nose, a small scab was all that was left of the cut, surrounded by red skin. The swelling itself had gone down, but the discoloration was another story. Worse than all of that was his cheekbone. It was still swollen, making the side of his face shiny. His eye was half closed against the skin, but he was thankful that it wasn't worse, knowing how awful face injuries can be.

"You just look like you got the shit beat out of you," he said to himself, fixing a loose hair at the top of his head. Sighing, Jeff said, "hope you're ready, Mal."

"What the fuc...hell happened to you," Mal said, looking back at her dad on the couch. His feet were planted on the coffee table across from the couch, the television on high volume, and his head bowed in his chest. "Come in."

She shut the door behind them and led him up the staircase, which was to the right of the front door. The living room, along with the stairs, were covered in burgundy red carpeting. The shades on the windows all drawn, giving the house an eerily sinister vibe. Jeff followed Mal up the stairs, making sure to step lightly because he did not want to deal with her father.

At the top, Mal's room was to the left, a bathroom directly in front of them, and to the right was the master bedroom. The door was left open and Jeff could see a single bed in the middle and nothing else. Mal pulled at his arm for him to come to her room; he followed.

Her room was the same as always. Jeff had seen it plenty of times on their video calls, but he had never been inside. Whenever he had come over to her house in previous years they were only allowed to play in the living room. No boys in Mal's room. Maybe that had changed, or maybe she had told her dad beforehand?

She took a seat in her leather desk chair. Unlike Jeff's room, her computer desk was set up so that the screen was facing the door with her bed sideways against the left side of the room. She had sliding doors against the right wall that opened up into her closet. The room itself was painted a bland white. There were a few posters pinned to her closet doors, and clothes lying strewn across the carpet.

"So," Mal said, her arms crossed as she sat. "Are you going to tell me what happened or am I just supposed to ignore your busted face, nose, and bruised neck?"

Jeff sighed, sitting on her twin mattress. "I'm not actually sick."

"Gathered that."

"Okay, well," he said, beginning from the text message in class and ending it with the suspension. She did not need to know about anything else, just what happened at the school. As he told her, her expression was hard to read, although stoic seemed a fitting way to describe her eyes.

When he was done, he waited for her to react. Anything. But she sat there, her hand resting across her jaw, squinting in thought.

"Okay," she said, meeting his gaze. "First things first, how are you? Are you okay? I'm so sorry that happened to you, Jeff. If I had known I would have helped, I could have helped."

"No, don't do that. Like I said, he was threatening to kill you. I couldn't…. you mean too much to me. I wasn't going to even risk putting you in danger."

"Yeah, but what if it went badly? Did you think it through?"

"I—"

"Sorry, that was dumb. Of course, you didn't have time to think it through." She sighed, shaking her head slightly. "How 'bout this? Next time you're in a compromising situation, and vice versa, we call each other. We're best friends, we have to help each other out."

"Okay," Jeff said smiling, feeling his shoulders ease. "But as for if I'm okay, I don't know. I can't really sleep that well and I have no appetite."

"I bet. I'd be traumatized."

"Yeah," he said, looking down at his lap. "Everyone just keeps trying to make it not a big deal, you know? Like, telling me it's okay, it was self-defense, he deserved it."

"Who said he deserved it?" Mal almost looked like she was going to laugh.

"The school nurse!"

"No!" Mal covered her mouth, but the crinkles in her eyes gave it away. "I'm sorry, I know it's not funny, but damn. The school nurse? That's cold."

"I know," Jeff said, a grin rising up his cheeks. "I was so surprised when she told me I did the school a favor."

"She said that?" Mal's eyes were wide, her jaw dropped open. "Remind me to never get on her bad side."

"What gets me is that if the school knew how bad he was, and knew he was this awful loose cannon, why didn't they kick him out? Why wait till he finally snaps?"

"Oh, you don't know? His dad is one of the biggest school donors. I don't know exactly what he does, but it's pretty high up security level stuff. My dad told me to stay away from Adrian because his dad apparently has deep connections with some sadistic businessman."

Jeff's smile faded away as his gut freefell. No one had come to him when he was in the hospital that would have hinted anyone knew he killed Adrian's father. Plus, he was rushed out of the shed so fast, if luck was on his side, none of those seedy businessmen would look into it.

"You okay?" Mal asked.

"I'm scared now! What if they come after me?"

"Who? His dad? Nah, you should be fine. He's always away anyways, doubt he even knows Adrian's dead."

Jeff didn't laugh.

"Sorry. That was a pretty shitty thing to say."

"It's fine," Jeff said, letting out a sigh. "I wish we never saw anything."

"Me too."

"Anyways," he said, standing up. "I told my mom I was just coming for my backpack. If I'm any later, she'll kill me."

"Oh, yeah, completely. Um," she turned around and reached for his backpack, which was under her desk. "Here you go."

"Thanks, Mal." He made eye contact with her and he stepped forward, arms open, wanting nothing more than to hug his best friend. They squeezed tightly, her hands rubbing up and down his back, lovingly.

"Anytime."

Pulling away, he wiped a tear from falling. "I'll text you. I know my parents won't let me out the rest of the week."

"I'll make sure to take notes for you."

"You're the best. Be safe."

"You too."

She walked him to the front door, her dad still in the same position. He must have been asleep. Jeff gave her one last hug before getting back into his car and heading home to his week of suspension.

Monday

Jeff [10:45am]: hows school?

Mal [10:56am]: the bathroom is still guarded with tape but otherwise nothing seems to have changed. Mr. Shan asked if you were okay. I told him you were pretty banged up hope that's okay!

Jeff [10:58am]: lol yeah thats fine. I cant believe he knows I dont want to go back imma feel like everyone is looking at me

Mal [11:14am]: don't worry no one is going to bug you about it. From what I can tell no one knows it's you. And he asked me in private so don't even stress about it. Just focus on getting better!

Jeff [11:15am]: haha I am. im literally about to take a nap lol talk to you later. be safe have a good day!

Marc [4:56pm]: May I come by tomorrow and see you?

Jeff [5:00pm]: yeah thatd be fine with me

Marc [5:01pm]: Be there at noon.

Tuesday

This was the first time that Marc had ever asked to come over. Usually he just showed up unannounced. But he asked, and Jeff had not talked to or seen him since Saturday. He knew they would need to talk eventually and figure out where they stood, he just figured it would be more unexpected and extra. Instead it was a simple text asking to come over. Maybe now that he had opened up to Jeff and drudged up his past, they could move forward. After all was said and done, there was a sense of longing to work it out, to somehow help Marc heal.

With a swipe of the ointment across his forearms, he peered over the wounds. They were grotesque looking scabs at the moment, but the fear of tearing them open was no longer a concern. The doctors were not lying when they said what they used would make him heal quicker. He had been able to take the ace bandages off the night before and sleep, arms free. By the time he actually went back to classes, the worst and most distinct feature would be his cheekbone, but even by then it would probably be less swollen. Maybe Mal was right that no one would know it was him. At the very least the thought eased his anxiety over the matter.

The doorbell rang at exactly noon; Marc was always right on time. It was impressive but at the same time semi-alarming. Jeff opened up the front door and let him in, leaning in for a peck. Marc's lips touched his and he could feel his boyfriend's mouth curl into a smile as they kissed.

"Hey," Marc said, placing his hand on Jeff's chin and looking over his face, surveying the damage. "You look much better. It's really healing great."

"Thank God," Jeff said, smiling. "I keep worrying I'm going to show up to school and everyone is going to know."

"So, what if they do? It means you aren't to be messed with. It'll help you survive the rest of high school."

"I guess. But I don't want to be known as that kid who killed another kid in the school bathroom."

"Who cares what people think. If I cared what everyone said about me I would never show my face. Just because people talk shit doesn't mean they know the truth. And you know the truth, I know the truth, your parents know the truth. Who cares if some random assholes in high school talk about you? The people who care about you know you."

Jeff couldn't help but smile. It was true, all of it. There was no disputing that. Marc gave him solid advice that did not rely on some form of murder, nor was it overtly aggressive in its form. It was truthful and exactly what Jeff needed in that moment.

"Thank you," he said, wrapping his arms around Marc.

"Anytime." Marc kissed his forehead and smirked. "You're not terrified of me after everything I told you?"

There was a level of fear that Jeff could register in Marc's voice, childlike. Even the idea of Marc sitting around worrying about if Jeff cares about him made him both joyous in knowing that Marc cares, but also empathetic knowing that he must have been worrying about it since he had told Jeff.

"Not at all," Jeff said, pulling away to make eye contact. "I'm honored that you trust me enough to tell me. It meant a lot."

"Yeah." Marc bit at his lower lip and stepped to the side, purposefully toppling over the back of the couch and landing in the pillows. "Just after I told you you got really pale and I took you home, so I just wanted to make sure."

"That was because of everything that had happened that day and the pain meds." Jeff sat down at the end of the couch, placing Marc's legs across his lap. "I care for you, Marc, and it gave me a better understanding of you. I'm glad you told me."

"What do you mean 'understanding?'" Marc asked, apprehension filled his eyes.

"I mean, like, for instance the bum fighting." Jeff shrugged his shoulders, hoping that would be enough, but by the look on Marc's face it wasn't. "You know what I mean? You said Willa introduced you to it. It just gave me more of a 'oh, I see,' type vibe. Plus, I don't know, hearing your childhood it kind of explains things in a way."

"Got it." The look of fear that maybe Jeff was going to say something that would be hurtful left and was replaced by a solemn still face. He simply nodded his head up and down.

"Are you mad?"

"No. I just didn't know that you thought there was something wrong with me and needed me to clarify that I had a fucked-up past to be able to accept me."

"No, what? That's not what I'm saying at all I —"

"It is, how can you say it's not! You said now you understand me better because of my childhood. Meaning, you thought I was fucked up and now that you have this tangible understanding of how I grew up, you can now associate that to anything remotely problematic that I do."

"But, that's not what I meant!" Jeff's face heated up as his cheeks flushed red. He didn't want to argue, about any of it. When he had said the comment, he did not think it would cause an argument. "Okay, well I didn't mean for it to sound like that but since you took it like that and are making this into a big thing, I'll say this — I have a right to be worried about things. You act like I'm this asshole who is constantly judging you but I'm not. In fact, I'm constantly trying to get to know the real you so that I won't be worried about us."

"What are you saying?"

"I'm saying," Jeff said, readjusting on the couch to turn his body and face Marc. "Me being upset about being taken to a bum fighting arena is valid. Or when we played that stupid game in that really creepy room at the party and you made that girl feel better about committing a mass shooting. These concerns I'm raising are fucking valid!"

"First of all, Jeff, you never told me how you felt about the party. All you said was you had fun. So, don't come at me with that after the fact. If you have a problem, speak up about it instead of being passive aggressive."

"I wasn't being passive aggressive."

"Yes, the hell you were," Marc said, rolling his eyes.

"I'm not trying to fight. Jesus." Jeff shoved Marc's legs off of his lap and stood up, briskly walking away and down the hallway to his room. He needed some painkillers to get through it. Not to mention his skull was beginning to throb.

"Wow, really?" Marc called out after him.

"I'm getting my pills!" Jeff barked as he made it to the bathroom and snatched the orange medicine bottle off think sink. He poured two into his hand and popped them into his mouth, leaning in and turning on the faucet. With a quick gulp of the cold tap water, he swallowed the two pills and turned around. Marc was sitting on the end of his bed, arms crossed.

"I don't want to fight either," Marc said, looking down and then back up. "I get defensive. I…" He trailed off, his Adam's apple jutting in his throat. "I just feel like you're constantly judging me. And usually I wouldn't care. Hell, I usually revel in judgment of my doings. But with you it's different. I actually care?"

Jeff took a moment to absorb it all before immediately replying. Maybe he just needed to listen better. With a half-smile, he walked to the bed and sat next to Marc, leaning his head on Marc's shoulder.

"I don't judge you." Jeff's voice was soft as he spoke. "But I'm also not going to pretend to be okay with things when I'm not."

"Fair enough." Marc's hand weaved into Jeff's as their fingers interlaced. They both squeezed as if to say sorry. "So, let's talk about it. I promise I won't get defensive, so long as you promise to hear me out."

"Deal." Jeff felt his cheek radiate pain as his lips curled into a full grin, but the feeling of togetherness outweighed any physical pain he was feeling.

Marc leaned back, and Jeff followed suit until they were lying on his bed, cuddling. Marc ran his fingers through Jeff's hair, planting quick pecks on his forehead, unbruised cheek, and lips. They didn't talk right away or delve into their issues. Instead, they lied in silence together, the sound of their breath and the wind swirling outside filled the room.

"So." Marc finally broke the silence. "Let's talk."

"Okay." Jeff nestled his head in the crook of Marc's shoulder and neck. "I guess we should talk about killing in general."

"What do you mean?"

"Well, this past week has been an eye opener for me. Not in a good way, but an eye opener nonetheless." Jeff let out a sigh. "I had this realization that you were right. Killing is a part or life now whether I like it or not."

"I'm glad you're starting to get it," Marc admitted, keeping his focus on the popcorn speckled ceiling.

"I do get it. But I also don't think killing is some end all to any problem or, like, chill to just do whenever. Just because it's legal doesn't mean it should be executed all the time, you know?"

"Sure, but also sometimes you need to."

"I can attest to that," Jeff joked, trying to lighten the mood.

Marc smirked. "Yes, you can."

"With that said, I don't like the bum fighting."

"I won't ever take you again."

Pausing, Jeff waited to see if that was he was all he was going to say about it. After a few seconds it seemed like that would be the only comment on the matter. But he wanted more. Somewhere deep inside him, Jeff wished that Marc would tell him he'd stop going, stop training, and leave it all together. There was this hopefulness that Jeff had not even realized was there until Marc said that.

"Would you ever stop?" Jeff asked, cautiously.

"I don't know. Maybe later on in life once I'm established and have moved up. I mean, I would never say never, so it could happen."

"It just makes me sad."

"Jeff," Marc said, rolling onto his side, his head leaning on his hand. "They choose it. None of them are forced into it and they all know the outcome. There's no surprise ending. They go into it willing because they need money just like anyone else."

"I don't know," Jeff said, turning on his side and facing Marc. "You don't personally kill any of them, right? They just fight each other?"

"Exactly." There it was again, that twinkle behind Marc's eye. Whenever the subject turned to anything remotely morbid, Marc seemed to come alive. The spark would appear in his eye and he would suddenly seem completely interested and ready to talk for hours. "I don't kill them at all. I train them, make sure they're ready to fight and know how to. Then from that point on it's all on them. I mean, yeah, I'm there cheering them on and watching it all happen, but I'm a fucking great trainer. My fighters hardly ever lose."

"Yeah, Gabbie told me you win most of the time," Jeff said, watching how Marc reacted to the information. His face didn't change much — there was still that twinkle in his eye — except that his teeth were engulfed by a straight-lined mouth.

"She talked about me?" Marc was speaking low, not angry, but not his normal voice.

"Just when I had met her at the bar when you left to go to the arena. She asked me who I came with and that she might know who and when I told her you, well, she told me you were the best trainer."

"What can I say," he said, rolling onto his back. One hand was under his head as he looked back up at the ceiling, his teeth becoming visible again. "She's not wrong. I know how to get someone to kill. I know how to kill." His voice came out almost sensual as he finished the sentence.

"Well, as long as you promise you don't go out and just kill people whenever, I'm okay. There were moments when I was worried you were a sociopath."

Marc laughed, the corner of his eyes crinkled together. "No, not a sociopath. Definitely not one of those."

They didn't say much after that. Jeff didn't need to hear anything else. Maybe in some twisted way, everything that happened to him over the past few days happened for a reason. He could have never had guessed that it would bring him and Marc closer, and yet as he lied there next to Marc, Jeff felt closer to him than ever before.

Wednesday

Jeff [12:34pm]: I forgot to tell you my parents are going to be out of town all weekend. we should do something

Marc [12:45pm]: Sounds good to me. I want to take you out to a nice restaurant and then have fun afterwards. Make it a great night after a shitty week.

Jeff [12:47pm]: yessss! if you want you can spend the night too?

Marc [12:50 pm]: As long as you're cool with it I would love to spend the night.

Jeff [12:55 pm]: id love it too

Thursday

The sound of forks clinking against porcelain plates filled the silence at the dinner table. Jeff had a jacket on, continuing his lie that he did not feel well. His arms were not ready to be seen by his parents. He moved his food around on the plate, not making eye contact with either of them. Across from him was his dad and at the head of the table sat his mom. They had come home from work with takeout and arranged it on plates to appear homelier. It had become a normality for most of their weekly dinners. Jeff didn't mind though. As long as the food tasted good he could not really care less who made it.

The sound from his mom's fork stopped and he knew what that meant.

"So," she said, "how are you feeling, Jeff?"

"Fine," he grunted, still not looking up.

"Oh, you're fine, huh?"

"That's what I said." Jeff was not in the mood to talk about how he was feeling because it was draining him to constantly try to distract himself from the flashing memories of the lives he took.

It was draining him to seem okay.

"I wouldn't know since you're mumbling." His mom always had a remark back to anything he said.

"Oh, okay, sure."

"Look at me when I talk to you." Her voice was not angry, but she probably wanted to assert herself as having the power in the conversation.

Jeff slowly glared up. "What?"

"What do you mean, 'what?'" She stared directly into Jeff's eyes, never looking away. "Are you going to drop the attitude?"

"I don't have an attitude," he said, rolling his eyes.

"Son." his dad chimed in. "You do."

"Wow, thanks dad," Jeff said sarcastically.

"Don't get mad at your father," his mom said. "I know you're going through a lot, but you need to talk about it so you're not bottling it up. It's not healthy."

"Can we not talk about this? Would that be cool?" Jeff averted his eyes back to his plate and moved the food around some more.

He didn't look back up, but the scraping of forks was gone. *Can this nightmare end,* he thought? Still keeping his eyes down, he imagined his parents making nods with their heads for the other to talk to him, but neither one of them wanting to because they had nothing that could make him feel better. No one could make him feel better. There was this feeling in the pit of his stomach that nothing would be okay and that made his chest tighten out of apprehension. This feeling was a constant throughout the day and at night when he lied in bed he would weep. Thoughts of his own mortality mixed with the gut wrenching knowledge that he killed and would never be the same person kept him awake. He had cried himself to sleep every night since, and inside he felt as though it was only the beginning, and life would never get better.

And really, how could anyone tell him anything that would ease his mind of that. His parents had never killed anyone, they made that a point to give him hope that the world is not an awful place where everyone kills. But in that moment their son, who they so desperately tried to shield from the world, had come face to face with reality and they had nothing to give him. Maybe they would spare them all the discomfort of the entire situation and leave Jeff to deal with it all on his own.

That is what he needed from them.

"I think we should cancel the trip," his mom said.

"No!" Jeff did not mean to say that out loud or in such a desperate way, but he had been looking forward to a weekend without his parents, without hiding Marc. They were going to go out and be a normal couple for once and he could not have his parents staying and ruining that.

"Oh, so now you're good to talk?"

"I just mean, I'm fine. I swear. You guys need to go to this." Jeff stopped moving his food around and let the fork fall against the edge of the plate. "I love you guys, but I really want to be alone and a weekend of just me by myself will be heaven for me."

"The same rules still apply. No going out while we're not here." His dad took a bite after the comment, his lips glistening with grease from the chicken. "We already have the fridge stocked."

"I know, I know. No one in and I am to stay in. No answering the door for anyone and no letting anyone know I'm home alone. I know guys. You do this trip every year."

"This years a little different." Jeff's mom reached out and placed her hand on top of his. "We just want you to be safe."

There were visible tears forming in her eyes but Jeff watched as she blinked quickly in an attempt to keep them from falling; it failed. A few tears streamed down her cheeks before she swiped them away.

"I'm sorry," Jeff said.

"You have nothing to be sorry for," she said, scooting her chair out and getting up to give him a hug. "We love you."

"I love you guys, too."

CHAPTER 19

The weather had taken an even further dip in temperatures as the day continued on. Fearing that it would begin to snow, and his parents' flight would be delayed, Jeff kept his sights on the weather app, making sure that there was not a single flake that could fall and ruin his weekend plans. Each hour felt like a day as the minute hand slowly ticked around the circle in a never-ending repetition. His parents' departure time was set for five in the afternoon, meaning they would leave for the airport around three. They needed to get to the airport an hour early and three was the perfect time in between traffic.

They hadn't talked much after the dinner the night before. Jeff had asked to be excused and left to his room where he lied in bed, headphones in, listening to mellow music. He would close his eyes as the beat coerced his mind, focusing on the lyrics as they filled his existence. Music was a place of solace that he went to when he was dealing with emotions he could not contain, or rather, emotions that were too immense for him to tackle. Ever since Adrian's death, Jeff had this pulling inside him, but he did not know what for. All he knew was that it was insatiable. As his eyes closed to sleep or as he awoke in the middle of night, drenched in sweat, his insides would not cease. Always in the back of his mind like a phantom ready to pounce and drag him kicking and screaming back into the depths of his mind, where a loop of Adrian, and his father's, lifeless bodies stayed cemented. There was no escape.

It was almost time for his parents to leave, and Jeff was sitting on the living room couch, watching them do last minute checks of everything. Their luggage was already set up next to the door, but his mom made sure that she kept her pills in her purse. She would slip them in her luggage before checking her bag in but needed the relaxers before she got on the plane. His mother was fearful of flying, it made her feel helpless in the middle of the sky. Jeff always found that funny. Flying was safer than a car, safer than walking down the street. Logically she knew that, seeing as Jeff made it a point to say it every time she left for a flight, but that did not stop her mind from deceiving her into a pit of anxiety. Maybe that's all the brain was good for: registering pain or fear and then forcing you to relive it over and over again.

"Jeff, sweetie, can you grab me a bottle of water from the fridge," his mom said as she rushed back down the hallway to her room. Another anxious trait of hers when she was to ask for help with simple tasks.

"Sure," he said, sighing as he got up and trudged to the fridge. He had on grey sweatpants and a pull over sweater, the bottom of his sweats were long enough for him to take the opening and put his foot in it like a onesie. He didn't care if it made them get dirtier, it kept his bare feet from freezing on the tile. Besides, he would only do it when he forgot to put on a pair of socks before leaving his room to get comfy on the couch.

With a quick pace he was back to the safety of the couch, his mom's water bottle on the coffee table. He could hear both his parents rummaging around in their room, an occasional few words would enter into the mix. The sound of his mom walking down the hopefully meant they had remembered to pack everything and were finally ready to leave. As much as he loved his parents, the anticipation of the weekend was making him eager for them to leave.

"Jeff," his mom said, stepping around the couch to stand in front of him. "You can't just leave water bottles like that without a coaster. I don't want any smudges, you know that."

"Oh my, god, mom." Jeff rolled his eyes and almost laughed. "I will have the house spotless when you come home. In fact, it'll be cleaner."

"Mhm." She reached out and grabbed her water bottle, putting her hand up to her mouth.

Jeff had not even noticed that she had been holding the pills. He watched as she took a large gulp of the cold water and swallowed two pills.

"This should last me a little bit," she said smiling. "Don't let anyone in. I swear, Jeff, if I find out you let someone in —"

"You are so dramatic." This time he laughed. "Mal was going to spend the night, you know how her dad is on the weekends."

"I…" His mom stopped herself and he watched her open her mouth and then close it on pursed lips. "Fine. Mal can stay over but no one else."

"Mom, you act like I have friends other than Mal."

"Jesus, Jeff, I'm talking about your boyfriend! I didn't think I'd need to spell it out for you."

"Oh." Jeff's cheeks flushed hot, forgetting that he had told his parents he had a boyfriend. "Yeah, um, no boyfriend." He avoided making eye contact after that, grabbing his phone from the middle pocket and unlocking it.

"I'm trusting you."

"I know, mom. Nothing will happen."

His parents left at exactly three. As they were leaving his mom was adamant to remind him a few more times no one could come over. It actually made him a little paranoid. The good thing was that he had already told Marc he did not want to hang out until after he knew his parents' fight had taken off. There was a worry they would, for some reason, decide to stay home with him instead. He could not risk his parents coming home, not even two hours after he promised no one would be over, to them meeting Marc — his twenty-four-year-old boyfriend. That was the one aspect of this weekend he knew he needed to solidify before he could go out and actually have fun without thinking about them.

Marc had booked a reservation at a restaurant for seven. He would not tell Jeff where it was or what restaurant, only that it was fancy. That had Jeff contemplating what to wear. The fanciest thing he owned was a black button up and a pair of black slacks; his grandmother's funeral outfit. It would have to do. Plus, he was almost positive that all black outfits were stylish no matter where you were. Either way, he had his outfit picked out.

Now all he had to do was wait.

Jeff had taken two Vicodin before Marc was on his way. That way the aches he still felt in his knees, face, and arms would hopefully dull out and he could have an enjoyable night without any reminders of what had happened earlier in the week.

Marc picked him up wearing a dark grey leather blazer on top of a black silk shirt. He had on slim fitting slacks that rounded the curve of his ass perfectly, along with his hair pulled taught into a back bun, not like the top knot he usually wore. Jeff could not help but gawk. That was his boyfriend and wow did he look incredible. His five o'clock shadow highlighted his cheekbones and Jeff wanted to yank him inside by that form fitting blazer and take him to his bedroom.

"You good?" Marc laughed, leaning forward and planting a soft kiss on Jeff's unbruised cheek. "You look surprised?"

"Sorry," Jeff said, realizing he had been staring without saying anything. "You just...you look amazing."

"Oh, well, I know how to put myself together from time to time." His smile was genuine as he stepped back for Jeff to walk out of the house. "You don't look too shabby yourself. Shall we?" He held out his arm for Jeff to wrap his around.

A smile rapidly grew on his face as he comfortably placed his arms in Marc's. Together they walked to Marc's car where Marc proceeded to open the door for him and even shut it after he sat down, making sure his feet weren't in the way first. This was a side of Marc that Jeff had never seen and he was loving every moment of it.

As they drove to the surprise restaurant, Marc placed his hand on the center console, his palms open for Jeff's hand. Jeff had not smiled that much in a long time. It warmed his chest and made him hopeful.

Unlike the last time Marc drove him to a surprise, this time the houses became increasingly more protected, and much bigger. Jeff had never really gone to the northern part of town. It was known to be where the grossly rich swarmed together. Besides his parents never went because the prices of everything were so inflated it was ridiculous. On top of that, they weren't shy of casting disgusted glances and making remarks when everyday teenagers showed up.

Jeff suddenly felt underdressed.

"Don't worry," Marc said, almost able to sense Jeff's unease. "It's not in the northern tip of hell. I wouldn't subject that on either of us. It's past these assholes and onto private grounds." He wiggled his eyebrows. "It's this exclusive restaurant where the inside is soundproof from the outside, bullet proof glass windows able to withstand basically anything. Guards protecting it. It's an oasis where you don't have to worry about the law. They check your weapons in before."

"Holy shit," Jeff remarked, not really knowing what to say. That sounded awesome, and extremely expensive. He didn't want Marc to go through that much trouble for him. "You didn't have to do this. I mean, it's awesome, but it sounds expensive?"

"Don't worry. There's a huge wait list to get in but the prices are chill. I just happen to know the owner, a big gambler. He's doing me this solid since I never let him down in the arena."

"Oh, well I guess it's cool to know it gets you perks." He had accepted that was part of the deal with dating Marc. So, he also had to accept he'd talk about it at times. Besides, it wasn't about the fighting, just explaining how he got in so Jeff wouldn't worry. It was kind of sweet in a weird way.

"Oh, you have no idea."

They continued their drive and made it past hell. As they moved on, the road became darker until they reached a large gate with a guard post for them to pull up to. A woman stepped out of the post, a machine gun hanging from straps, right in hands reach.

"Name?"

"Marc Salguero."

She turned back without saying anything and clicked a button that opened the gate inward. They drove up a graveled path that became lit with small lights along the sides. There was a lake to the right of them and Jeff could see the building in front of them. It almost looked like a castle, just miniature. It was grey and made of rock. It even had a point on the top of it. It was beautiful.

There were windows where Jeff could see people sitting down enjoying their meals, and a valet at the front. The restaurant had hanging lights that led from the building to trees surrounding it. It looked like something out of a movie.

Marc chuckled and then lifted Jeff's hand to his mouth and kissed it. "You're cute when you're really surprised."

"Shut up," Jeff said, smiling. "This is beautiful."

"Now do you see why there's a wait list." Marc smirked as they pulled up to the valet.

The two of them got out of the car and Jeff could hear the rustling of all the trees collectively speaking as the wind blew through them. It was calming to hear. A twig snapped in the distance and he saw a man standing there with a gun. His first instinct was to panic, but he realized it was the same gun as the guard at the front. Marc had told him it was guarded.

As they walked forward, they were ushered in by a young man with a tuxedo on. His hair was trimmed short, but he had a luscious beard that filled his face well. He looked like a Greek god and Jeff had to force himself to not stare.

"Follow me gentlemen," he said, waving them in. He opened two big wooden double doors that he then closed behind them. The moment they shut all the noise from the outside was silenced. In front of them were lockers and a man standing with a metal detector in hand. "So, he will take your weapons and I will then take you into the restaurant."

"We don't have any," Marc said, smiling. "But obviously swipe us down so we can get to eating."

"Very nice, sir. Most people think they can somehow slip some in." The usher laughed, gesturing for them to step forward.

The guard had them spread their arms and legs as he checked them up and down. Jeff was lucky his arms were healed enough to stretch out like that. Once they were cleared they followed their usher into the main dining area. It was through bright red doors, leading into a very lit room. There was a chandelier right above them as they first walked in, which then led down a walkway — Christmas lights covered the borders of the hallway — and to their table.

Each table was spaced from each other, with a personal candle in the middle. It was all so romantic, and Jeff had never felt so fancy in his life. Marc pulled his chair out for him when they got to their table, taking a second to squeeze Jeff's shoulders. The usher simply smiled and waited. Marc sat down across from Jeff as the usher placed two menus in front of them. After wishing them a good evening he left, and they were left to dine in peace.

There was a screen at the head of the table that was blank, but when they were ready they would order their food and drinks through it. The idea was to have a very intimate dinner with as few distractions as possible. The waiter only came if you clicked that you needed something, and that was all. Jeff actually really enjoyed it.

The closest table to them was still spaced pretty adequately away from them, but the couple at the table were very loud, or better yet the man at the table. He looked in his late twenties, greased back blonde hair that was cut almost bald on the sides. The man had on a navy-blue blazer with a white line bordering the collar, a white button up underneath, and a red and blue striped tie in the middle. He looked like something out of a fraternity, but older.

The woman across from him looked bored. She sat there with her chin resting in her palm as he continued on with his story, slurred speech and all. Her hair was straight down and platinum blonde, bangs going straight across her forehead. She had really thin lips but filled them in with a lot of lipstick; Jeff had seen videos online on how girls do that. A red dress hung loosely against her pale skin, the left strap hanging down off her shoulder. Her eyes were bloodshot, and she appeared to just be staring off into space as the guy across from her continued on.

Marc turned his head around and glared at them, pushing his seat back against the tile.

"Marc, it's fine," Jeff said, reaching his hand and grabbing Marc's. "Seriously. Look their plates, they already ate. They'll be leaving soon."

Marc let out a loud sigh. "You're right," he said, sitting back down, his tongue swiping across his bottom lip, a look of frustration on his face.

"Hey." Jeff smiled and looked him in the eyes. "I love this."

"I'm glad," Marc said, letting out a less angry sigh and smiling back. "I thought you would like a place where you didn't have to worry."

"I do."

"Real quick though," Marc said, pointing a man standing by the entrance to the kitchen. "That's the owner. I'm gonna go thank him really quick. Be right back."

As Marc headed across the room, Jeff kept his gaze on the couple at the table. The man was no longer yelling because she was talking now. He could see her eyelids at points drooping as she spoke, and he had a realization that she was high on something. Maybe they both were? At the very least the man was drunk. But Jeff could not help but continue to stare at the woman. Her face was slender, but in an unhealthy manner. There were dark circles under her eyes, and Jeff almost felt sorry for her. She looked lost.

Marc sat back down across from him, Jeff's focus shifting back to his boyfriend.

"You ready to order?" Marc asked, taking a once over glance at the menu. "Or do you trust me?"

Jeff squinted his eyes in a joking way, "what did you have in mind?"

"He just recommended that we order the steak special, said it's to die for."

"I'm cool with that." Jeff's mom didn't make steak often, but he loved it when she did. It was one of his favorite dishes his mom made.

"Awesome," Marc said, reaching over and clicking the menu button the screen. He picked their order on the screen and then asked, "how do you like your meat?"

"Well-done," Jeff said.

"Well-done? Baby, you're not living until you've had it rare."

"Nope, I'm good living just the way I am, thank you." Jeff laughed. "I like my meat well."

"I bet you do," Marc said, raising his eyebrows as he sent their orders in. "I like mine as close to raw as I can get it."

"So why not just have it raw?" Jeff asked, meeting Marc's gaze.

"Illnesses, possibly?"

"I don't know, I think it depends on what meat you're enjoying raw."

Jeff felt Marc's foot slide up his calf. As he slid it back down, Jeff bit his lower lip and smirked.

"I'm hungry," Jeff said.

"I'm starving."

The air was palpable between the two of them as they sat with their eyes locked onto each other. The rest of the world was tuned out, as if a spotlight was only on them and everything else was dark. Marc's eyes had that sparkle to them, only this time it wasn't about killing or anything morbid, it was flirting.

"I gotta go the bathroom really quick," Marc said, standing up and leaning in, planting a quick kiss on Jeff's cheek.

Before Jeff had time to react, Marc was up and rushing off. He must have really had to go. Jeff grinned to himself, wondering if the night could get any better. His gaze wandered to the table where the couple was, only they were no longer there. Jeff had not even realized they had gotten up and left. There went his entertainment.

It had been five minutes and Marc was still not back. Maybe he really needed to go, Jeff couldn't know. But that made his mind wonder if it could be for other reasons. He had read articles online on how to have safe clean sex, but did that mean Marc would bott—

"Hey, sorry!" Marc shot back at the table, sitting down and looking out of breath. "So I went to the bathroom and then the owner pulled me aside into the back room to talk to me about some business. I rushed back after I realized I had left for a long time."

"Oh," Jeff said, feeling his face flush. "I thought you just really had to go."

Marc let out a loud bark of a laugh before quieting it down and shaking in his seat. "That's so funny! Could you imagine, our first romantic date and I spend almost ten minutes shitting."

Jeff realized how funny it did sound and started to laugh also. "You're right," he said, "that would he pretty weird."

"And unromantic as hell."

"Let's get off this subject," Jeff suggested, still chuckling.

The waiter came with their steaks. It was easy to tell who's apart by the amount of red liquid surrounding the piece of meat. There was a creamy butter that had green chopped up herbs on top of it. For the side, there were garlic mashed potatoes alongside steamed vegetables. It looked incredible and Jeff did not even stop to wait. He unwrapped his cloth napkin, placed it in his lap, grabbed his fork and knife and started carving. The two of them remained relatively quiet while they ate, only occasionally making a comment on how good the food tasted.

"Just wait till dessert," Marc said, stabbing his fork into a bloody piece of meat and eating it. His potatoes had been stained red on the sides where it touched the meat.

"What's for dessert?" Jeff scooted a few vegetables into his mashed potatoes and put them together on his fork, loving the mixture.

"It's this lava brownie cake that has hot fudge in the middle, ice cream on top, and I wanna say more chocolate on top? I'm not a hundred percent sure but I know it's gonna taste great."

"Just a plain brownie with ice cream would have got me going. That sounds so good."

Dessert was amazing. The brownie was cookies n' cream, which made it even better in Jeff's opinion. Once they were done with that, Marc called for the check, paid, and they left the restaurant. It was chilly outside, and the sound of trees was welcomed. Jeff paused and inhaled, letting this night soak in.

He expected Marc's car to be brought and for them to leave, but Marc informed him that they were now going to go walk by the lake. There was a bench that sat in front of it, a street lamp was directly next to it, only lighting the bench and nowhere else. They sat down together, Marc putting his arm around Jeff and pulling him in close. They stayed like that, Jeff snuggled into Marc as they stared off at the lake. The moon reflected off the still water, the smell of wet grass filled the air.

"I'm having a really great night," Jeff said. "Thank you."

"You're welcome," Marc said, leaning his head in and kissing Jeff.

They stayed in each other's embrace, kissing under the moonlight. Jeff never really thought he could have moments like this in life. He always chalked it up to some pipe dream that Hollywood sold to the public, knowing damn well that the reality was much different. But in that moment, Jeff realized someone just needed money or connections to live a carefree life. All the people here are protected, enjoying themselves without any fear, while just across town someone is probably fearing for their life. The juxtaposition of situations in such a small area of space was an eye opener.

After that they got into the car and drove back to Jeff's house. Marc pulled up in the driveway and shut off the headlights.

"So," Jeff said, contemplating the entire drive if he should do it. "Do you want to come inside?"

"I would love to," Marc said, "but I have some things I need to get done tonight so that tomorrow I can take you out to a party. And before you object, it won't be at the house I took you to before, and there won't be a lot of people."

"Okay," Jeff said, semi disappointed.

"Tomorrow night for sure, though," Marc said, leaning in and resting his elbow on the center console. "It'll be worth the wait."

"I don't know," Jeff said, feeling his jeans tighten.

"Trust me," Marc said, his hand sliding up Jeff's thigh until his grip tightened. "I'll make it worthwhile."

Marc's hand started palming up and down on Jeff, while he leaned forward and kissed his neck, moving up to his earlobe and biting softly. Jeff let out an audible moan as Marc's mouth came over his and they started to kiss. Marc's lips were soft, but his facial hair was rough and would rub against Jeff's skin. It didn't matter though, in a way it felt good.

Jeff felt his pants unbutton as Marc slipped his hand in. Jeff leaned his head back against the chair, his breath visible in front of him. He felt Marc's mouth sweep across his neck and down to his collarbone; he unbuttoned the top few buttons, giving Marc more access. His entire body was buzzing as Marc's hand picked up the pace. Jeff's breathing became more and more ragged as his muscles began to tighten.

"You're so hot," Marc said, as Jeff let out a final moan.

His body was electric as Marc slowed his rhythm and tightened his grip.

"Oh my, God," Jeff said, breathing in and out heavily.

"That should hold you off," he said, licking his thumb, "till tomorrow."

"What about you?" Jeff asked, gazing down.

"I'm good. I like making sure you're having a good time," he said, starting the car and turning the heater on. "So, tomorrow I'll pick you up. It's just a party so you don't need to dress fancy or anything."

"Got it," Jeff said, opening up the car door. "Thanks again."

"Anytime."

CHAPTER 20

Jeff had gotten the best night sleep in a while that night. For a few brief hours he forgot about all his problems and was able to enjoy himself. He woke up around noon, sleeping dead through the night; he needed sleep. The bags under his eyes were not as dark, and his skin had more color to it. The house was warm because he had remembered to turn on the heater before bed, and it felt cozy to lie in bed and not be icy.

He walked on the tile barefoot and went into the kitchen. Grabbing the peanut butter and the raspberry jelly, he made a quick sandwich before taking his pills. Then it was time to get prepared for tonight. There was a definite unspoken feeling from the night before that they were planning on taking their relationship further, but Jeff did not know how far that meant. Just to be sure, he groomed everywhere while in the shower, making sure he was ready for anything. Logically he knew it would not change anything but attempted to do sit ups to make his abs look a little tighter, hopefully. As for eating, that sandwich was all he was going to eat. He did not want a full stomach going into tonight, plus his nerves were starting to rise up and the first thing to always go when he was nervous was his appetite.

Jeff [2:23pm]: Hey! I didn't know when you were coming to get me but I'm ready whenever :)

Marc [2:28pm]: Look at you continuing on in perfect grammar<3 The party is gonna start around 6 so I'll get to yours at 5.

Jeff [2:29pm]: Only for you<3 Okay sounds good, see you then.

Jeff saw Marc's headlights shine into his room as he hopped out of a quick once over shower just to make sure. He took another pill, slipped into a pair of black jeans, a navy-blue hoodie, with a white undershirt. The doorbell rang right as he slipped his sneakers on his feet. Nothing was even happening yet, and his heart was already banging its' drum.

Marc had on a grey beanie, jeans, and a black coat. "Okay," he said, walking in and giving Jeff a peck. "So, I want to drink tonight. Well, rather, I want us to just have a fun night out and drink and just loosen up."

"That sounds fun to me," Jeff said, "but who's driving then?"

"Already taken care of. I ordered us a ride with 'Nywhere.'" Marc grinned. "That way we can drink and still get back to your place later on." He stepped forward and had Jeff against the wall, his hands on Jeff's waist. "And then," he said, their mouths almost touching, "I can sleep over."

Marc lifted Jeff up and pushed him against the wall, the pressure holding him up. Jeff wrapped his legs around Marc's waist, running his hands through the back of Marc's hair. Before it could go any further, a honk from a car was outside.

"That's our ride," Marc said, stepping back and letting Jeff step down. "I love how it's literally just a robot car driving us places. It's the best app."

"I haven't used it before," Jeff admitted, knowing all about it but never needing it. "Is there like an actual robot in the driver seat?"

"No," Marc laughed, straightening his jeans. "It's just the car. It's really cool."

They went outside, and Jeff saw that it was a sleek looking silver car with tinted windows and scissor doors. They opened for Marc as he typed the command into his phone. The inside was spacious. Two seats in the middle with cup holders on both sides, a mini fridge at the front, and neon lights that bordered the roof on the inside. Jeff went in first and sat down in the white leather seats. The seat itself was really comfortable and he could recline it all the way back if he wanted.

The front simply had a dashboard with a screen that awaited instructions. Marc typed in the address and Jeff watched as it showed up on the screen, along with a map showing where they were going. A part of him was nervous to have a computer drive him, but that was also how most people got around, so it could not be that dangerous.

The car ride was smooth, with no jerky stops or sudden accelerations. It was actually much better than most people drive. They arrived in front of a large gated house. Marc clicked something on his phone and the gate opened. The two of them got out of the car and walked up the driveway to the bright red front door. The house itself was a two-story white wooden house with a wraparound porch, and pillars. It was quite beautiful.

Marc did not ring the doorbell or knock but rather just opened up the door. Jeff immediately saw Alena, causing him to catch himself before he rolled his eyes. As much as he knew how much of a messed-up life she had, she seemed much more enthralled with killing. She even had tattoos to remember it by. Next to her were Peter and Robyn. This time they looked much less dressed up. He should have known it would have been them and — that is when he saw Gabbie and his face lit up. She was walking over to the three others with shots in her hand.

The house was very spacious, with a living room to the right — which had a foldable table set up in the middle — and behind the group of friends was a hallway that led into the kitchen, which also connected to a game room. The staircase was in the middle of the hallway. There were people standing on the steps drinking, a few other's playing beer pong at the table, and Jeff could hear more conversation coming from down the hallway.

"What's up," Marc said, striding over to them. Jeff followed behind him.

"There he is," Peter said, reaching out and pulling Marc in for a one-armed hug.

Gabbie turned and met eyes with Jeff. He saw as they immediately softened, and she smiled.

"Glad you're looking better," she said sincerely.

"Yeah modern medicine does some crazy stuff now," Jeff joked.

"It really does, though," Gabbie said, nodding her head. "I've been to the hospital a few times."

"When have you ever been to the hospital?" Robyn asked, taking the shot without so much as batting an eye. "Aren't you all about what motivates people to stand on the sideline and observe?"

"First off," Gabbie said, "was that even English." Everyone in the circled collectively laughed. "And trust me, Robyn, I've had moments where I've been involved."

"So ominous."

"You know me," Gabbie said, raising her eyebrows. "Better than most."

"You guys need a room?" Peter asked. "At least usually it's further along into the party before you guys jump each other's bones."

"We're just talking," Gabbie said, rolling her eyes.

"Yeah, Peter, shut the hell up." Robyn turned to Jeff and rested her hand on his shoulder. "For real, though, sorry you had your first kill. They're the hardest."

"Yeah," everyone said together.

"Here," Peter said, handing Jeff his shot. "You deserve it more than me."

"Hold on," Marc said, rushing over to a table that was set up alongside the hallway, next to the kitchen. An array of alcohols were laid across the table and Mar made enough shots for everyone. "Okay," he said coming back. "On three, to Jeff."

"To Jeff," Gabbie repeated softly.

"One, two, three," Marc said.

"To Jeff," they all said.

Jeff tilted his head back and took the shot, that way he could blame his watery eyes on the burning of the alcohol in his throat. Marc wrapped his arm around him, patting him on the back.

"Tonight's gonna be amazing." Marc kissed his cheek.

"There's too much lovey dovey shit going on," Alena said, already looking drunk. Her eyes were plastered with red veins, as her eyelids hid half. "Let's play beer pong or something. We only have this house for four hours, remember?"

"Huh?" Jeff said, not understanding what she meant. Why would they only have the house for four hours? Had they broken into it?

"Have you really not heard of renting a secured house out for a party?" Alena smirked. "You are just as naive and ignorant as they get. It's adorable."

As she finished her sentence she left and sauntered over to the table to pour another shot.

"Ignore her," Marc said, whispering the next part. "She gets like this when she drinks."

"She does have a point, though," Peter said, shrugging. "We really only have, like, a good three and a half hours left. I say we go make the most of it."

"I'm always down for a good time," Robyn said, grabbing Gabbie's hand. "If we're playing beer pong, Gabbie is my partner."

"Of course," Peter said, grinning. "I take it I'm Alena's partner then?"

"You did just side with her, so," Jeff interjected, hoping his joke would land well with everyone.

"Damn," Gabbie said, covering her mouth and laughing. "He got you good."

Peter's smirk remained, and he nodded his head. His eyes looked warm as he shrugged. "All right, I see you, Jeff. You have a point."

"That's my man," Marc said, wrapping his arms around Jeff and lifting him off the floor, planting a kiss on his lips.

Jeff landed on his feet with a smile on his face. His chest soared as he grabbed Marc's hand and whispered, "let's take another shot." Only he bit Marc's earlobe on the last word.

"Let's."

The two of them made their way to the drinks while the others went to the table in the living room. There was a couch in the game room also, with a few people sitting down with red cups in hands. Jeff saw someone sitting there with beautiful dark skin, a form fitting blue tank top on, with a thigh high black skirt. They were staring off and Jeff could see their eyelashes were perfectly curled upward and looked like something out of a magazine. A thin gold necklace hung against their collarbone, landing directly in the middle of their chest. They were beautiful.

"Okay," Marc said, holding two small plastic shot cups. "I made us each two. This one is tequila, and I figured we can chase it off with this baby." He pointed to a bottle of regular plain old vodka.

"Jesus," Jeff said, laughing. "Let's do it."

Marc handed him the first shot. He could smell the tequila before he even put the shot near his face. This was going to be strong, he knew it. Marc did a countdown and Jeff tilted his head back and tried his best to swallow it all in one gulp without coughing any back up. The fire liquid filled his mouth, burning down his esophagus and into his stomach. His eyes were squinted, and his mouth was pursed, but Marc handed him the second one and there he went. Jeff felt his stomach try to reject it as it came down, but he forced the alcohol down. Across from him, Marc's face was also scrunched up.

"Jesus," he coughed out, "maybe having that as a chaser wasn't a good idea."

"No going back now," Jeff said, clearing his throat, hoping the pain would subside soon. "You good at beer pong?"

"I've never lost," Marc bragged.

"Good, because I've never played before."

"The safer you live," Marc said, leaning in and whispering, "the less you experience."

"I'm seeing that." Jeff smiled and wrapped his arms around Marc's shoulder. "See, and we haven't killed anyone, or anything. 'Cause we don't need to unless attacked."

"Yes," Marc said, hugging Jeff and leaning his head on his shoulder. "You taught me that one."

"Marc? Hey, man!" A girl in the kitchen said. She had brown hair that was styled in a faux hawk, with a blazer on that buttoned in the middle. She did not have any shirt on underneath that, so her beige tawny skin was the main aesthetic on her front. With skinny black jeans and pair of black shiny shoes, she looked almost business casual, but for a party. She had a beer in one hand and a joint in the other.

"Leila! No way," Marc said, bounding across the island in the middle of the kitchen to grab her into a bear hug. "I miss you."

Jeff looked around and saw that there was a cooler next to the table. He opened up and looked inside. An array of different beers and wine coolers were placed together in the ice. Jeff decided that he wanted a fruity drink and grabbed a dragon berry wine cooler. To his luck, there was a seat open on the couch. He twisted off the top of his cooler, stuck the aluminum in his pocket, and strode to the couch to get it before anyone else sat down. He didn't mind that Marc went to go talk to the girl, he just did not want to stand awkwardly by the alcohol. At least sitting on the couch wasn't awkward.

"Is this seat taken?" Jeff asked.

"No, you're good," they said, scooting over ever slightly for Jeff to fit in comfortably.

Jeff took a swig of the drink, still feeling the after burn of the two shots.

"So, let me guess," they said, looking Jeff up and down and grinning, their cheekbones high up, shaping their face beautifully.

"You don't like the taste of beer?" They were holding an IPA in their hand.

"I don't mind it," Jeff said, shrugging. "I just figure, if I'm going to drink, I'd rather have it taste like something really good."

"Okay, I can get behind that." They tilted their head back and put the bottle up to their mouth, taking a sip and turning back. "Hi, my name's Yvette." They held out their hand for Jeff to shake.

"Jeff," he said, letting go and taking another drink. "Listen, before we keep talking, I just want to ask what pronoun you prefer? I'd rather know now than misgender you in conversation, you know?"

"Well, thank you. I go by she or her," she said.

"Got it," Jeff said, giving a genuine smile. He could feel the alcohol was kicking in as he sat there, his cheeks heating up.

"How do you know this crowd?" Her eyebrows furrowed with a questioning glance. "I haven't ever seen you at one of the parties before, or at the fights? But seeing as you have that bruise on your cheek I guess you must know someone. Let me guess," she turned her head and scoped out the party going on around them. As her head turned around to face the kitchen, she gasped and turned back to him. "No. You can't be the one that Alena's been talking about?"

Jeff could not help it, he rolled his eyes. Yvette laughed and clapped her hands together.

"Don't worry," she said, winking. "I won't tell her."

"What did she say?" Jeff wanted to know what she was saying behind his back. If he wanted to be petty he could talk about her seeing as knew a lot about her life that he doubted anyone else did. He had a temptation deep down inside of him to tell, but knew he couldn't, at least not for Marc's sake. The idea of her being affected didn't faze him, but he did not want to add any stress for Marc.

"Just that she didn't see what Marc saw in you because you're so innocent." Yvette cocked her head as her eyes surveyed him again. "I don't know, you don't look too innocent to me."

"Thank you!" Jeff exclaimed, his hands flying into the air. "I don't know why she thinks that, but then again she always seems drunk, so."

"Damn," she said, taking a sip and widening her eyes. "You're not entirely wrong, though."

"Sorry," Jeff said, realizing he was coming off a little too strong, especially not knowing if Yvette was close with Alena or not. "She just says things that...I don't know."

"Get under your skin? Trust me, I get it."

"Are you close with her?" Jeff asked, trying to gauge how much damage he had done within those brief minutes.

"We kind of grew up together, or better yet, she was the older sister I never wanted."

"Wait, you grew up in that house with John and Lucy?" Jeff had flashbacks to the horrors that Marc had told him.

"Who? No," she said. "Willa. She took me in and taught me how to protect myself and got me on my feet. I was eleven when Marc and Alena came to stay with Willa, and let's just say, she was much more volatile back then."

"Yvette," Marc said, walking up and standing in front of them. "How you been?"

"I'm good," she said, smiling. "Just getting acquainted with your boo." A teasing tone found the end of the sentence.

"Isn't he adorable?" Marc reached down and grabbed Jeff's hand, yanking him to his feet. "Now, Yvette, stay out of trouble."

"Look who's talking," she scoffed, rolling her eyes. "You guys have fun now."

"It was nice meeting you," Jeff said, beaming as Marc pulled at his arm for them to go to the beer pong table.

The rest of the night devolved into a drunken mess. Marc and Jeff played against Gabbie and Robyn, where just as Jeff expected, he did horribly. The ping pong ball flew past the cups and bounced off the wall behind the girls. Marc made up for it though, sinking every single shot. Only thing is, they switched the rules on them, and each cup had a mystery alcohol. By the end of the first game, and on an empty stomach, Jeff was drunk, along with Marc.

Marc's cheeks were rosy as he beamed, his teeth the most visible thing on his face. His eyes were drooping, and his speech was slurred, but so was Jeff's and he was having the most fun. Gabbie and Robyn were on the couch, making out. Peter and Alena wandered off somewhere, and by the looks on their faces, they were the most hammered.

Marc was wobbling in front of Jeff who was leaning against the wall by the front door. He placed his arms next to Jeff to hold himself up, but also to lean in. The two of them began to drunkenly make out, sloppy and hot. Jeff forgot for a moment they were not in private as he rubbed his hand against Marc's crotch.

"Let's get out of here," Marc said, almost frantically.

"Yes," Jeff exhaled out.

The car ride home was spent with Jeff lying on top of Marc in their reclined chair, their mouths and bodies inseparable. The idea of using this service to go everywhere was tempting as Marc's hand gripped the nape of Jeff's neck and pulled him, sucking on his neck.

They barreled through the front door, only stopping for Jeff to enter the alarm code. That didn't stop Marc from standing behind him and kissing his earlobe while he typed in the code. Jeff turned around and was pushed against the wall. In his drunken stupor he did not even feel the alarm box against his back.

They went from the hallway to the bedroom — colliding with each part of the wall as they went. Jeff's eyes would close as they kissed, tongues exploring each other's mouths. One moment he would slam into something hard, then something that made a lot of noise until he was shirtless and thrown on the bed, pants unzipped.

This was it, finally.

"You good?"

"Yeah."

CHAPTER 21

Jeff squinted, the sunlight spreading into his room like a virus. He had never blacked out before, and as he tried to remember everything from the night before, it was all quick flashes in between nothing. He remembered them coming in and drunkenly making it to the bed, then his memory came back with Marc underneath him, face in a pillow, moaning.

Through half closed eyes, Jeff turned to his side and saw Marc lying shirtless on his stomach. The sheets covered the lower half of him; Jeff was also shirtless. He burped, and it burned his stomach. With a grimace, he closed his eyes and took a deep breath, hoping the hangover would not last all day.

He had never seen Marc's bed head before, but it was cute. The hairs were tangled together on the top like a mop. Jeff surveyed down and saw that he had a skull tattoo that covered his right shoulder blade. A quick flash of a memory came back to him and Jeff remembered leaning forward while Marc was under him and kissing the tattoo.

On the left side of his back, there were scars. Small lines that started right at the top of his left shoulder blade. There were rows and Jeff couldn't count exactly how many lines there were – at least twenty – and two of the scars were fresh and still scabbing. In his drunken haze, Jeff couldn't remember if he had seen those the night before and he wasn't entirely sure what they signified, but something inside him knew he wasn't going to like the answer. Although, that feeling inside could also be the ear-splitting headache that was worsening with each ray of sun that shone in.

Turning to see why his blinds were not keeping the light out, Jeff realized that they had bent the blinds the night before. That would explain the noise he heard as his back hit something. His brain seemed to register pain in that moment because it was then that the middle of his back began to ache.

"I'm never drinking again," he said to himself.

Jeff's mouth felt like a desert and tasted awful. Smacking his lips together, he got up quietly. Tiptoeing to the bathroom, he turned on the sink and leaned his face in lapping up water. With a sigh, he came back to bed and lied down, closing his eyes as his head hit the pillow.

Jeff lied there quietly smiling. He didn't care that his first time was when he was drunk because in a way that probably made it easier. Knowing himself, he would have been nervous the entire time and asking if it was good. From the bits and pieces he was remembering, he definitely was not nervous or shy.

With heavy eyes, Jeff began to feel himself drift back off to sleep. Marc shifted next to him in bed and made a half grunt half snore.

"Love you," Jeff whispered, not even sure if he actually meant it. But the thought of having even just those two days without trouble made him thankful. And with that he drifted back to sleep.

There was a loud knocking at the front door. Jeff popped up and his head punished him for it. They had not turned on the heater before getting to it, so the house was cold. He shivered and looked for his shirt, which he remembered Marc pulling off of him. It was lying on top of the lampshade next to his bed. He grabbed it and slipped it on, crossing his arms to warm himself up.

"It's freezing in here," he mumbled while grabbing a pair of socks from his dresser.

Another set of knocks broke the silence of the house, this time louder than before. Jeff looked behind him and saw that Marc was still asleep. He thought that maybe he should get Marc up in case something happened but shook the thought from his mind. After all he had been through, he could take care of himself.

Tiptoeing down the hallway, Jeff held his breath as if whoever was outside could hear him. Before he reached the front door, he ducked and brought his face up to the peephole, peering through.

"Shit," he hissed.

"What?" Marc's voice sent a chill down to his bones.

Jeff jumped back and bit his knuckle to make sure not to scream. "You scared me!" Jeff surveyed Marc who was standing at the end of the hallway in nothing but black boxer briefs, tapping the barrel of his pistol against his thigh. Jeff didn't even know Marc had his pistol on him but was not surprised. In any other circumstance Jeff would have probably laughed at how ridiculous he looked.

"It's the detective," Jeff whispered. "I got this. Go back to the room."

Marc nodded in agreement but didn't budge. Jeff's eyes widened as he nudged his head for him to go back. Marc rolled his eyes and backed up into the hallway. Jeff had no time to make sure he actually left as another knock – or rather banging – came from the door, startling him and forcing him to deal with the immediate issue at hand.

Jeff's door had a chain that they hardly ever used, but before unlocking the door he put it in place. He didn't trust that man. The door creaked open enough for Jeff to peek through. The icy wind whirled past him and filled every space available in his living room.

"Hello, Jeff," Detective Seymour said, his voice sounding as devious as ever. He was wearing exactly what Jeff would expect an asshole detective to wear. He had on a black coat that covered him down to his knees, where it met his black slacks. His hands were covered in leather gloves and his neck was wrapped with a wool scarf. "May I come in?"

"No." Jeff kept his left hand on the door knob in case he needed to slam the door shut.

"It's pretty cold out and I think it would be nicer for both of us if you let me in, so we could talk."

"You came to talk to me in this weather. I'm not letting you in my house."

"Fine." Jeff could hear his leather gloves tighten. "You see, I find myself constantly coming back to your statement that day and something just doesn't seem to be adding up."

"Well, I told you everything that happened so if something isn't adding up that's not because of me." Jeff focused on his breathing, trying to remain calm. His hand was white knuckling the doorknob.

"Yes, of course. But we both know you already lied because the rope was cut, remember? So, I think it's safe to say I have some more questions."

"I didn't lie," Jeff said through gritted teeth.

With one swift movement, Detective Seymour glided his hand up to the door and leaned on it, making the chain pull taut. Jeff worried it would break under the pressure. "Humor me?"

"Fine." Jeff mimicked him.

"So, according to you, you went to the fighting arena to see if it was actually a thing? You heard of it and just wanted to see if it was real. You still sticking to that?"

"I'm not sticking to anything," Jeff said, his voice rising. "That's what happened."

"Okay." Detective Seymour raised his hands and the pressure on the chain eased up. "So, you go there and what? You could've just seen that there were people at the warehouse and left, why go up to it?"

"I was –"

"Celebrating? I mean what better way to enjoy a week off of school after murdering a classmate than watching men fight to the death."

"That's not how it was. We already went over this at the hospital." Jeff's tongue flicked across his lower lip in frustration. He could feel the hairs on his arms standing up from the cold and his breath was clearly visible in front of his face. "Besides, we both know whether I did go there to kill his dad or, the truth being I got attacked, it's still legal."

"I was hoping you'd bring up legalities." Detective Seymour smirked, and Jeff wanted nothing more than to punch him in the face. "Since you've murdered two people already, I'm sure you're fairly familiar with the law."

"Both of those cases were self-defense. I'm not a killer." He wasn't even sure he knew where the detective was going with these questions but there was an uneasy feeling in the pit of his stomach, twisting inside him like the knife he'd twisted in Adrian's throat.

"Okay." Detective Seymour reached into his pocket and pulled out the same notebook he had in the hospital. With a few flips in, his finger landed on a page and he began to read to himself. "So, self-defense. But that's not really my point. My point is, if you know the law, then you know that gambling is illegal, and gambling on human life, well, that's a felony."

"I wasn't gambling." Jeff huffed and closed his eyes, trying to understand why this detective was even back questioning him. That had been one of the worst days of his life; he was sure he was going to die tied to that chair. "I already told you. I walked up and before I could even get in, Adrian's dad hit me over the head and dragged me into that horror shed."

"I just can't wrap my head around that story."

"Well, it's what happened!" Jeff didn't mean to raise his voice but the fact that he had already lied before was now forcing him to continue. He knew it would look worse if Seymour found out he lied to him, although he felt like giving up at that point. It seemed the detective knew already that he was. But then he thought of his parents. He didn't need them to go through any more trouble on his behalf. Plus, he knew if he told the truth, Marc would be arrested, and he was not going to have that.

"Then where was your car?" The Detective's eyes did not shift away from Jeff — he did not even blink — and Jeff could feel the blood drain from his face. His cheeks felt like pins were being poked into him. "What's the matter, Jeff? Saw a ghost?"

"No," Jeff said, trying his best to come up with a lie.

"While you rack your brain with ideas and excuses, let me tell you how this is going to go." Detective Seymour slammed his hand into the door and the chain snapped. Jeff jumped back as it swung inward and hit the wall, making a mark. "I know you didn't go alone. I know it probably wasn't even your idea. But here's my issue, Jeff. You're the only one who was left after the police raided the place. Your car was never there. We know that for a fact, and I highly doubt your parents dropped you off to have fun at an abandoned warehouse. Now, I need to know who brought you."

"Excuse me?" Jeff took a step forward and the detective shifted his arm to show his gun in its holster on his hip.

"Careful, wouldn't want you to get hurt." The detective's voice coiled around Jeff's throat and stopped any sentence from forming. "Now, you're going to tell me who took you. This homeless death-fighting epidemic needs to stop and I need names. Someone brought you and if you don't tell me who I'm going to— "

"Kill me?" Jeff didn't back down, he stood his ground. His heart was racing with adrenaline and his body felt like it was vibrating. "I know how much you police love to kill people."

"Is that what you think?" Detective Seymour leaned in until his face was mere inches away from Jeff's. "You should be much more afraid of police who follow the law. Trust me," he said, a toothy grin filling his face. "The criminal justice system is worse than death."

"Must make you proud working for it then."

"It does, when I can put scumbags away. Now if you don't give me names, I'm going to make sure I go after you, and arrest you for lying to a detective in an investigation."

Jeff tried his absolute best to not react to, but a mixture of fear, anger, and adrenaline got the best of him. "How about this? Get a warrant or get the fuck off my property."

With that final sentiment, Jeff slammed the door shut and held his entire body against it while twisting the deadlock. He had his ear to the door and he listened for a few seconds before peeking out.

Detective Seymour was a small figure all the way down by the end of the sidewalk. He let out a sigh of relief and slid his body down the edge of the door until he was sitting on the tiled floor.

"Wow," Marc said as he walked out from the hallway. "Who are you and what have you done with my boyfriend?"

"Shut up," Jeff said, grinning. "Were you listening the entire time?"

"Is the earth round?" Marc, still in just his underwear, sauntered over to Jeff. "That was hot the way you told the detective to fuck off."

"Shut up," Jeff said again as Marc straddled his waist. "I don't get why he's so adamant about coming after me."

"Don't let it get to you. Cops have nothing better to do than harass people. He has nothing on you. Just forget about it," Marc said, kissing down his neck. When he reached Jeff's collarbone he bit it playfully and suddenly nothing mattered. Marc pinned his arms above his head and moved across to his other collarbone, nibbling.

"Let's take a shower," Jeff said in Marc's ear, biting his earlobe. He had become increasingly aware that neither of them had after the night before.

Marc gripped the nape of his neck and got a handful of hair, yanking Jeff's head back and exposing his neck. "That would require us to move and I don't know about you," Marc pulled a little harder on his hair. "But I like it here."

"I like it here, too," Jeff said, running his hands down Marc's back, suddenly remembering the scars as his hand glided against them. Marc winced.

"Sorry, it hurts."

"Oh, yeah. I saw those this morning." Jeff saw Marc's eyes shift to the side. "What do they mean?"

"Nothing," Marc said, keeping his gaze averted.

"Marc, come on. We're finally being honest with each other. Don't push me out now."

"I can't." Marc stood up and ran his hands through his hair, straightening the small knots as he went. "Just trust me, it's not important."

Jeff began to rack his mind as to what it could be. They were obviously a tally system of some kind, but what would he be marking down. There was a moment when Jeff thought he knew what they were, what they signified. Since there were two new ones, and Marc was not talking to him about the fighting arenas, they were most likely a scar for every win. Jeff stood up and put his hands on Marc's shoulder, turning him so that they were making eye contact.

"Is it one for every win at the fights?" His gaze did not falter as he watched Marc's eyes shift again.

"Can we just not do this right now?" Marc shrugged Jeff's grip off him and turned away.

"Tell me." Jeff's chest was getting tighter with each passing moment while his insides felt like they were plummeting. There was something deep down inside him that knew what the answer was, maybe he did all along, but he needed to hear it. He needed Marc to look him in the eyes and tell him.

"No. I'm not telling you."

Marc turned on his heel and walked to the hallway. Jeff dashed after him and latched onto his shoulder, spinning him around.

"You're going to tell me, right now." His voice was level as he said it, even though he wanted to shout it at the top of his lungs.

"No, I'm really not." Marc's eyes had an anger to them as he shoved Jeff back and away from him. "Now fucking drop it."

"I'm not gonna drop it." Jeff took a step forward and instinctively puffed out his chest. "God, we're finally good, finally talking and you're gonna throw it all away because you still can't just be honest. It's pathetic."

"What'd you just say?" Marc moved in, making them mere inches apart. "Call me pathetic again and see what happens."

"Are you threatening me?" Jeff was not sure if it was the hangover or simply that he was fed up with lies, but he was getting angrier with each passing moment. Why was Marc picking a fight after the night they just shared?

"Are you trying to get a rise out of me?" Marc's tongue flicked across his bottom lip as he glared at Jeff. "Because trust me, babe, you're not going to like it."

"There you go with your empty threats." Jeff rolled his eyes. "You really are pathet—"

Before he could finish his sentence, Marc slammed his back into the wall, knocking down a picture frame. The glass shattered on the floor, but Jeff was more focused on Marc's hand as it snaked around his neck, his mouth hot against Jeff's ear.

"You done?"

"Gabbie was right about you," Jeff snarled, knowing that it would get under Marc's skin. Sure enough, the grip around his throat tightened.

"What did that bitch say?" Marc's other hand closed into a fist and he held it at bay. "Tell me!" His hand collided with the wall, leaving a hole.

"Get the fuck out of my house," Jeff said, raising his head high, keeping his eye contact with Marc.

"Not until you tell me what she —"

"Said?" Jeff laughed. "So, I'm supposed to tell you everything, but you can't even tell me what the hell the scars on your back mean? How do you expect this relationship to work? Me follow everything you say?"

"You really wanna know?" Marc pushed the weight of his body against Jeff, pinning him to the wall.

"Yes," Jeff said, fearing what the answer was going to be.

"One for every person I've killed."

Jeff tried his best to not react, to not show Marc that he felt like he had been stabbed in his heart and repeatedly kicked in the gut. Two fresh scars. That meant Marc had killed two people recently, if not within the last few days. And even as his brain processed what he had just heard, it somehow already knew. He should have known.

"When did you?" Jeff's voice shook as he tried to get the sentence out, realizing in that moment that Marc was never truthful with him, not entirely. The entire foundation that they were building their relationship on was a lie. "When did you kill two people recently?"

"That's not important."

"Like hell it isn't," Jeff said, pushing forward, trying to get unpinned from the wall. "We talked about not killing anymore. I need to know. Was it after we talked? After you said you wouldn't go out and kill if you didn't need to."

"I have a better idea," Marc said, pushing his hand upward, forcing Jeff to raise his neck to avoid choking. "You tell me what Gabbie said."

"Not until I know," Jeff's heart was racing in his chest, his palms were sweaty, and his knees felt like they could give out at any moment, but somewhere inside him was a fire that would not go out. He was not going to let Marc switch the subject or lie anymore. He needed the truth, deserved the truth.

"Don't make me do this," Marc said, although it was not threatening. There was a moment where his face quit harboring an angry expression, and his eyebrows arched up, his eyes looked vulnerable. "Please, don't make me." Jeff could see that his eyes were getting watery, as his grip loosened.

"Tell me. I deserve to know the truth." Jeff dropped his fed-up tone, trying to be as sincere as possible. "Marc, please."

"I don't want to hurt you."

Jeff almost laughed. How could he say that when he had Jeff pinned to the wall, lying to him. The trust that they had built together was slowly diminishing in front of Jeff's eyes, and somehow Marc did not seem to grasp that. If he didn't want to hurt Jeff, maybe he should have thought it all through before lying and killing.

"Too late," Jeff said, feeling a tear fall from his eye. "Tell me."

"I…" Marc let go of Jeff's throat and backed up, until he was leaning against the wall opposite Jeff. With a swipe of his hand down his mouth and to his chin, Marc sighed. "It was when we went for dinner."

Jeff's face went slack, his eyes burned, but he forced tears from falling, forced back the ball that was rising in his throat, and tried his best to not let Marc have any more control over his emotions. The entire two days had been a break from pain, but that's all it was, a pit stop before the truth came out. Marc hadn't changed. He killed people when they were at dinner. How did he even have time?

"What?" Jeff gnawed on his lower lip. "What do you mean when we went for dinner? I was with you the whole night!"

"Why are you doing this?" Marc pushed off the back of the wall and strode forward, pushing up against Jeff and wrapping his arms around his waist. "It's not a big deal, please, you're overreacting."

"I'm over— are you fucking kidding me," Jeff shouted, shoving Marc back with all his strength. "When?"

"You're such an asshole," Marc snarled. "You think you're better than me. I see it on your face whenever I tell you anything new about me. You stare at me like I'm this piece of shit lost soul who needs to be saved."

"That's not true, and you know it." Jeff had his hands in fists by his side, not sure what Marc would do. If what Gabbie said was true about his old boyfriend, he had to be ready for anything.

"Like hell I do." Marc paused, tilting his head to the side and pursing his lips together. "Fuck it. We're gonna break up anyways."

The words sliced into Jeff as the air escaped his lungs.

"Maybe it's best it happened now." Marc glared, his eyes full of darkness. "I can't keep acting like I'm this holier than now guy when I'm with you. Yeah, I killed those two obnoxious drunks who were ruining dinner, and I'd do it again."

"Wha—"

"Shut up!" Marc screamed, the veins in his neck popping out. "You wanted to know, well here you go. I didn't go up to the owner to thank him. I told him to make sure they didn't leave. Then I said I needed to go to the bathroom and got up."

Remembering that night, Marc had a twinkle in his eye right before going to the bathroom. Jeff had assumed it was because they were flirting and having a great night but now he realized that it was about killing. It always was. He only looked alive and joyful when murder was involved.

"That's why you had that look in your eyes." Jeff let out an audible sigh, shaking his head slightly. "You weren't happy because of me, you were excited to kill them,"

"Don't act so surprised," Marc said, rolling his eyes. "Did you really think I'd just change because my high school piece of ass was upset? I've been killing since I was nine years old and no one, not even God himself, will change that."

"Get out," Jeff said, warm tears fell down his cheeks.

"Not until you tell me what Gabbie said."

"It doesn't matter because I'm done. We're done."

"Is that so?" Once again Marc rushed forward, but this time Jeff was ready and punched him in the jaw. His knuckles hurt as he pulled his hand away, but there was a feeling of satisfaction that trumped it all.

"I'm not going to just take your shit. Gabbie told me the rumor about your last boyfriend and I'm not going to be some toy you can get rid of when you're done." Jeff was fuming. "Now get the fuck out of my house!"

Marc had stumbled back and caught his balance, looking back up at Jeff. There was blood in the corner of his mouth. He took his tongue and slowly licked it, not moving his gaze from Jeff.

"Big mistake," Marc growled.

"Just leave."

"You're gonna regret this." And with that Marc turned and went back into Jeff's room.

Jeff could hear him rummaging around for his clothes; he did not move. There was broken glass next to his feet, in fact, he had not realized that in the moment he stepped on a few shards. He would have to take them out after. Marc appeared at the edge of the hallway, a silhouette against the light coming from Jeff's room.

Keeping his chest out and his head held high, Jeff stood his ground, watching Marc as he walked by him and to the front door. Everything Marc was wearing from the night before no longer gave Jeff any other feeling than disgust. As soon as he heard the door close behind Marc he hobbled over to the door, trying not to put too much pressure on his feet. Locking the deadbolt, Jeff slid down and felt his body give in to his emotions. His shoulders dropped, his eyes welled up, and his throat felt like it was closing. Before he could stop it from happening, the floodgates opened, and he began to weep.

After the initial breakdown, he was able to get his breathing back in check and focus on what he needed to do next. First, he needed to go clean his foot off and get the glass out. Then he needed to clean up the hallway. His parents were coming home that night and he had no idea how he was going to explain a hole in the wall, a broken chain on the front door, and the broken picture frame.

With a heavy sigh and a wipe of his eyes, Jeff looked at the bottom of his foot and pulled out the few small pieces that were lodged in his skin. There was not a lot of blood, mainly just minor cuts, but somehow little wounds seemed to hurt more. He grabbed the broom and dust pan from the laundry room and swept up the remaining pieces on the floor. It was his parent's wedding picture; he was screwed.

His mind was too tired, too hungover, too sad to think of an excuse for all of the things his parents were about to come home to. So instead of stressing over it, Jeff took three Vicodin, hoping it would simply knock him out so he did not have to deal with life for a short while. He trudged into his room and stopped at the doorway. The bed was unmade, the under sheet coming up from the corners, but he did not care. He grabbed his comforter, lied down underneath it's warmth, and closed his eyes.

As his mind slowly winded down and his breathing got shallower and calm, Jeff thought about the fact that he had to go back to school the next day. His first day back in over a week, and he had to go under these circumstances. A part of him wanted to laugh because it felt like a joke. But it wasn't. The next day he would go back to class and move on with his life as though nothing happened. At least his arms had healed up and his gashes were now scars. He was still going to try and keep that fact from his parents for as long as possible.

A heaviness set in on his eyelids and he finally closed them. He heard his phone buzz but ignored it, figuring it was Marc. With one last deep breath, Jeff drifted off to sleep.

CHAPTER 22

"Get up!"

Jeff squinted, seeing his mom standing in front of his bed, hands on hip. He had no idea what time it was, but from the amount of darkness his room had succumbed to, he figured he had slept clean through the entire day. His mom was tapping her foot as she waited for him to get out of bed, but he really did not want to. There was no getting around that he was going to be in trouble, but couldn't he just stay in bed and get yelled at?

"Hey, mom," Jeff said, rubbing his eyes.

"Jeffery, get the hell up!"

Looked as if that was a pipe dream. Jeff let out a long sigh and threw the covers off himself. He hadn't eaten before taking the pills and his face was being antagonized by small daggers as he stood up, feeling the blood rush from his cheeks. His eyes drooped as he placed his hand onto his nightstand to hold himself up.

"What happened? There's a hole in the wall, and our wedding picture isn't hanging up?"

All Jeff took away from that was that they had not seen the broken chain yet.

"And why the hell are your blinds so smashed!?"

"I messed up?" At that point, he was not sure if it was the drugs or not, but he could not seem to care at all. It all just felt so trivial to him. The fact that he was getting yelled about blinds and broken frames when people were being killed, when the world they lived in was so utterly despicable.

"You messed up? That's all you — that's it, you're grounded. I don't know what's gotten into you, but you better get your act together. Do you understand me?"

"Yes," Jeff said, sitting down on the edge of his bed before lying back down. "Sorry."

"I…" Her finger was pointed out until she closed her hand into a fist and shook her head, storming out of his room.

"Okay," he said to himself, going back to sleep.

There was a tapping sound that would not cease. Jeff opened his eyes and looked around. His room was completely dark, along with the hallway outside. He had no idea what time it was or what that sound was, but it was getting irritating. With a frustrated swing of his arm, Jeff grabbed his phone off the nightstand and checked the time.

His screen showed that it was almost midnight, and that he had a text from Gabbie.

Gabbie [2:17pm]: wtf did you tell marc??? he just left me this really scary voicemail!

Jeff [11:48pm]: omg im so sorry I took a bunch of vicodin after me and him got into a fight and then I just knocked out I just woke up! call me

His phone lit up with Gabbie calling him right after he sent the message.

"Hello," Jeff said, his entire body waking up as he scooted himself up against the bedpost. "What happened?"

"Dude," Gabbie said, sounding like she did not even know where to start. "Did you tell Marc that we kissed in the hospital?"

"What? No," Jeff said, "me and him got in a fight and then he got physical, so I made a comment that you were right, and he freaked."

"Oh, that explains it," she said, sighing. "He was yelling on the voicemail about how I ruined your guys relationship by getting close to you. I just assumed it was about the kiss."

"No, we're safe when it comes to that," he joked. "But honestly, he was so mad. He told me I was going to regret breaking up with him. It was scary."

"Yeah, it wasn't peaches and rainbows on my end either. At least for now we just have to be careful." Gabbie took a pause and as she did, Jeff heard the tapping still, only this time it got louder, and he could now pinpoint where it was coming from; his window.

"Gabbie," Jeff whispered, dread latching onto his heart. "I think there's someone at my window."

"Don't go look," she said. "Even if it's not Marc, who would be tapping."

"The lights aren't on." A brief amount of relief eased his heart. "That means no one's there," he said, standing up. "I'm gonna go look at what it is."

"Okay," she said, "be careful."

"Gabbie, there's no one —" Jeff dropped the phone and covered his mouth from screaming as he peeked through the blinds to see Marc's face leering at him. "Oh my — shit," Jeff hissed, looking back at his open door.

He could hear Gabbie calling out "hello" as he watched Marc shake his head no while wagging his finger. Jeff stood trembling as he watched Marc mime for him to open the window. There was no way he was going to let him into the room, let alone even open it a crack. Jeff shook his head no and watched Marc snarl and cuss, reaching into his pocket and yanking his phone out. Pointing at Jeff's phone, as he clicked on his. An incoming call from Marc showed up, his screen still in the call with Gabbie.

Jeff leaned down and picked it up, quickly saying, "I'll call you back, Gabbie," before swiping to accept the call.

"Open the window, now." Marc's voice was low and full of rage.

"No," Jeff said, backing up to close his bedroom door. "Did you cut the power?"

"No, I just turned the sensor earlier. Let me in, Jeff."

Jeff closed the door and turned back to see Marc pacing outside of his window. He knew his parents bought the best bullet proof window there was on the market, so he was safe in that sense, but Marc turning the sensor and showing up made him fearful. Is this what he meant by Jeff would regret it? Or was he trying to make up?

"What do you want?" Jeff asked, walking back to the window, one arm crossed while the other held the phone.

"Just open the goddamn window!"

"No" he hissed, "I'm not letting you in."

Marc's lower jaw went back and forth as he swiped his hand through his hair. "Fine, have it your way." His eyes were bloodshot and puffy, a mixture of melancholy and rage filled them. Jeff watched him close his eyes and tilt his head, nodding.
"You might as well just leave because you're not coming inside."
"Okay, Jeff," he said, opening his eyes and glaring, a sinister smile eroding. "Okay."

And with that Marc hung up, walking away from the window and into the darkness of Jeff's front yard. A breath that he had not even realized he was holding came blowing out, his shoulders lowering. He backed up until his leg hit the side of his bed, then he climbed in and lied under the covers, not looking away from the window.

Redialing Gabbie, he waited for it to only ring once before she picked up.

"You okay?" She sounded worried which made Jeff feel in some way better. She was one of the only people who knew what was going on with him and it was nice to know she cared.

"It was Marc," Jeff said, lying on his back, not moving out of fear. "He turned the sensor off earlier today, I guess. I don't know, it was scary."

"He's a psychopath," she said. "I know we're friends, me and him, but he's so controlling and really seems to get off on killing people. I know we're are all products of our upbringing and I know Marc had a screwed-up childhood, don't get me wrong, but at some point, you need to heal and move forward. He never did, and he's been fighting it since."

"Yeah," Jeff said, "I can tell." He let out a sigh and felt his eyes starting to burn and his throat begin to tighten. "I'm going to go to bed," he said, knowing he was about to start crying and didn't need her hearing. "First day back to school tomorrow."

"All right. Be safe, okay?"

"You too."

As soon as he hung up his face melted in on itself as he began to cry, latching onto the blanket and shaking. He did not think it was possible to cry even more after all he'd been through and yet, there he was, bawling. Everything around him felt like it was out of his control and he was drowning in it. The idea of having to show up at school and be okay was giving him anxiety, along with not knowing what Marc was going to do next.

As he tried to get a grip on himself and steady his breathing, the outside light turned on and shone into his room. There was a shadow outside and Jeff stayed perfectly still, petrified. The shadow left but the light remained on for another three minutes, as programmed. When it turned off, Jeff was holding his breath.

That continued on for hours. Each time Jeff's eyes would start to weigh down and he would just be going to sleep, the outside light would turn on, with that same ominous shadow. On the last time it turned on his phone also buzzed with a text from Marc.

Marc [2:33am]: sweet dreams

His alarm blared in his face and he felt like he was going to die of exhaustion. The moment he shut it off his mom opened up his bedroom door with a pot and pan, banging them together. Jeff covered his ears and shouted but his mom continued to hit the two of them together. Jeff angrily kicked his blankets off and got out of bed, flouncing past his mom as she finally stopped.

"Rise and shine," she said, straight faced. "Eat your breakfast and get dressed. I'm driving you to school."

"Mom, what?" Jeff asked incredulously. "This is so unfair. Plus, I drive Mal."

"Mal's been getting to school fine without you for a week, she can manage it while you're grounded."

He didn't say anything just stormed down the hallway and into the kitchen. There was a bowl of oatmeal on the table. With an audible huff, he sat down and ate the food as quickly as possible. He did not want to have to sit with his mom while eating. After breakfast he showered and got ready, at a slow pace. His mom was shouting for him to hurry up, but he purposefully took his time, changing outfits, going to the bathroom — where he really just sat on the toilet seat to make his mom wait. Anything to frustrate her more somehow made him feel a little better.

The car ride to school was silent. Jeff kept his gaze out the window as his mom turned up her oldies. There were only so many times he could hear Rihanna's classics. She sang along, and he sat seething, actually looking forward to school. As they pulled up, Jeff opened the door immediately and closed it while his mom was saying something. With a fast step, he stomped his way into school, through the double doors, and away from her.

Mal and him had texted earlier to meet up at the front inside. Sure enough, she was standing to the right of the doors, smiling.

"It's so good to have you back," she said, walking forward and hugging him. Her arms rubbed up and down his back and Jeff could feel his eyes beginning to water. "I missed you."

"I missed you, too," he said, squeezing. "Marc and I broke up yesterday."

"Good," she said, rubbing his shoulders. "I didn't like you dating a twenty-four-year-old. It was creepy, Jeff."

"Yeah," he huffed, the two of them walking towards their first class. "I really did like him, though. Like a lot."

"I know. Didn't help that from the pictures you've shown me he's pretty attractive."

"Also, we kind of, had sex?" Jeff waited as he watched Mal stop, pivot, and face him with wide eyes and a look of shock.

"What? When?"

"Saturday. He took me to this party and we got drunk and kind of just did it."

"Jeff!" Her jaw dropped, and she hit his arm lightly, smirking. "Was it good?"

"I think? I was really drunk I don't remember it fully. I hate this. I wish I never did it."

"That's why I'm all about cuddling. You can't go wrong with it and can't not remember if you were even good."

"Yeah well, duh, you're ace."

Mal rolled her eyes. "And you're bi, so? Besides, that doesn't mean I don't want to go on dates. I just have to wait for when I finally move out and can go on them without my dad being, well, my dad, I am going to love it. Eat out, or in, it doesn't matter and then just hang out, cuddle, watch a movie." She let out a long sigh, a smile plastered on her.

"That does sound pretty nice," he admitted.

"Exactly," she said, "and it has nothing to do with what I like, asshole. I just know what a good date is."

"Sorry," he said, realizing that came off pretty rude. "I'm just…" He thought if he should tell her about Marc showing up at his window last night. Last time they talked they did agree to tell each other when they were dealing with something, but there was something in the back of his mind that warned him against it. It was this feeling that somehow getting her involved would put her in danger, and that keeping it from her was best. He hated it, hated that he was listening, but his mind did have a point. "I'm just really tired."

"Yeah, I can tell," she said, a tone of sympathy. "Your eye doesn't look too bad anymore, you just look like you haven't been sleeping."

They reached the door to Mr. Shan's class.

"I really haven't been."

Jeff pushed opened the door and walked into class, keeping his head down. His teacher was not in yet, so he could avoid having an awkward conversation, but he could feel other kid's eyes on him as he made his way to his seat. He looked up and saw the bookcase where he hid the knife. His palms started to sweat, and his lungs felt like they were constricting. It felt like his mind was back in time, while his body was in the present. The same fear that he experienced when Adrian threatened him was now surfacing as he remembered, in vivid detail, the events.

"You okay?" Mal asked, interrupting the image of the hilt of the blade twisted.

"Yeah, just light headed." Jeff sat down, tapping his leg rapidly and trying his best to focus on his breathing.

Mr. Shan entered and the two of them made eye contact. Jeff was afraid he would say something, but instead he simply nodded quickly, before addressing the class. At least that went better than expected, but Jeff's chest still felt like it was being compressed, and he didn't know why. He only knew it felt like the walls were getting closer and he needed to get out.

"Okay," Mr. Shan began, "where did we leave off?"

"Bum fighting," a girl said.

"Ah, yes, the homeless death rings." Mr. Shan began to talk, write on the tablet that projected onto the wall, teach, but none of it was comprehensible for Jeff.

The moment he heard the girl say that, his world felt like it was going to collapse around him. He was trying to take in deep breaths but the most he could inhale was a small amount at a time. Each breath felt like it was becoming more rapid as he started getting dizzy.

"They shoot them at the end," Mr. Shan's voice cut through and Jeff was back at the bar, back watching the two men duel to the death, back to that day.

He shot up without warning, alarming — from the looks on their faces — everyone.

"I need," he couldn't get the sentence out. "I need to.... I...."

"I'll take him," Mal said, standing up and grabbing Jeff's forearm.

"Okay," Mr. Shan said, a worried look on his face as Jeff tried his best to walk past him without falling. "Take all the time you need."

Jeff simply bobbed his head as Mal led him out the door and into the hallway. The moment they were out of the classroom he collapsed, finally giving in to his body's demands. His lungs were refusing to work, his heart felt like it was being put on overdrive, while his mind worked against him every step of the way.

"Jeff," Mal said, squatting down next to him. "Listen to my breathing and just focus on it, okay? You don't have to talk or anything, just mimic along."

With everything he had, Jeff focused on his hearing, listening to her inhale, holding it for three seconds, and then exhaling. He tried to follow along, but it felt the like air was hitting speed bumps on its way down to his lungs, shaking his body. Mal didn't say anything about it, just continued breathing. After a few times it was improving, and he was able to take in more air.

"Good," she said, lightly placing her hand on his back. "You just need to breathe."

"I can't walk past the bathroom," he said, not wanting to even think about.

"Totally, we will avoid it."

They sat outside of the classroom together until the bell rang. Jeff went in after most of the kids had left to grab his backpack. Mr. Shan was sitting at his desk when Jeff walked in, and he stood up immediately. With a quick step he strode forward and stood in front of Jeff, placing his hand on his shoulder.

"If the content is too triggering for you I understand completely and will be willing to let you sit out of the lectures about the law."

"Really?"

"Yeah, after this week the class is going to take a test and then we'll move on. I wasn't expecting you to take the test anyway, but I don't want you to have to sit through content that can be upsetting."

"Thank you," Jeff said, wanting to give him a hug, but knowing that would be weird.

"Of course," he said, letting his hand drop and stepping back towards his desk. "I'm always here if you need to talk."

"Noted," Jeff said, walking back to his desk and grabbing his backpack.

As he was making his way out, Mr. Shan said, "hey. I'm glad you're alive."

Jeff paused, and then walked out, not entirely sure if he could say the same.

As he exited school at the end of the day, he saw that his mom was the first one parked out front. He could see her pointing for him to come to the car. Rolling his eyes and sighing, Jeff walked heavily towards the car, his shoes scraping the concrete with each step. The only pleasant thing was the heat in the car which was a nice contrast to the temperature outside. He closed the door behind him and strapped in, immediately looking out the window and away from his mom.

She did not say anything at first, and Jeff hoped it stayed that way.

It didn't.

"I did not appreciate you slamming the door in my face this morning," she said.

"Yeah, well I don't appreciate listening to 'We Found Love' for the five millionth damn time." The words shot out of his mouth with anger in them, and not even anger directly at his mom, just an overall feeling of rage. "I mean honestly, that song is literally thirty years old, Jesus."

"I've had it up to here with you."

"The feeling's mutual."

The two of them did not talk after that. His mom got out of the car first, shutting it with all her might and briskly stomping to the front door. Jeff shook his head in disbelief and got out. As he started walking towards the house he remembered Marc and got paranoid that he was going to be there. With a quick glance over his shoulder, Jeff half jogged to the front door, closing it behind him and twisting the lock.

The sound of his mom's pill bottle rattling came from down the hallway.

"Of course," he mumbled to himself, kicking off his shoes and going to his room.

Jeff closed the door and lied in bed. He had no energy, he didn't have an appetite, and the only thing he really wanted was to just sleep. That would have been ideal, but as his eyes were closing, his phone buzzed.

Gabbie [3:17pm]: marc just called me and said for me to meet him at this place tonight at like eleven. he sent me the pin drop and he told me not to tell you otherwise hed kill me and then you! but i have to let you know in case he does kill me and i cant warn you

Jeff [3:19pm]: omg! im coming with you if thats the case!! im not having anyone else get hurt because of me. maybe if im there and talk to him he will calm down?? I just need this whole thing to end already

Gabbie [3:20pm]: no I cant have you come!

Jeff [3:21pm]: remember when you said marc thinks things out. well I doubt he thought youd tell me so he wont expect me to be there which means we can catch him off guard and hopefully get him to chill

Gabbie [3:21pm]: idk jeff

Jeff [3:22pm]: trust me. just pick me up tonight around 10:30 that way my parents are asleep and I can sneak out

Gabbie [3:23pm]: fine, see you then

CHAPTER 23

His phone buzzed with a message from Gabbie saying she was outside. Jeff had already disarmed the alarm system, so he could sneak in and out without waking his parents. He had done it plenty of times before with nothing happening, and he was not going to let Gabbie go alone. His parents would not even know, and he would be back in time to wake up and pretend like nothing happened. That felt like all he was doing lately. It was taxing.

With a flick of the switch, the outside light was off, and Jeff was quietly opening his window. Gabbie was not parked directly in front of his house, but he could see her black car across the street. He briskly jogged to the passenger side door and climbed in, rubbing his hands together for warmth.

"You sure you want to come?" Gabbie asked before putting the car in drive.

"Gabbie," Jeff said, turning in his seat and facing her. "I am not letting you do this alone."

"I brought this just in case," she said, reaching under her driver seat to reveal a silver gun that shone off the dashboard lights. "You never know."

"Let's hope we don't need it."

"That all hinges on what the hell Marc wants." Gabbie let out a long sigh as they drove, her navigation telling her where to turn. "He sounded like he was sad to be honest."

"What did he say exactly?" Jeff, no matter how much he did not want to admit it, felt bad for Marc. As much as he said he was putting on an act, Jeff could see that there were moments when he was being genuine and caring. There was no faking those emotions. And there was no denying that Jeff had fallen for him, even if he only said it in secret.

"He sounded winded when I picked up," she said. "Then in this low voice he said that he needed to talk to me tonight. Told me he needed to clear things up because he didn't get what I said that caused it all. Said he would send me a pin drop and that if I told you about it he would kill me, and then," she paused, shaking her head. "He told me that after he killed me he'd go and kill you."

Jeff groaned, looking out the window, seeing snow fall. "Why does everything need to be life and death with him?"

"I'm telling you," she said, making a left down a dirt road surrounded by trees. "He's a psychopath. I looked it up online and he has to be. I've seen him, he gets off on killing. That's not normal."

"I told him I thought he was a sociopath," Jeff chuckled, shaking his head. "I should have known something was off. I should have listened to you when you warned me."

"Don't beat yourself up," she said, reaching over and rubbing his shoulder. "He can be very convincing, trust me."

"He would get this twinkle in his eye whenever the subject was about death."

"I know exactly what you're talking about!" Gabbie shook her head and bit her lower lip. "It was like he was all there in those moments, you know? Like any other time, he's totally in control of what he's putting out there, but when it came to death and carnage, he came alive."

"When we went on a date and were flirting, I saw that same look and got happy." Jeff felt dumb saying it out loud, admitting that he got joy from the thought of his boyfriend looking at him that way. "I thought it was because of me, you know?" His voice quaked. "He told me yesterday it was because he was going to go kill a couple while we were at dinner."

"Jesus," she said, "he's got issues."

"Isn't that sad? To want someone to look at you the way they look at killing."

"No. It's sad that he can't look at anything like that besides murder. Nothing about wanting your partner to look alive when they're with you."

"Does Robyn look at you like that?"

"Robyn?" Gabbie laughed. "No. No, we're not a thing. We just hook up from time to time. She's not really the commitment type and I'm not looking for a relationship right now. It works out."

"Oh," Jeff said, feeling his cheeks heat up. "I just assumed."

"I would have if I were you too. But nope, just good friends."

Jeff turned to survey their surroundings. Trees. That's all he could see from the headlights. They were the only ones on the path, leading to wherever Marc wanted Gabbie to go. Her navigation said that they were a mile away from the destination and Jeff had no idea where they were, let alone why they were in the middle of the woods. Gabbie slowed down, as they approached a cabin. It was completely dark, except for a light that they could see on in the second story.

"I didn't know Marc had a cabin," Jeff commented, seeing the dark wood through the headlights.

"He doesn't," Gabbie said, reaching down and grabbing the pistol.

The two of them were trudging through the snow on their way to the front door. Gabbie was in front of Jeff, handgun by her side as they made their way. The wind was working its way into Jeff's clothes and chilling him to the bone. He really hoped the inside was warm and that nothing bad happened. His hope was that he would somehow be able to talk to Marc, let them have some type of closure without any violence.

He wasn't holding his breath.

Gabbie reached the front door, twisting the handle slowly to test if it was unlocked. Sure enough, it was. The door creaked as it opened, the moonlight from outside filling the darkness. Jeff saw a staircase directly in front of them that lead to the second story. The house smelt of burnt wood and was accompanied by an eerily quiet atmosphere. Taking out his cellphone, he turned the flashlight on and peered around.

A wooden fireplace — with a bear's head plastered above it — was to their left, dying embers still flickering. An uneasiness settled in the pit of Jeff's stomach. Gabbie had her pistol aimed in front of her as he closed the door behind them. They stayed still for a moment, listening. Besides their breathing, Jeff could not hear any other noise that would give reason to suspect anyone was in the house. The stairs were wooden, creaking with each step they took.

The staircase did not go up directly but turned left in the middle and led them up. As they turned the corner, Jeff saw a light coming from underneath a closed door directly across from the top. His heart rattled in his chest as they took each step, tiptoeing up.

"You good?" Gabbie asked as they reached the top.

"I'm nervous," he admitted, wiping his sweaty palms onto his pants.

"Me too."

They were standing in front of the door, silent. Jeff wanted to fling it open and get the night over with but was unsure as to what even awaited the two of them. Knowing Marc, it would most likely be something dramatic, but there was hope that maybe he would just be sitting down and want to talk. There was always that voice in the back hoping for the best. Gabbie turned the knob, the latch making an audible click as she pushed the door open with one hand, gun pointed out in the other.

The light filled the space around them and made Jeff squint for a second as his eyes adjusted. That is when he saw Marc, and all the hope left his body.

Marc was lying in the bathtub, head sunken in chest. One of his arms was hanging over the edge of the ghostly white porcelain tub, blood dripping down from his wrist and off the tips of his fingers, collecting in a small pool on the tile. Gabbie covered her mouth, handing Jeff the gun and rushing forward. She was saying something, but Jeff's hearing stopped in that moment and everything slowed down. Marc was dead? Guilt coated Jeff like a cloak.

"I did this," he whispered to himself, backing up as he watched Gabbie grab Marc.

Jeff felt his head spinning and as he stepped back, away from the door, his foot slipped in something wet. He looked down and saw blood streaked down the wooden floor and leading down the hallway. The light from the bathroom only lit up so much of the hallway, so Jeff took his cellphone out and turned the flashlight on again, keeping the pistol out. Cautiously he stepped forward, avoiding the crimson blood trail as he walked.

It led to a closed door at the end of the long hallway. There was no way that it was Marc's blood, and that made the hairs on Jeff's arms stand to attention. All his focus was on the door as he reached out and turned the knob, slowly pushing it with an open hand. The room was completely dark, but Jeff heard something shuffle in the corner and he held out the gun, pointing.

"Hello?"

Before he had time to react, a shadow came lunging forward. Jeff had no time to think and pulled the trigger, the flash from the shot lighting up the room for a brief second. His arms coiled back, and he instinctively shot again, the shot illuminating the room again. Whoever was rushing at Jeff collapsed as they made their way forward. His hands were shaking but he kept his arms out, stiffly holding the pistol in front of him.

He waited a second before lowering the gun to his side and reaching for his phone to see who it was. As he turned on the flashlight, Jeff dry heaved at the sight in front of him. On the floor were four bodies, three piled on top of each other. On the bottom, he could see a woman in pajamas, her eyes and mouth sewn shut, throat slit. On top of her were two children, both the same.

"What the —" Jeff stopped and saw that there was a man lying face first on the floor, two exit wounds in his back, also in pajamas.

Nothing was making sense to Jeff. It almost felt like his mind stopped trying to make sense of the world and he could physically feel the Earth spinning on its axis, feel every molecule in his body, feel as his stomach retched, and vomit came careening up his throat. He closed his mouth and slammed his hand over it, forcing the puke back down.

"Well, well, well," Marc's voice came creeping into his ear from behind. Before Jeff could turn around something connected with the back of his head and his vision cut out.

Jeff opened his eyes, slowly. The light burned his eyes and the back of his head was throbbing. It took him a moment to realize what had happened, or what he thought happened. He definitely heard Marc's voice and judging by the fact that he was lying in the bathtub now, Marc was alive. Jeff reached behind him and touched the back of his skull, wincing. His fingers felt dry blood that had stuck in his hair.

"He's awake," Marc said, and Jeff turned to the side, seeing him standing against the door. "Finally, am I right, Gabbie?"

He stepped over and Jeff saw Gabbie hunched over on the toilet, her right hand was handcuffed to a pipe behind her on the floor. Her face was bruised, and Jeff could see blood dripping from her slack lips.

"Now I can ease up on you, isn't that great!" There was a sadistically happy tone to his voice as he stepped to Gabbie and roughly grabbed her by her cheeks.

"Stop," Jeff croaked out, trying to push himself up. "Marc, please just—"

Before Jeff could finish, Marc bounded towards him, grabbing him by the collar and dragging him out of the bathtub. His shoulder blades hit the edge as Marc slammed him on the ground, the back of his head hitting the tile. Jeff's vision spotted as Marc snarled in his face, landing a kick into his ribs. Coughing out in pain, Jeff looked up and saw Marc's foot as it came barreling towards his face, connecting with his jaw and making his neck snap back, the metallic taste of blood filling his mouth.

"Oh, no, Jeff," Marc said, grinning from ear to ear, eyes sparkling. "You don't get to talk. You have been revoked of that privilege. And I know it's so sad for you," he said, leaning forward and pulling Jeff's head up by his hair, causing Jeff to shriek in agony. "Seeing as you're a privileged little bitch." With that last comment Marc shoved Jeff's head back.

"Please," Jeff said, spitting blood up.

"Please, what? Please don't kill you?" Marc almost twirled as he stood up and walked to the counter where the sink was. The gun Jeff had earlier was one end of the sink, a knife opposite. But Marc went to neither and instead pulled his phone out and started scrolling.

Jeff turned his attention to Gabbie. Her face was still hanging there, blood had stained onto her jacket, but he could see that her chest was still rising, giving him some hope. He needed to talk to Marc, somehow convince him to at least let Gabbie go. Whatever this was, whatever Marc was doing, she did not need to be involved. This was between him and Jeff.

"Need to set the mood," Marc said, switching a song onto his phone, filling the silence. "Marilyn Manson's cover of 'Sweet Dreams' always puts me in the right mood."

With a toothy grin he bounced back over to Jeff, squatting in front of him. Jeff had not realized that Marc had grabbed the pistol as he was watching Gabbie, but now Marc had it aimed in his face, cocking his head. Jeff's eyes burned, and he could feel tears starting to drop without him even blinking, making Marc's leer somehow grow.

"You want to know something, Jeff?"

Jeff did not say anything, simply held his chin up high and glared.

"I was never going to stop killing. Ever. I just saw that it made you happy, so I hid it from you." Marc let out a chuckle, swiping his hand down his mouth and smirking. "Shit, I even killed Julian while you were getting your prescription filled and you were so gullible. I mean, really? You believed I gave him my jacket? Come on."

"You're such a piece of sh—"

Marc's fists connected with Jeff's gut as the air exploded out of him, causing his body to fold in on itself.

"What was that?" Marc asked, laughing. "What? Did you think because I opened up to you that somehow I was going to get better, work on my issues and me and you could have some happy bullshit life? Wake up, Jeff. It's 2040, there is no happy ending, there is no normal life. There's survival and that's all."

"No," Jeff coughed out, tilting his head up.

"You just shot and killed a man because you were afraid," Marc said, licking his bottom lip. "How does it feel to know you killed a defenseless man?"

"You're sick," Jeff said, remembering the shots as the man fell to the floor, remembering the corpses of the family, still and cold. "How could you kill kids?"

"Easy," Marc said, "they're smaller. It's literally easier to kill them."

Jeff felt sick.

"Oh, don't give me that look," Marc said, tilting the barrel of the gun and placing the cold tip against Jeff's bruised cheek. "I saved them a world of pain. We both know growing up sucks. Only one of us is just now realizing it a little too late." Making a mocking sad face, Marc lifted the butt of the gun to hit Jeff, but he raised his hand just in time and yelped as the pistol collided with his wrist, a loud popping filled the air.

The pain radiated up his bones as his hand hit the floor. Before Marc could raise his hand and do it again, Jeff kicked his leg out and connected with Marc's shin. It did not cause Marc to fall but forced him to stop before he could hit Jeff again.

"Fuck!" Marc shouted at the top of his lungs, standing up and twisting around to face Gabbie. "How 'bout I just kill her now?" He pointed the gun and Jeff felt his heart stop in his chest.

"No!" Jeff screamed at the top of his lungs, the taste of his salty warm tears found their way into his mouth. "Marc, please!"

"Okay," Marc said, lifting the gun upwards and placing the barrel next to his temple. "Lay down."

"What?" Jeff said, his hands shaking, his entire body was.

"Lie the fuck down," Marc barked, pointing the gun back at Gabbie.

"Okay," Jeff said, his lips quivering as he lied himself down against the frigid tile, arms by his side. "Now what?"

Marc strode over to him, standing with his crotch above Jeff's face. "Now," Marc said, smirking. "Now I do whatever the fuck I want." Before Jeff could react, Marc shifted and pointed the gun directly down at him. "Don't move. If you move, I'm going to make the last moments of your privileged life a literal hell."

Marc did a quick laugh before he positioned himself above Jeff's chest. With his arms by his side, Jeff watched as Marc lowered himself, straddling onto Jeff, pinning his hands to his side. With a cock of his head, Marc glared down at Jeff, triggering flashbacks of Adrian holding him down on the bathroom floor. Only difference was, Marc had a gun and Jeff had nothing to defend himself.

Unless he could make it to the knife on the counter somehow.

"Look at me," Marc said, his face directly above Jeff's. "I really liked you. I really, really liked you." As he said that, he rubbed the tip of the pistol down Jeff's cheek and towards his pursed lips. "Remember when we were on that date," Marc said, shifting his weight so he was almost sitting on Jeff's crotch, with the gun at the opening of his mouth. "Remember when we," he said wiggling his eyebrows, pushing the tip of the silver barrel against Jeff's lips. "You were so good for a virgin."

Jeff's mouth was quaking as the gun was placed against it. With everything he had, he forced himself not to talk.

"Open up," Marc said, licking his bottom lip. "Open your mouth for me one last time."

"Don't do it, Jeff," Gabbie's voice broke through the tension, both relieving him and also adding more worry to his heart.

"Open. Your. Mouth." This time it was much more aggressive in tone, and his lip curled up in an insidious manner.

Jeff didn't want to, but he knew he had to. If he didn't listen to Marc that would mean he was responsible for Gabbie's death, atop all the other lives that he blamed himself for, atop the man he murdered just earlier. His stomach twisted in knots as he slowly opened his jaw, feeling and tasting the cold metal against his tongue, against his teeth, against his life.

"That's it," Marc said, pushing the barrel in, making Jeff gag. "Oh, no, I know for a fact you can take more than this."

Tears were falling down Jeff's temples as Marc moved the gun in and out, a look of pure pleasure on his face. Jeff was almost positive he was going to puke.

"Stop!" Gabbie shouted, and Jeff could hear her banging her arm around, the metal from the handcuffs making noise as it scraped against the pipe. "Marc, stop! You've made your point."

"Have I?" Marc asked, taking the pistol out — Jeff gasped, immediately shutting his mouth — and then leaned in, biting Jeff's lower lip. "I just want to remember you, Jeff, that's all. I killed my last boyfriend before I even had some fun. Blue balled the shit out of me." He was practically lying on top of Jeff, and he could feel Marc's hand sliding up his chest to his throat. "Showed up and stabbed him so quick I didn't even get a chance to say goodbye, to have one last moment."

With that last word, his grip coiled around Jeff's throat.

"I don't want that for you. I want to remember you."

Marc tilted his head back, rotating his neck in a circle as the music continued to play in the background. His grips stayed constant, with his thumb rubbing up and down against the side of Jeff's throat. The gun was no longer directly pointed at his face and Jeff had needed to figure out a way to get out from underneath him. His arms were a no go, but maybe he could lift his leg up like he did with Adrian and knee Marc.

"You're pathetic," Gabbie said, still trying to her best to break the pipe.

"What was that?" Marc asked, letting go of Jeff and standing up.

Now was the moment.

As Marc started to step forward, Jeff quickly grabbed onto his ankle and yanked backwards, watching Marc fall face first onto the tile. The gun slid across the tile and smacked into the corner of the bathroom, almost close enough for Gabbie to grab. Before Marc could get himself up, Jeff did exactly what Adrian had done to him and pulled Marc back by his legs.

Marc twisted around, and Jeff could see his nose was bleeding.

"Oh, you fucked up," Marc said, blood staining his teeth.

"I fucked up the moment I dated you," Jeff snarled, yanking Marc back, trying to squirm his way on top. Marc swung, missing Jeff's face but hitting his shoulder; it hurt but he forced himself to ignore it, balling his fists up and slamming them down onto Marc's lower back. With all his strength, Jeff continued to lift both his hands up and rain them down onto Marc.

Out of the corner of his eye Jeff could see Gabbie trying her best to get the pistol. She had her leg out as far as she could, hanging off the seat with her arm stretched out.

"I'm going to take my time," Marc growled as Jeff pulled himself up and was able to pin Marc's arms down.

Jeff glared down at Marc underneath him as he watched his hands wrap around Marc's throat, squeezing with all his might. "It didn't have to be this way," Jeff said, unable to stop tears from falling.

"Yes, it did," Marc said, his face beginning to redden. "Just know, Jeff, you kill me, and your life is going to get a hell of a lot worse."

"Is that so?" Jeff said, gritting his teeth and shoving his body weight against Marc, feeling his throat closing under his fingers, hearing the air getting caught in his throat as he tried to breathe in.

Marc had a grin spread across his face. "Kill or be killed," he said, as his eyes became increasingly more bloodshot, his face becoming almost purple.

Jeff did not let go, he kept his grip steady. There was an anger bubbling inside of him and he could not contain it, could not stop himself. He jerked forward again, looking directly into Marc's eyes as he watched the twinkle leave it, as he watched Marc's lips go slack, as he felt Marc's throat no longer attempting to breathe, as he felt relief fill his bones at the sight of Marc's dead body.

CHAPTER 24

"Jeff."

Gabbie's voice broke through the silence he experienced as he continued to stare into Marc's lifeless eyes, hands still enwrapped. Jeff looked up and saw that Gabbie had a frantic look on her face.

"We need to go," Gabbie said, shaking her wrists.

"Sorry," Jeff said, pushing himself up, feeling his legs wobbling underneath him. His body was vibrating as he walked over to Gabbie. "Do you know where the key is?"

"Check his pockets," she said, no longer desperately hanging off the toilet trying to get the pistol.

Jeff rushed over to Marc's body and reached into his pant pockets, digging around until his fingers touched what felt like a key. He pulled it out and looked in the palm of his hand to see it was. Relief filled his lungs as he sighed, stood up and unlocked the handcuffs on Gabbie. Without skipping a beat, Gabbie stomped up, walked over to Marc's body and kicked it. Jeff did not even question it, he understood. They had been through hell together and lived. It was only natural she was mad, he was too.

"Let's go before we get in trouble for breaking and entering," she said, walking to the gun and picking it up.

"He killed the entire family," Jeff said, watching as Gabbie took the sleeve of her jacket and started rubbing all the spots she had touched. He followed suit, realizing their prints would be there. As they walked out of the bathroom, taking one last look at his lifeless body before turning off the light and shutting the door. "He killed kids."

"Jesus," she said, as they made their way down the creaky stairs. Each time they walked past anything they had touched earlier they would wipe it down.

The house had taken on the environment from outside and was freezing. The fire that had been on before no longer even had embers. The entire house felt like death to Jeff and he needed to get out of there and go home, shower, and try to forget all about it.

As the two of them drove back from the cabin it was mainly silent. Jeff did not have much to say, and he could sense that Gabbie was the same. She drove, and he watched as the trees whipped by them, the gravel under the tires the only noise that filled the void. Closing his eyes, he felt like it was finally over, that now — unlike before — he could completely move forward and put this all behind him.

Marc was the constant in every problem since Adrian, and he was gone now.

As they turned onto Jeff's street, he said, "park a few houses down. I don't want there to be any way my parents can see us."

"Okay," Gabbie said, parking and shutting off her headlights. She turned in her seat and faced Jeff. "Are you okay?"

Jeff did a half smile and shrugged. "I don't know how I am, to be honest." He sighed, "are you okay?"

"My face has seen worse," she said, a quick chuckle. "I'll be okay."

"I'm sorry this happened."

"It's not your fault," she said, reaching out and placing her hand on his. "Marc was a loose cannon. If it wasn't us it would have been someone else. Just look at it that way. We saved someone else the pain."

"Yeah," Jeff said, nodding, not wanting to tell her about the man he shot. "I guess I should go inside. School tomorrow."

"Good luck," she said, reaching out for an awkward car hug; he obliged and the two of them remained locked in each other's embrace for a while. "Call me whenever, okay? We've been through this together, we're bonded now," she laughed, but there was solemnness to it.

"I will," he said. "Same to you."

With one last nod, he opened the car door and stepped out into the coldness. Jeff flipped his hood up and started down the street to his house; her headlights shone the way as she drove past him. He made his way up the driveway and went up to his window, pulling on it just to feel resistance. With a confused look, he tried again, knowing he left it unlocked.

It was locked.

"Fuck," he said, realizing his parents probably woke up. "This night just keeps getting better."

With a heaviness filling the pit of his stomach, his heart began to race as he made his way up to the front door. Luckily, he had brought his house key with him. There was only one problem, the front door was cracked open. Jeff's insides felt like they were free falling as he pushed the door open and called out for his parents. There was no reply.

Jeff started to walk towards the hallway, each step feeling like he was in cement.

"Please be okay, please be okay," he kept saying over and over as he moved forward.

The hallway was only lit from the moonlight that came in from his open door. He could see that his parents' door was cracked open also. Each moment felt like an eternity as he closed in on their door. With an apprehensiveness he had never experienced before, Jeff pushed their bedroom door open and turned on the light, feeling the entire world fall out from underneath him.

His mom and dad were both sitting up against their bedpost, hands nailed above their heads. Jeff could see both their throats were slit as his knees buckled underneath him, vomit poured out of his mouth and onto the carpet. Without being able to control his breathing, his body shook as his vision blurred through the tears.

Two hands gripped onto his back and Jeff was ripped from his mind and slammed against the wall.

"Jeffery Braen," a similar voice said. "You are under arrest for the breaking and entering of Patrick Rodchester's house. My partner's house," Seymour snarled, closing the handcuffs tightly around Jeff's wrists.

Jeff could barely understand what was happening, all he knew was his entire life was over. Seymour roughly yanked him by his elbow, slamming him against the wall, his fingers getting pinched as they were handcuffed behind his back. His vision was a blur, snot and tears accumulating in his mouth as he choked out coughs of agony.

"You sick fuck," Seymour said, jutting forward and punching his fists in Jeff's gut, knocking the wind out. "You even killed his family."

"What are you—" Jeff was cut off with another punch to the stomach. His feet gave out and he fell to the floor, landing on his tailbone.

"Get up," he snarled, kicking Jeff's leg.

His body felt unusable. Even if he wanted his legs to move they would not respond. It felt as though he was in a state of paralysis, his gaze hanging on where his parents could be seen bloodied on the bed. Nothing really mattered at that point. He was getting arrested and it would all be over from there.

Jeff was utterly and completely alone.

To Be Continued...

www.ingramcontent.com/pod-product-compliance
Lightning Source LLC
Chambersburg PA
CBHW030559180626
46816CB00005B/1603